D

The Turning of the Tide

OTHER BOOKS BY SAMUEL LEWIN

In Yiddish:

A Sreifah (Conflagration; drama)
Far Sint (Sin and After; drama)
Gesang vun Doires (Song of the Generations; fiction)
Kegn Himl (Storming the Heavens; fiction)
In Guleth (In Exile; drama)
Der Hoifsinger (The Courtyard-Singer; fiction)
Chesjoines (Visions; poem)
Tsvishn Tsvei Tehumen (Between Two Abysses; fiction—a trilogy)
   Vol. 1: Dos Groisse Morden (The Great Carnage)
   Vol. 2: Shvartse Berg un Bloie Toln (Black Mountains and Blue
           Valleys)
   Vol. 3: Wolkn-Gedrang (Massed Clouds)

In English:

The Impatient Sages (fiction)

In German:

Chassidische Legende (Chassidic Legend; fiction)
Daemonen des Blutes (Demons in the Spirit; fiction)
Zeitwende (Changes; fiction)
Nacht am Hellen Tag (The Rise of Satan; drama)
Gesichte (Visions; poem)
Und er Kehrte Heim (And He Returned Home; fiction)
Im Wandel der Generationen (Metamorphoses; fiction)

In Hebrew:

Ben Shene Tehomoth (Between Two Abysses; fiction—a trilogy)
Lo Hegeah Hashaah (The Time Has Not Arrived Yet; fiction)

In Czech:

Chassidská Legendá (Chassidic Legend; fiction)
Generacnı Proměni (Song of the Generations; fiction)

In French:

Légende Hassidique (Chassidic Legend; fiction)

The Turning of the Tide

A novel by
Samuel Lewin

Translated from the Yiddish by
Joseph Leftwich

South Brunswick and New York: A. S. Barnes and Company
London: Thomas Yoseloff Ltd

© 1978 by A. S. Barnes and Co., Inc.

A. S. Barnes and Co., Inc.
Cranbury, New Jersey 08512

Thomas Yoseloff Ltd
Magdalen House
136-148 Tooley Street
London SE1 2TT, England

Library of Congress Cataloging in Publication Data
Lewin, Samuel, 1890–1959.
  The turning of the tide.
  I. Title.
PZ3.L5844Tu [PJ5129.L47] 839'.09'33 77–89644
ISBN 0–498–02087–8

The illustration for the jacket was drawn by the author's son,
ISAIAH S. LEWIN.

Foreword

What can a man write about with better knowledge than his own life and his own surroundings, the happenings he witnessed and the people to whom he saw them happening? It could be straight autobiography, or it could be put in the form of fiction, a story where the people are not portraits and the events need not have happened just as they appear, but the people are real and alive and the events ring true nevertheless, as though they could have happened. Freed from the straitjacket of fact, the truth grows and fits into a wider, larger pattern, becomes an allegory—a fable pointing to the moral—applicable to the whole period and milieu.

It is that once-upon-a-time fairy-tale way of telling his story that is so attractive in Samuel Lewin's novel *The Turning of the Tide*. It is not for nothing that Franz Werfel called Lewin a "poet." There is no involved plot—the story is as straightforward and simple as a folk tale. It is indeed that—a folk fairy tale. It begins with a legendary poor tailor in his humble home, and his wife, who was ugly but had a beautiful soul. And this poor tailor becomes revealed and venerated as a saint.

Peretz wrote a short story called "Revelation," which stems

basically from the same folk legend—of a poor man and his wife, held by their neighbors of little account; and suddenly the poor man is revealed as one of the saints, one of the great Hasidic rabbis. It is part of the Jewish folk mythos, of the Jewish ethical folk literature. It is the background to the Jewish belief in the thirty-six unknown saints, the just men for whose merit the world is preserved. The important thing about them is that their identity must not be known—one must respect every poor and humble man because any one of them may be one of the thirty-six!

It is a universal theme, worldwide in international folklore and fairy tale. It is the story of the ugly duckling, the story of beauty and the beast, the story of the enchanted frog who became a handsome prince, the story of the beggarman who, when treated kindly, reveals himself as a noble sage. It is the special Jewish point of view that turns the hero of the story into a saint and a rabbi.

The moral is the same for them all. As G. K. Chesterton said: "A promise is broken to a cat and the whole world goes wrong. A man and a woman are put in a garden on condition that they do not eat one fruit; they eat it, and lose their joy in all the fruits of the earth. All ethics should be taught to this fairy tale tune—that if one does the thing forbidden one imperils all the things provided."

The fairy-tale motive is behind all of Samuel Lewin's considerable corpus of novels, all picturing the way life developed in his own small town, typical of the entire Russian-Polish Pale of Jewish Settlement toward the beginning of this century, from a quiet, humble, pious hamlet to a bustling industrial town, with masters and men, capitalist and proletariat. That is his theme—industrialization destroying the old simple faith, the trust and innocence of the people.

It is the passion of Ruskin and William Morris and Tolstoy and the others who hated and feared the spread of industrialization. Samuel Lewin renders one of his people coming from his early simpler life to the factory: "He wasn't happy. The huge machines terrified him. And he hated getting up in the winter before dawn to walk to the factory."

In the factory he learns of the new faith that is taking the place of the old religious faith that the young people are discarding: "He made friends with some of the workers in the factory. They told him about the Labor and Socialist movement, which was trying to abolish the long working hours, and in time to abolish masters and employers, and establish Socialism, which would make the workers the masters."

Side by side with the decline in religious faith there was this new faith growing up, the faith in Socialism, in social and economic justice. Lewin depicts this growth, this transition, powerfully and poetically, most of all in this novel, *Turning of the Tide*—for it is the turning of tides, seemingly inexorable, that concerns him in all his portrayals of that life which he viewed at close quarters, which he shared with his readers in book after book, illuminating all the different aspects of the process as he saw it and painting the people he had seen involved in it, as it affected them and theirs.

There was cruelty and suffering in the earlier life, too. The rich landowners had serfs, and the former oppressed the latter. The landowners ill-treated their Jews. There were pogroms. "But the Jews were pious and trusted in God. They prayed in the synagogues. They studied the Talmud. They read Psalms. They took pride in their work. They were skilled craftsmen who loved their work, tailors and shoemakers, carpenters and joiners and carvers and goldsmiths."

Then, with the coming of the factories, "The town moaned and groaned, because life had become hard." The legend of the little tailor, the saint, remained an inspiring memory, and when his great-grandson grew up, a handsome young man, full of idealism, the people began to hope that he would take the saint's place, and comfort them and guide them.

But—and this is the tragedy that obsesses Lewin—the saint's great-grandson has a different ideal: Socialism. "There was a complete revolution in the Jewish life of this town. The old beliefs and the old ways of life were being abandoned. And the little tailor's great-grandchildren had not escaped. It was not a wayward revolt by a few young people—it was a complete change on the part of the entire young generation."

Yet the little tailor's great grandson has a foreboding—there is still something of the old faith in him, and he concludes that "the best Socialists were the old Hebrew Prophets, who had roused the people against oppression and injustice, against those who laid field to field and ground down the face of the poor and robbed the fatherless and the widow." He was afraid that "the new Socialism, with its dogmas and divisions and its antilibertarian doctrines was establishing a new orthodoxy, and a new heresy-hunting, the 'crime' of 'deviationism'; he feared the priests of Marxism would not be different from any other priests. They would want to stamp out opposition and independent thought, and impose a bureaucracy to enforce adherence to their dogmas. Instead of freedom it would bring a new slavery." The fairy tale is beginning to show its demonic side.

There is the once-upon-a-time fairy-tale atmosphere in these books too, in the way they recall a life that has passed, that has been throttled out of existence by those who followed Hitler. Samuel Lewin has not turned all his human beings into saints—he shows them as real living characters, with faults as well as virtues, thieves as well as honest men, but they are all seen with love and are painted with affection for their authentic way of life, the old modes of Jewish behavior and of folk tradition. Lewin's novels are monuments raised to a people who are no longer here, the millions of Jews of the towns and cities and villages of what used to be the Jewish Pale of Settlement, who were exterminated in the ghettos and the death camps and the crematoriums. Samuel Lewin sees them with the eye of one who knew them closely and loved them and has the artistry to bring them before us as living people.

And he ends his book as a fairy tale ends, with the modern young man, the descendant of the legendary saint, going back to his roots: "his saintly great-grandfather—he was telling them about the poverty that people had suffered here years ago, when the town had been a small place."

Samuel Lewin has painted unforgettable scenes and portrayed remarkable people, a gallery of characters, all real, each with his or her own story involved in the pattern of the whole. It is a beautifully written book. In many places it has the authentic fairy-tale, folk-tale magic. And the sheer story-telling power holds the reader's attention throughout. Like Franz Werfel, "I venture with calm assurance to name Samuel Lewin as a poet."

Joseph Leftwich

The Turning of the Tide

Note: A Glossary of Yiddish and Hebrew terms employed in *The Turning of the Tide* begins on page 229.

1

On *both sides* of the River Vistula scattered towns and villages, water mills and windmills. A lot of roads and neglected paths cutting through and across the fields, winding and twisting to reach the highway linking Lublin with Warsaw, those two noble Polish towns. Railways were still unknown then in those parts. Jews and non-Jews both lived simple, poor lives. But many lovely tales were told there about great rabbis who worked miracles, and big landowners who farmed out to Jews their spirit distilleries and breweries, timber forests and charcoal kilns, taverns and inns, and all sorts of financial and commercial enterprises. But most of these territorial magnates were also cruel to their Jewish tenants; they whipped them and humiliated them in all sorts of ways to satisfy their savage lusts. They made them dance like bears, climb up trees and from the branches sing down to them or crow like cocks. Many of these lords, together with the Catholic clergy, oppressed and afflicted the Jews, darkened their lives, hurled the most terrible accusations against them, like the infamous blood libel. And they incited the populace to program the Jews. The peasants were at that time serfs.

But the Jews of those days were entirely different Jews. They were pious and put more trust in God. They rose very early, while it was still dark, and by the light of a tallow candle read psalms and followed them with their morning prayers. These were the ordinary Jews. The scholars sat day and night in the *Beth Hamedrash*, the House of Study, over books of sacred lore. Their voices rose sweet and sad with the plaintive Gemara chant, obstinately trying to pierce the meaning of a difficult chapter of the Talmud. Most of the artisans, plain, simple, honest folk, started work before dawn. The tailors sewed with strong thread silk and satin and damask, velvet and broadcloth and cheviot, alpaca and linen and calico. Some as they worked sang snatches of the liturgy to the tunes the cantors sang in the synagogue, some sang folksongs or the merry melodies of the wedding-party musicians, and made small close stitches so that the garment should be well tailored. There were such who enjoyed their work, took pride in a well-done job, who admired their own craftsmanship. The same with the bootmaker and the carpenter, the joiner and the carver and the goldsmith and all the other craftsmen. There were good, honest, God-fearing Jews among the shopkeepers, who were mostly poor. And among the big merchants who traded with Leipzig and Danzig and other faraway places. Also among the carters and the water-carriers.

In that part of the country, beside the Vistula, there lived a tailor, a thin little Jew with a scanty beard something like a billy goat's, and he was terribly poor. The community had married him to an old maid who had no parents or relatives, and not a penny to her name. She was also a hunchback and very ugly; but she was a pious woman, and she had a gracious look in her big sad eyes. They lived in great poverty, but with willing acceptance of their hard lot. There was peace and content in their home; they were like a pair of quiet doves, so that people might think they were rolling in wealth. She couldn't do enough for him. He was the apple of her eye. She walked on tiptoe in his presence. She spoke to him as one speaks to a king—such was her reverence of him. And the little tailor called his wife "my prophetess," not only because her name was Miriam. She bore her husband one son; and at his circumcision they named him Melech, which means *king*. Nasty people in the town made fun of the little tailor. They mocked him and mocked his wife—laughed at them. They didn't know who the little tailor was, and that Heaven might punish them for their irreverence. They would have got their retribution, if the little tailor had agreed to it. He knew what they were saying about him and about his wife. It hurt him, but he forgave them with all his heart, and prayed for them to God.

They lived on next to nothing, for the little tailor's earnings were not much. He wasn't really a good tailor. It was only because he was no good for anything else that he had decided to try his luck with the needle. And of course his materials were not silk and satin. Reb Feivel—that was his name—went around among the peasants in the neighboring villages mending their smocks and their coats and spencers. Before his marriage he had sometimes sat studying the Mishna—but nobody in this small town knew whether he was anything of a scholar. He was a silent humble man. He would certainly have preferred to sit and study the Torah. But he knew how hard it was to earn a living. The wags in the town laughed and scoffed at him—"Some tailor! Just the man to make the Emperor's clothes!"

But gradually some people in the town had their eyes opened and they suddenly saw that this little tailor was a hidden saint, one of the thirty-six. "What fools those scoffers are!" they said. "They don't realize that he is a saint, who has not yet revealed himself."

The little tailor went his usual way, appearing not to notice and not to hear. He continued doing his work as best he could, plying his needle in the villages and also in his home, where his hunchback wife Miriam, with her beautiful sad eyes, helped him with his work. And those same Jews who had suddenly seen that the little tailor was a hidden saint now realized too that Miriam was no hunchback at all. She only

15

carried a small pack on her back, in which she collected all the sins committed in the town, and then flung them into the river. So that none should see what she did.

Those Jews who had been the first to see these hidden things kept quiet about them. They understood that the time had not yet come to reveal them.

But one day, shortly before the tailor was due to reveal himself, a wag stopped him in the market, and jeered: "Wouldn't you like to make me a sheepskin coat, Reb Feivel!"

And Reb Feivel smiled, like a fond father, and answered: "Why not? God will help you! You will prosper, and you'll have a sheepskin coat made! Only you won't come to me to make it. You'll go to a very good tailor! To the best tailor in Warsaw!"

And the wag mocked the little tailor, and made bleating noises at him like a sheep.

Before three weeks had passed the young wag found a hundred gold pieces in the market place, tied up in a cloth. And he went to Warsaw, and bought himself a completely new outfit, like a lord, and he had a fine sheepskin coat made, and he came back to the town, unrecognizable. Everybody in the town proposed their daughters to him and he married a beautiful rich girl.

But his punishment soon came because he had jeered at the little tailor. He fell seriously ill. And when he got better he was no longer rich. And he couldn't speak as he had spoken before, like a human being, but he bleated like a sheep. His wife demanded a divorce. So he went to the little tailor, flung himself at his feet, and begged him for forgiveness. And the tailor forgave him, and blessed him, so that he talked like a man again, and became rich again. The blessing was fulfilled immediately.

The news soon spread. The little tailor was revealed for what he really was. It was against his wish, because he in his humility wanted to remain hidden and unknown, and he still went on plying his needle, going to the villages and mending the peasants' smocks and coats and spencers, and earning in that way his poor crust of bread. Often he came home only for the Sabbath. For the rest of the week he ate and slept in Jewish inns or in the huts of Jewish farmers.

But almost everybody now knew that the little tailor was one of the secret thirty-six. It revealed itself even in his work. Every garment he mended, however old and worn and torn, looked like new. That was because tailoring to Reb Feivel was not just a job to earn his living, but a way of serving God. Every stitch he made was a prayer, a word of the Torah.

The Jews of the town and from neighboring towns started going to the little tailor to ask for help. Hasidim, followers of other rebbes, came to him, and scholars came to him, learned men and rich men, from everywhere, more and more. Yet some still scoffed. And these were the top Hasidim, the richest men in the town. "The rabbi with the needle!" they jeered.

Reb Feivel knew it, and once smiling in his fashion, he said to his Hasidim: "I could stab them with my needle; but they are poor blind fools. That's enough punishment for them!"

But the richer men, the more prominent people among his Hasidim, didn't like their rabbi continuing as a tailor. They pleaded with him: "You needn't and you mustn't remain hidden any longer, Rebbe!"

Reb Feivel acceded to the wish, not of the Hasidim, but of Heaven, and he was revealed for what he was.

Now his Hasidim went a step further, and wanted him to appoint a gabbai to serve him and to arrange his affairs—as was proper for a rebbe. So Reb Feivel sent a call to the fence, the local receiver of stolen goods, a Jew with a long beard who was known in the town not as Mechel but Reb Mechel, and who was given much respect by everybody, though all knew that he bought the stuff the thieves in the town brought him, and that these stolen goods had made him rich. But Reb Mechel came from a fine respected family, and he considered himself a pious Jew.

The Hasidim were surprised by their rebbe's choice, for they knew that nothing was hidden from him, and he knew

17

who Reb Mechel was and what he did. Yet they also knew that their rebbe did nothing without some deep purpose. So they didn't question him, but they waited till he himself would tell them why he had done this. And the little tailor—which was the name they gave their rebbe—told them, smiling in his quiet way, that he had meant to achieve two aims—for the sake of his honest and pious parents to redeem Reb Mechel from the sinful trade into which he had fallen, and also to save the town from thieves. Because if there would be no receiver to buy the stolen goods the thieves wouldn't steal.

◆━━◆━━◆━━◆━━◆━━◆

Reb Melech, the little tailor's only son, wouldn't take over his father's legacy and position, though the whole town begged him to. He was a great Talmudic scholar. But he became a timber merchant. He bought tree felling rights in big forests, and he became very wealthy. One legacy he did take over from his father, his greatest, his most essential legacy—he was a humble man, with a warm heart. He appreciated only the things of the spirit—moneyed worldly pleasures were to his mind worthless. His wealth was important only as a means of giving charity. He helped the Jews—and the non-Jews too—in the town with a generous hand. With timber from his forests, to build, or repair a house. And with money, to pay the builders, and to buy what was needed. Those who could repay, and were honest, repaid the money he lent them, over a period of years, as they could manage it, without interest, of course. And those who couldn't or wouldn't had no need to worry. The debt was canceled. The result was that many poor people in the town became quite well-to-do.

Everybody in the town respected Reb Melech. And many loved him. But nobody could understand why he had refused to succeed his father as the rebbe. Stranger still—he didn't like Hasidim. And yet he—judged by his conduct—was himself a true Hasid. The question was put to him once by a close friend; Reb Melech's answer was: "I don't like rebbes, and I can't abide the flocks of sheep that run to the rebbe for help, no matter who and what the rebbe is. Put a *shtreimel* on a horse, and he'll preside at the rebbe's table, and take gifts and petitions for help. Much better for each Jew to try to reach God himself, and to pray to God direct for whatever he wants."

Reb Melech did not hold aloof from the ordinary folk. He was an easily accessible man. Anybody could come to him, and he listened and did what he could. Even those with whom others refused to consort, the outcasts, were not repulsed. Indeed, he sometimes did more for these, because he was sorry for them, and he prayed to God that they should find the way back to the straight path. And he tried to win them back with kind words and with help. What he hated were those who prided themselves on distinguished ancestry, or learning or wealth. He wouldn't have anything to do with such vain people.

Reb Melech had a big staff of clerks and bookkeepers, and overseers in the forests. There was a young bookkeeper in one of his forests who was the son of a poor tailor, and he was himself poor, because what he earned he sent to help his parents. His name was Abraham. It so happened that one day Reb Melech took his only daughter with him to the forest where Abraham was a bookkeeper, and he noticed that when Abraham came near she blushed. It happened several times. And when he spoke to her about it she told him that she loved the young man. Reb Melech also liked the young man, and he agreed to their betrothal.

But his wife Sheindel, who came of a rich distinguished family, opposed the match. "He's poor," she objected, "a tailor's son!"

Then Reb Melech rebuked her: "I am also a poor tailor's son, yet your parents, for all their wealth and their fine descent, took me as their son-in-law. Our daughter Rachel is a beautiful girl, but you were at her age more beautiful, and you still are. He's poor? So was I. What is more important is that

Abraham, the poor tailor's son, is a very fine young man. He is quite a Hebrew scholar, and he has taught himself Russian and Polish and some German. His arithmetic and his accountancy is better than that of any other of my bookkeepers. And he is pious and God-fearing, and he keeps the Law. He is honest and good and gentle. He's a good clever lad. And he can carve beautiful things out of wood with his penknife. I used to do that when I was young. But never so good as what he does."

And Sheindel, his wife, no longer opposed the match.

Abraham was no great scholar. He liked—when he had time—to sit under a tree, or to shut himself up in his office, and think, or dream, or read learned books. Reb Melech had caught him at it several times; both before the marriage and afterwards, when he was already his son-in-law. But he didn't say anything, because he believed that a man should study when he wanted to. It was a good thing to have knowledge. And he admired the carvings that Abraham made out of blocks of wood—beasts and birds, people and angels, and fantastic creatures of his imagination. Reb Melech spoke to him about these, and once he said to him:

"The soul of each person seeks its fulfilment. Each seeks something else. But not everybody has the time to devote himself to what his soul desires. And not everybody understands, what his soul desires. There are also the souls of the wicked, whose desire is wickedness, and there are souls that want the gross pleasures of the flesh. And there are dead souls, that have no desires at all. It is good to find a soul that longs for Torah and desires good deeds. Such a soul, even if it has not attained what it seeks, has eternal life. And beauty is itself a high stage. As we see from the fact that Bezalel Ben Uri is praised in the Torah for what he did to beautify the Sanctuary. We have many words in our sacred tongue for beauty. And if a soul longs for beauty it means that its source is beauty—and therefore its seeks to find its fulfilment in beauty."

Reb Melech had high regard for good breeding and good

family. But not for outward distinctions, only for the spirit. He didn't make much of the fact that he was the son of a rebbe. But he tried to follow in his father's ways. He thought deeply about his business transactions, and tried hard not to commit any dishonesty in his dealings. He never forgot that "My father was a poor man all his life. When he became a rebbe he refused to take gifts. And if any rich people insisted on giving money it usually remained with the gabbai. 'I took payment for my tailoring,' he used to say. 'I won't take money for praying to God to help anyone who is in need.' "

Reb Melech began to think, "Perhaps I should distribute my wealth among the poor. Why should I be rich, and they poor? Where's the justice!"

Many people in the town couldn't understand why the rich Reb Melech had taken a poor penniless tailor's son, one of his own employees, to be his son-in-law, to marry his beautiful daughter Rachel. Evil tongues wagged; some said it was probably because there was no other way—he had to marry her, to save her from shame. . . .

This talk came to Reb Melech's ears. He took no notice. He loved his daughter dearly, and he loved her even more when he found that she had fallen in love with Abraham, the poor tailor's son. "She takes after her grandfather, the saint," he said to himself, and he was more proud of it than he was of his wealth.

The wedding was held in the forest, in that forest where Abraham worked, keeping the books. It was on a Tuesday, after Pentecost. There were three bands playing. The tables were laid with the best of everything. The whole town came to the wedding, and rabbis from all the places round about, and they spoke Torah. Wine was drunk from gold cups, and the wedding presents were precious stones. The tailor's Hasidim danced and celebrated all the seven days of the wedding feast. It was the Tailor's granddaughter's wedding. . . .

When Reb Melech died, and his wife after him, the town felt the loss bitterly. Life in the town had generally grown more drab and dull since the little tailor had died. Reb Melech's wealth went to his daughter, and her husband, Abraham, ran the affairs of the forests. He sold some, or he had them felled, and he bought others. Rachel bore him two children, a girl and a boy. They named the girl Miriam and the boy Joseph.

Many Jews in the town wanted to see Abraham succeed to his father-in-law's fine ways and habits. Some even hoped that he might do what his father-in-law had refused to do, take the little tailor's place as their rebbe. The town remembered the little tailor, and still repeated the stories that had been told about him. They had created a legend round him, had embroidered it lovingly like a *paroches* over the Ark of the Law.

Bu the *paroches* was beginning to fade, was losing its bright colors. Life in the town was growing to be more drab and humdrum. It became like a stagnant pool, like a swamp. Not so much because of the poverty, which had always existed, but because a sadness had descended on the town after the little tailor's bright presence. As though the skies had darkened. As though the sun had gone out.

When the little tailor had been their rebbe, a poor pious Jew could, after a week's hard work and trouble and worry, go to him on the Sabbath, sit with the others round his table and fill himself with new spirit, from the rabbi's words of Torah and from the communal singing of hymns after the meal. It gave him fresh strength to shoulder the burden of another week of the daily grind. Now that Reb Melech had died there was no one left in the town to comfort them and to bring ease to their heavy hearts. They had respected Reb Melech. And now they respected Reb Abraham, because they saw in him also something of the little tailor, and they knew he was trying to walk in the ways of his father-in-law, Reb Melech. But he only showed himself generous in the matter of charity. He gave them no spiritual comfort.

And the town moaned and groaned, because material life

22

had become harder. The artisan worked from morning till night and didn't earn enough for dry bread. The rooms were small and damp and dark. The tiny windows were kept fastened most of the year and were plastered outside with clay to keep out the wind and the cold. When a pane got broken it was stuffed with rags or cardboard because they couldn't pay to have a new pane put in. The kitchen was full of smoke, the roof leaked and let in the rain. The people who owned the houses were most of them no better off than their tenants. Often two families with their children lived in one room; and many rooms were also used as workshops—sometimes two workshops, when both occupants were "master" artisans.

Obviously such homes could not be kept clean; they swarmed with vermin. The beds were bedding put down on the floor or on benches. In winter the people froze. Where the womenfolk helped their husbands by trading in the market the room was also littered with baskets of eggs and vegetables and fruit, and sometimes they actually kept fowls in the room. Under such conditions the children inevitably were neglected and were sickly, suffering all the diseases of poverty and dirt—rickets and scabies and tuberculosis. Epidemics like scarlet fever, even the dread cholera, were not infrequent. There were many deaths. Fewer people sat studying in the Beth Hamedrash. Piety and trust in God diminished.

It became intolerable. Those who considered themselves Hasidim of the little tailor, Reb Feivel—they used to go to his grave to pray there—held a meeting and decided to have a Sepher Torah written in the name of Reb Feivel, who had been their rebbe. That would remind the town of the saint, and might revive their faith and trust in God, so that their life would again become what it had been in his time.

Two Hasidim went to the scribe, Reb Itzik, and said: "We have come to you about a great and holy matter. We want to ask you to write a Sepher Torah for the saintly Reb Feivel, our rebbe, of revered memory."

One of the two Hasidim was Reb Abraham, the husband of the little tailor's grandchild. Out of humility he let his companion, Reb Pinchas, do the talking. For Reb Pinchas was an older man and was reputed to be a great scholar and a pious man. And this is what Reb Pinchas said:

"The town has forgotten the holy tailor. The number of scholars in the Beth Hamedrash has grown very small. True piety and trust in God is now found in few hearts. Therefore life here has become unbearable. Grief and despair increase daily. It is too much!" He paused. "You can save us, Reb Itzik!"

The scribe was an old man, weak with age, and he spent more time in bed than up.

"I can save? How?"

"By writing a Sepher Torah."

Reb Itzik waved away the idea with his hand. He didn't like people suggesting that he could work miracles with the scrolls of the Law he wrote, or with his mezuzahs or tephilin.

"I can't work miracles!" he cried angrily. "Only God can save!"

Reb Itzik was a frail old man, except for his gray-blue eyes, which had remained youthful. He ate little—not because he was poor, but because food didn't interest him. A wheaten roll, a glass of milk, a bowl of gruel, some fruit, and that was enough for the day. He never touched either meat or fish, not even on the Sabbath. Not because he was a vegetarian, for he knew nothing about vegetarianism. It was his way of living. For the same reason that he made his own special fast days. His wife had tried at first to persuade him that a Jew must eat meat on the Sabbath. His answer was: "There are greater satisfactions for the Sabbath than eating meat. There is studying Torah!"

He lived in his own house, which he had inherited from his parents. It consisted of one room, a smaller side room, and a kitchen. The house leaned on one side, and was propped up with poles, so as not to fall. The outside walls were pitted with tiny holes, out of which came a constant yellow dust.

Reb Itzik wouldn't sell a mezuzah to anybody who just came along. He looked the man up and down, and if he got the impression that he didn't fear God as much as he feared the devil, he said to him: "I don't write mezuzahs as charms and talismans, to ward off evil spirits." And if a scoffing unbeliever pretended that he wanted to buy tephilin, Reb Itzik would storm at him: "You can't even fool me! So how do you suppose you can fool God Almighty!"

He refused to write amulets; no amount of money could tempt him. He laughed at the man or woman who asked him to—"There are no evil spirits! If you want to be healed from your illness, see a doctor!"

All his life he had written very few Sepher Torahs. And now when he was old and ill, and spent most of his time in bed, he was unwilling to write any at all. His hand was no longer so steady to write the sacred scroll as it should be written.

But he agreed to write the Sepher Torah for the little tailor. He had suddenly felt a new surge of strength going into him; his fingers felt fresh and young again.

The Scribe rose the next day before daybreak, and as in past years, after he had washed and said his prayers and broken his fast, he sat down to write the Sepher Torah. So day after day, week after week, till he had completed his sacred task.

The same two Jews, Reb Abraham and Reb Pinchas, came to take away the Sepher Torah. They arrived dressed in their festive best, wearing satin caftans, with brandy and cake, and fine gifts for Reb Itzik. They put the brandy and cake down on the table—and the gifts also: a new satin caftan, and a new tallith with a silver neck-band. The old Scribe looked at the gifts, looked at Reb Abraham and Reb Pinchas, and said: "Who are these for?"

"For you, Reb Itzik."

The scribe flew into a temper. But he mastered himself, and said as quietly as he could: "Do you think I am a young man? What do I want with a new caftan and a new tallith? Am I going to get married under the canopy?"

"You're going under a canopy, all right!" said Reb Pinchas. "With the new Sepher Torah that you have written!"

"And you will live to see Messiah!" Reb Abraham added.
He poured three glasses of brandy, passed one to Reb Itzik
and one to Reb Pinchas, and said: "Good health! *L'Chaim!*
Long life!"

All three repeated the blessing, sipped at their glasses, and
said:

"*L'Chaim! L'Chaim! L'Chaim!*"

Wearing his new satin caftan and his old *shtreimel*, with the
new Sepher Torah wrapped in the new tallith hugged to his
breast, escorted by Reb Pinchas and Reb Abraham on either
side, and his gray-blue eyes shining brightly in his old, lined
face, Reb Itzik the scribe made his way through the street to
the house where the feast for the new Sepher Torah was being
given.

The town was on holiday. As for a big wedding. And most of
the rejoicing was that of the ordinary folk, the pious artisans.
They felt particularly close to this celebration, for the rabbi in
whose honor the Sepher Torah was written had been one of
their own, the little tailor.

Reb Abraham's front door stood wide open all day. The
whole town came, men and boys, women and children, even
such who cared little for the tailor's memory, for the Torah
means something to every Jew, even the heretics.

Rachel was delighted. It was her celebration—her grandfather! She didn't walk—she floated through the air. She saw
to everything—brandy, cherry brandy, wine, cake, biscuits,
fruit pies. "Please help yourselves!" she kept repeating, going
about among the people with a tray laden with good things.

Every room was crowded, and more people kept coming.
At dusk big tallow candles were lighted and set in silver candlesticks on the white-covered tables, in the sconces and in
the hanging candelabras. The big oil lamps were also lighted,
so that the brilliance was dazzling.

The women had put on their Sabbath and festival clothes,
silk and satin, velvet and brocade, and in all the colors of the

rainbow, but most in bordeaux, like the red wine of that name, blue like the sky in July when there are no clouds, green as the fields in spring, and in lilac, yellow, gold, white, and also black—in all the different shades of all these colors. Some had Brussels or Venice lace on their dresses. Some of the older women had put on their white wedding dresses, which they wore only to go to synagogue on Rosh Hashanah and Yom Kippur. And they wore their jewelry, gold bracelets and gold rings, pearls, brooches, watches on chains. The men, too, wore their best clothes, silk and satin caftans, all with girdles round their waists, and *shtreimels*. There were beards, black and red and grey, long and short, all tidily trimmed and combed, earlocks curled or straight, broad or narrow, long or short. Some with shining top boots, and some with delicate gentlemanly shoes. The young men were all dressed like bridegrooms for their wedding. And the heder boys were all dressed up. Some parents had got their children new clothes for the occasion, as if it were Passover. The young girls all looked like brides. Of course, the sexes were divided, in separate rooms. But the doors were kept open, and the girls and boys shyly exchanged glances.

When the afternoon prayers, the Mincha service, had been said, they started auctioning the letters in the final verses to complete the scroll. They had a table in the middle of the room, on which lay the new Sepher Torah, with two big lighted candles on each side.

Reb Israel Tocker had brought the rollers that he was donating, and fastened them to the Sepher Torah. Then Miriam, Reb Abraham and Rachel's daughter, the little tailor's great-grandchild, brought in on a silver tray the sash to bind the Sepher Torah and the mantle to wear over it, which she had made and embroidered herself.

Miriam was very beautiful. She wore a white dress, and her black hair hung down in two long plaits. When she appeared in the open door people gaped. There was a hush as she advanced towards Reb Itzik, holding out the tray to him.

Reb Itzik took the sash and the mantle from the tray, looked closely at the mantle, and asked: "Is it silk or satin?"

Miriam was no longer a child, but she blushed, with so many eyes, men's eyes, on her, and she answered shyly: "It is Turkish velvet, edged with Spanish satin."

Reb Itzik held up the mantle, admiring it, showing it off to the others: "Isn't it beautiful! I've seen so many mantles, but never anything so beautiful."

People kept coming up to look, grown men, and young men still unmarried, and the mantle passed from hand to hand. And many admiring glances were turned not only on the mantle but on Miriam who had made it. Some of the older people thought of her great-grandfather, the little tailor, in whose honor this Siyum Hasepher was being held. One pious old man, also a tailor, told this story:

"It was in the days before anyone knew who the little tailor really was. A poor widow woman was getting her daughter married, but she had no wedding dress for the bride, not even an old dress that could be made over, only her own wedding dress, which was old and torn. So she took it to a tailor, and he laughed at her: 'I can't do anything with that rag! Take it to the little tailor with the billy-goat beard. He'll make a royal robe out of it!'

"The poor woman went to the little tailor, and he made a beautiful dress out of the old rag. The whole town admired it. It was so beautiful. . . ."

Finally the mantle, passed from hand to hand, came back to Reb Itzik, the scribe. He held it up again, admiring it, and then he said to Miriam:

"May you stay always as beautiful as the mantle you have made for the Torah! And may your soul be always as pure as the memory of your great-grandfather, the holy little tailor!"

Her mother, Rachel, standing near, heard and hugged and kissed Miriam, and said with great fervor, "Amen! Amen!"

When the mantle was held up it looked from a distance like a deep blue sky at evening with the edges roseate from the setting sun. The Shield of David in the middle was embroidered with silver thread. Inside the Shield of David there were two embroidered lions, erect, facing each other, with a gold crown set with diamonds over their heads, and under the lions, embroidered in all the colors of the rainbow, the words: "Gur Aryah Yehuda," "The Lions of Judah." Round the Shield of David was an embroidered wreath, with green leaves and yellow roses, made so that they looked absolutely real.

The women were then asked to put in the final stitches in the scroll parchment. Reb Itzik, the scribe, explained that this honor had been reserved specially for the women, so that they should have their share in the Sepher Torah. First Rachel, then the other women were given the needle threaded with sinew, and after they had made their stitch they got a glass of cherry brandy, and drank it, wishing and being wished everything good.

Rachel looked young and beautiful, like a bride on her wedding day.

Next it was the men's turn—the final letters of the scroll were put up for sale. Everyone tried as far as he could to outbid the others; the one who gained the privilege was called up, with all the formality of the Reading of the Law in the synagogue.

Reb Itzik had outlined each letter on the parchment. Now he handed the quill pen to the purchaser of the letter and showed him how to ink it in. And then the man was given a glass of brandy and a *Mazel Tov*. So it went on. Everybody got a letter, even those who couldn't afford to buy one.

The last who was called up was Reb Abraham, the host. He had been left the last three words of the Torah to write in. These three words, these last letters had not been put up for auction. They were reserved as his privilege.

It had been so intended, and so arranged, yet Reb Abraham was taken aback that this honor should be bestowed on him. "The honor belongs to Reb Israel Tocker!" he stammered. He was thinking of the beautiful rollers Reb Israel Tocker had made and given for the Sepher Torah. He held Reb Israel in high regard, because though he was a wealthy man, a big timber merchant, he was very friendly with the artisans of the town. His own father had been an artisan, a tailor. His grandfather too. He was proud of his long line of artisan forbears.

The artisans appreciated it. Just as they did when the shammes calling up Reb Abraham mentioned first among his titles of honor that he was the son-in-law of Reb Melech, the holy tailor's son, and that the saintly rabbi whom they were now honoring had been a poor tailor, an artisan. "One of us!"

There was a hush at the mention of the little tailor, a hush of reverence and awe. The simple pious folk thought that the flames of the candles burned higher and dipped lower in deference. As though the little tailor's soul had come in and stood beside the Sepher Torah that had been written in his name.

On the same silver tray on which Miriam had brought the mantle for the new Sepher Torah, and the sash to bind it, her brother Joseph, the son of the house, now brought the jewels for the new Sepher Torah, a silver crown, ornamented with gold, set with precious stones, a silver hand to guide the reader and a silver breastplate with gold chains. Reb Itzik, the scribe, stood admiring them. He lifted them one by one, to show to the crowd jostling to get near. "Look at this Crown, Keter Torah . . . The Crown of the Torah . . . Lovelier than the crown worn by a bride. You could place it on the top of Mount Sinai where God gave the Torah—it flamed there like the flames through which God spoke from the Mount . . .

"Wonderful!" said Reb Itzik the scribe. "Tell me, who made all these wonderful things?"

"I did!" said Joseph, who was only a youngster, delighted at this opportunity the old man had given him to explain. "I made all the designs, and they were given to Reb Zorach, the goldsmith, and he made them all according to my designs. Exactly as I had drawn them. I've kept all the drawings. I took them back when he had finished. I can show them to you!"

Reb Abraham listened proudly to his son. It made him think of his own wood carvings that he had made as a boy and as a young man, even after his marriage. He was glad that Joseph was taking after him.

Joseph's mother, Rachel, too, looked at her son with fond pride. So did some of the other women standing round her. Joseph felt embarrassed.

"Clever boy!" said Reb Itzik. "You deserve a pat on the cheek for that!"

When Reb Abraham had written in the last three words of the Sepher Torah with the quill pen, and the cantor from the Beth Hamedrash had chanted the final portion, concluding with the three closing words, "Leini Kol Yisroel," "In the sight of all Israel," and the people had responded "Chazak, Chazak," the band struck up a merry tune and they all went off to the synagogue.

Jews walked through the streets with lighted plaited Havdalah candles of all colors. Young boys carried paper lanterns, shining red and green and yellow and blue. Joseph had made all these paper lanterns—not just paper cutouts, but decorated with all sorts of drawings made with colored pencil—trees, flowers, houses, sun and moon and stars, even illustrations of the Pentateuch.

Then came something unexpected that the common folk, the artisans, the carters, the carriers had arranged quietly, without telling anyone outside their own circle. They suddenly appeared in the streets in masquerade, warriors with wooden swords and pikes and flaming torches, on horseback. They rode in front of the bridal procession, in front of the new Sepher Torah that was being carried to the synagogue under the new bridal canopy of white silk made specially for this occasion. Four tall men held the poles of the canopy. Under the canopy walked Reb Abraham, holding the new Sepher Torah, royally adorned and bejeweled. He held it tightly clasped in his arms, against his breast. On his right walked Reb Itzik, the scribe, and on his left Reb Pinchas.

The riders were headed by three "Generals" on white horses. The one in the center was in blue uniform; the other two in white. All three held blue and white flags. The flag in the middle bore in gold lettering the words "Degel Machne Yehuda," "The Banner of the Army of Israel." The flag on the left was inscribed "Gibori Yisroel," "The Heroes of Israel," and the one on the right "Dovid Melech Yisroel Chai Ve-Kaim," "David King of Israel Lives For Ever!"

Behind the riders came the band playing. And after the canopy with the new Sepher Torah under it the whole town of Jews, men and women, the young people, boys and girls, children. Big lighted candles shining from all the windows. Every Jewish house astir. From the windows and balconies of the rich they had hung carpets and tapestries. The lighted candles in all the windows, the burning Havdalah tapers, the torches and the paper lanterns all together, with the flashing of the women's jewelry and the shining stars made a blaze of light. The band didn't stop playing. The men and the boys danced alongside, singing, and clapping their hands. The women and girls who were not allowed to sing wove in a dance in and out behind the horses, clapping their hands.

Suddenly there was a cry of alarm. The synagogue on fire! But it was only the Jewish fire brigade doing lifesaving exercises.

As the crowd came toward the synagogue, Jews poured out from everywhere, dancing toward them, with scrolls of the Law in their arms. And so, singing and dancing and clapping their hands they all entered the synagogue.

Hundreds of candles and all the bright lamps in the synagogue had been lighted. The four men carrying the four poles of the canopy and the three men under the canopy, Reb Abraham, Reb Itzik, and Reb Pinchas, went up on the *Almemor* with the bride, the new Sepher Torah. The band stood under the Almenmor playing. Men with scrolls of the Law, youths with Gemaras and heder boys with *Chumashim*, danced in a ring round the Almemor. The women and girls stood against the walls clapping their hands, crying: "Next year may we go to meet the Messiah!"

The riders on their horses and the crowds for whom there was no room in the synagogue remained outside, and danced round and round in the snow, under the frosty sky and the dancing stars.

In the Beth Hamedrash they danced on the tables and on

the benches, round the Almemor, forgetting all their daily cares and worries, dancing, singing, and the little tailor, their rebbe, the saint, danced with them, and a host of angels danced with them.

After midnight the band played the "Vehi Binsoa," "And it came to pass when the Ark set forward," the opening words for the Reading of the Law, and the cantor read the first portion of the Book of Genesis from the new scroll. Then the crowd dispersed.

The new scroll stayed in the Beth Hamedrash, which bore the name of the little tailor, because it was here that he had prayed and studied.

2

But this Siyum Hasepher was about the last merrymaking the pious Jews of the town had. For soon after there was a big fire, and many houses were burned down; and then the whole town was changed.

There were also Germans living in the town, weavers working hand-looms, though in the large towns like Lodz they already had modern power-looms. After the war a tall German came to the town with a lot of money and built a power mill—nothing as big as those in Lodz, but it had a tall chimney, and it had a siren that sounded three times a day. Before long a rich Pole built another power mill, and then Reb Zalman Finkelstein sold his brewery, and he too built a power mill. Overnight the town became an industrial center. The old poverty disappeared, for almost the entire population, Christians and Jews—many peasants from the villages as well—went to work in the mills. On the sites of the small, dilapidated, wooden shacks that had been burned down there were soon several fine new two- and three- and four-story brick buildings and modern shops and hotels, and restaurants and dance halls. And with them came new openings for employment—forwarding agencies for goods, travel agencies, insurance brokers, and insurance agents. Luxury articles appeared in the shops. All the artisans had plenty of work, and some of them had to engage workmen and apprentices. And the railway was extended to the town.

The whole way of life in the town changed. And when the old rabbi died they replaced him—it was now a much larger town—with a modern crown rabbi, a tall, middle-aged man with a golden beard, cut short and neatly trimmed, and with intelligent brown eyes. The truly pious Jews, who were not so many now—though a great number had not changed outwardly and still pretended to be as pious as before—were not very happy about this rabbi because he hardly ever interfered with their private lives. He didn't worry, as the former rabbi had, whether the Jews of the town lived pious Jewishly observant lives according to the Shulchan Aruch. Before long it was common talk that the rabbi was reading Zionist literature, that he taught everything upside down, that what mattered to him was T'nach and Maimonides' *Guide to the Perplexed*—he was a philosopher, a "German." He walked along the street erect with head up, a proud man. Those who didn't like him grumbled—"Thinks he's a Duke, or the Emperor himself!"

The young people divided into two sections—most of them became proletarianized, on modern lines, like in all the big towns. These were openly irreligious. Among those who remained religious there were also two trends—those who continued the old ways unchanged, and those who took up modern education and began to form the Jewish intelligentsia, the Jewish intellectuals, with the emphasis on the "Jewish." Some of them frequented the new rabbi's house.

Then suddenly, as suddenly as the fire had broken out before, an epidemic struck the town. It was mostly young children who died. It caused a panic. It was just after Passover, when the ground is growing green and the trees bloom and the sun shines warm—spring! And at that moment of growth and blooming, the streets and the alleyways of the town resounded to the cries of despairing mothers—"Help! My child is dying!" Pious women rushed to the synagogue and sobbed and prayed before the Holy Ark of the Law; they went to the little tailor's Beth Hamedrash, lighted candles there, assembled Jews to sit and read Psalms. They ran to the cemetery and pleaded at the grave of the little tailor and the graves of the other dead to intercede for the town. It didn't help.

Lag B'Omer arrived. The teachers in the heder gave their boys wooden swords and bows and arrows, and they all went to the forest outside the town, and split into two "armies"— one was called "Life" and the other "Death." The two "armies" waged "war" against each other, and "Life" won. "Life" routed "Death." Even that didn't help.

People began to say that the epidemic was a punishment for the sins of its inhabitants; that when innocent young children die, it is because of the sins of their elders. "It's because of the rabbi and his modern ways," the pious Jews said. "He has led the whole town off the right path." Others said that it was "the new factories, the big power mills, all this modern way of life." And "flouting religion, the open defiance of the laws of Judaism." The pious women blamed the young girls, "the shameless hussies who go about with boys and sin flagrantly!" The community leaders summoned the parents of these young sinners, and these pleaded that it wasn't their fault, that they couldn't do anything with their growing children. The younger ones listened, but the older defied their parents openly, and sneered at them and called them fools and fanatics.

Then something unexpected happened again. A rabbi, a rebbe, passed through the town. He stopped there for only a few hours, and it was announced that he would speak between Mincha and Maariv in the little tailor's Beth Hamedrash. The pious men and the pious women waited for dusk to fall, for the time for Mincha to pass, so that they should hear what the rebbe had to say. A spark of hope had kindled in the hearts of those mothers whose children lay ill. Nobody knew who this rebbe was, or where he came from. They wondered. . . . An angel from heaven. . . ?

36

The sun had just set. The Beth Hamedrash was packed tight with people. They stood in the gangways and at the back and in the doorway. The rebbe in his tallith stood on the Almemor, and spoke—about the epidemic in the town. Women sobbed as they listened; the men sighed and groaned.

"When young children die in a town it is because the town is full of sin!" the rebbe thundered.

That made the women in their part of the synagogue cry and weep aloud.

Then the rebbe started talking about hell and about the punishment that awaited the wicked there. He pictured the flames, the barrels of boiling pitch, the red-hot pincers with which the tongues of the blasphemers were torn out, the vipers and scorpions that attached themselves to shameless hussies and bit into their hearts. And he concluded with these words: "I command the plague to cease, to leave this town!"

A sigh of relief passed through the crowd. Some people looked up in the air, expecting to see the Angel of Death fly past on his way out of the town.

As soon as the rebbe had finished he descended from the Almemor. The people drew aside to let him pass. But no one saw his face, which had been hidden in the tallith, and he and his gabbai who had accompanied him vanished before anyone realized that they had gone. Into thin air.

The talk in the town was that it had been the little tailor who had come back to help them. But it turned out that it was neither the little tailor, nor as some said an angel from heaven, but a real rebbe who had passed through the town on his way to another town. And this is the way it all came out.

A young woman in the town was in labor, in great pain. Her husband had determined to ask the rebbe to help her. But the rebbe had vanished. The young husband ran through the town trying to find some trace of him. At last he discovered the coachman who had taken the rebbe and his gabbai to the railway station. He drove to the station and found the rebbe still there, waiting for his train. But the gabbai tried to keep him away from the rebbe; he said he mustn't be disturbed.

The young man pushed the gabbai aside, and fell to his knees before the rebbe, and begged him to help his wife in her difficult childbirth.

The rebbe said to him: "The fact that my gabbai tried to prevent you reaching me is proof that the Adversary in heaven doesn't want to let your prayers reach God's Mercy Seat. But if a man perseveres, the walls of obstruction must fall. Go home to your wife, and before you cross the threshold cry out as loud as you can 'The rebbe said that if you don't have the child at once, he will come with his stick and chase you out of bed!'"

The young man did as the rebbe said, and the child, their first, was born immediately.

The news spread rapidly, and several leading men drove at once to the station, where they found the rebbe still waiting on the platform, and they begged him to come back to the town and "be our rebbe!"

The rebbe refused. But the men were persistent. "Rebbe, we won't go away till you agree to become our rebbe!"

Then the rebbe agreed. "Firmness conquers!" he said.

It was a hot summer. The rebbe stayed at first in the big inn owned by Reb Ozie, one of the most pious and strictly observant Jews in the town. All the time the rebbe lived there the place was packed with people, men and women, who came with written petitions, asking him for help. And still no one knew who the rebbe was, not even his name and the place from which he came. Some people found it strange; then they said, "One doesn't question God's messengers! Hasn't he proved himself by his actions? He said the child would be born; and he said the epidemic would go, and it went!"

There were two long tables in the inn, on which lay the books that the rebbe had written and had brought with him to sell. Two young men, the sons-in-law of rich homes, were the salesmen. They couldn't serve their customers quickly enough. People pushed the money into their hands. Everybody wanted the rebbe's books, especially those books which described in Yiddish all sorts of ailments, giving their names and their symptoms, and saying how they should be treated—with charms and spells and prayers. Some of the books were about demons and evil spirits, dybbukim and the like.

The town was agog with the rebbe. The doors of Reb Ozie's inn never closed. The pressure of the crowds tore them off their hinges.

After he had spent several weeks in the town the rebbe revealed to the people who he was, and gave his distinguished lineage for the past ten generations. Everybody begged him to remain in the town and to be their rebbe. "God sent you to us," they said, "to save our town from sin."

Again the rebbe agreed. The town gave him a fine house. And the rebbe's wife came with their children and their furniture, and the rebbe settled in the town for good.

Now there was together with the stir and bustle of the new factory life also the passion and the zeal of the new Hasidic revival. The rebbe attracted Hasidim from towns and villages from many miles around, even from very great distances. The pious Jews began to think that the old religious life that had been largely swept away by the new factory ways was returning, that the rebbe's presence in the town would banish the forces of evil that had taken possession there. He would make the factories stop. They would sink into the ground. Neither the blast of the sirens nor the thick smoke from the factory chimneys would disturb their old ways if only the rebbe said to them, "Depart!"

The upheaval that had transformed a poor small town into a big industrial and commercial center had still left it very provincial. The old artisans and the new factory workers grew to become distinct from the bourgeois middle class. A differentiation of classes developed. A cleavage between the factory proletariat and the emerging bourgeoisie, and between the free-thinkers, the God-deniers (mostly very naive and ignorant), and the religious Jews, both genuine and hypocrites.

Before long the workers and artisans began using new words that they had not known before—*Socialism, Karl Marx, International, Revolution.* Many merely repeated the words without bothering to discover their meaning. Some couldn't pronounce the words properly. Some wags deliberately mispronounced them, thinking it funny. But there were others who began to philosophize about these words, to read additional meanings into them. Karl Marx became a prophet to them, something like Moses. He had a face like a rabbi, with a big beard and stern yet kindly eyes, and his Torah, his teaching, was justice for the oppressed and the exploited, and liberation from slavery.

In the same way as the rebbe had suddenly arrived out of the blue for the religious Jews of the town, so now not one but two "rebbes" arrived for the proletariat. Two strange young men turned up one day; they had thin pale faces and long black hair, and they wore Russian blouses.

People said that they had come from Warsaw, and were the kind who wrote the books that the atheists in the town had been reading. Philosophers. But the workers knew them as "the delegates." A few knew that they were teachers and had come to open a school in the town.

This was true. The religious Jews promptly declared that they wouldn't allow a "Goyish" school for Jewish children. There was a buzz of angry talk in the little tailor's Beth Hamedrash:

"We're not going to stand having a school here where the children will be taught to be atheists! We want our children to be Jews!"

No school was opened yet, but there was talk of an application having been made to the authorities for permission to open the school. Meanwhile the two young men were giving lessons to small groups of workers. There were many in the town whose parents had been too poor to send them to heder, and they couldn't read or write even Yiddish, let alone Russian. All they knew was a little Hebrew, enough to read the prayers. Now these young people, young men and women, even some who were married, took eagerly to their lessons. And before long the authorities gave permission to open an elementary school for the Jewish population. The religious Jews had tried hard to prevent it, but had failed. The story went round that the "German" rabbi had been responsible; that he had written to the governor supporting the idea of the school.

Very soon after a second school was opened, where the instruction was not in Yiddish, but in Hebrew with the Sephardic pronunciation.

Now the town was really divided; the modern-educated rabbi against the Hasidic rebbe and his Hasidim (with the support of all the "enlightened" people in the town), the modern schools against the old-fashioned heder. Besides Karl Marx there was now Theodor Herzl, besides Socialism there was Zionism, and besides the International there was Hatikvah.

And now the workers were talking of a strike. They were holding secret meetings in the woods outside the town, with impassioned speeches about Socialism; there were heated discussions, and they sang revolutionary songs.

And young men and women of the bourgeoisie sang Hebrew songs and spoke nostalgically of Zion.

All sorts of newspapers were being read in the town—Yiddish, Hebrew, Polish, and Russian. And pamphlets and books, some of which had to be hidden from the police—and Zionist literature, which had to be hidden from pious parents.

The eyes of the workers flamed with revolutionary fire. The eyes of the Zionists burned with hope that the end of the Galut was in sight.

41

Reb Abraham and his wife Rachel had no other children besides Joseph and Miriam, who were now both grown up. Rachel had indeed had another child, but stillborn, and she had nearly died in childbirth. It had left her ailing.

Though they had a big rich home they lived modestly. They did not show off, with fine furniture or luxurious living. But there was something they missed and longed for. To Rachel it was the sadly beautiful chant of the Gemara she had been accustomed to hear in her father's house. Reb Abraham was no great Talmud scholar, and even if he sat over a Talmud folio sometimes, his voice was not heard. He liked to read with his eyes, not aloud, and to meditate silently. Both Reb Abraham and Rachel felt sad and oppressed because of something they couldn't define. They couldn't say what it was that frightened and saddened them. Rachel sensed it first in her husband before he sensed it in her. He didn't question her, and she was too shy to question him. So they both went about sad and hurt. She thought it might be business difficulties that worried him. But she had never spoken to him about his business affairs. She didn't attempt to understand them. So she didn't speak. And she suffered in silence.

Joseph took after his father in many ways—he also liked to meditate, to dream, to draw, to make carvings in wood, little figures of people and of animals. He had also inherited some of his grandparents' characteristics, through his mother—he was humble, he loved truth and justice, and he felt drawn to the poor, those who worked hard and suffered want. He worshipped the memory of his great-grandfather, the little tailor. He was tall and handsome, and he had brains. He studied in his great-grandfather's Beth Hamedrash, and he was at first a religiously observant Jew.

But later he had begun to waver and doubt. He still went to the Beth Hamedrash, but not to study. He still sat over a Gemara, but he had different thoughts in his mind. He always had his penknife with him, and he carved bits of wood at the table where he sat. At home he stayed up half the night drawing and carving wood. He imagined King Solomon's

42

palace that the master builders of Tyre had constructed, and the Temple. He got the idea into his head that he would decorate the outside of his father's house with paintings and carvings, to make it look like a palace. The thought of King Solomon began to dominate his mind. He read Proverbs and Ecclesiastes over again, and he searched in the Midrash for every mention of King Solomon. He was fascinated by the Haggadic tales about the wise king, and his love for beautiful things.

Joseph imagined how the Jews lived in those days, what the Holy Land had looked like then, especially Jerusalem. And the hills, the valleys, the gardens, the fields, the woods. But most of all his fantasy was busy with King Solomon's palace, and with his Temple. His imagination played with the pictures of the palace, all glass and mirrors, where the wise king ruled over all the seventy tongues of the earth, and understood the languages of the birds and beasts, and how he tricked the Queen of Sheba in front of everybody. He saw King Solomon's throne, which he had himself fashioned, and on which he sat and ruled—all of gold, with birds and beasts of gold, with living birds and beasts on each of the steps of the throne. When the king mounted the first step the bird and the beast on either side of that step bowed to him; the same on the second step, and the third and the fourth—on each of the twelve steps of his throne. The bird on the top step was an eagle, and the beast a lion. They set the crown on the king's head, and placed the gold scepter in his hand. The crown was studded with jewels; there were twelve big rubies in it representing the twelve tribes, and on the top of the crown a huge diamond, the largest in the world, that radiated so much light that no one could look at it.

Joseph painted the lower half of the front of his father's house like a blue sea, so that it looked from a distance as if the house stood in the water, in the midst of the waves. And he painted the upper part like white marble, with gold columns, and trees with leaves and vines with clusters of grapes, and the moon and stars. It looked wonderful. People came from ever so far away to see it, and his parents were proud of their son, and placed great hopes in him. His mother hoped he would become heir to the lttle tailor, with his piety and goodness. His father wasn't sure what he hoped for from his son, but he saw him as himself over again, when he had as a young man loved to carve figures out of wood.

The hopes of both were disappointed. Suddenly Joseph began to frequent the house of the crown rabbi. At first he concealed it from his parents. But the change it made in him was too great to hide it or to want to hide it for long, especially from his father. The pretense weighed too heavily on his soul. So he finally confessed to his parents:

"It would have been wasting my life to sit all the time studying Gemara," he said. "I feel that I am only now beginning to live."

Rachel wept, and Abraham bowed his head.

Joseph kept bringing books home now; he literally devoured them. He read day and night. His father didn't try to stop him. He had also when he was young read profane literature. But it didn't please him. He kept silent only because that was his nature. The older he became the more silent he grew, more thoughtful, more sad.

Rachel mutely sought her husband's and her son's eyes; she couldn't penetrate to their souls. How can I, a simple woman, know what is going on in their hearts? But a much greater fear assailed Rachel's mind when she heard what people in the town were saying about her daughter.

"It isn't true!" she told herself. "Enemies have spread lies about my child! Evil tongues have said these things! They said the same about me when I was young. They said my parents had to marry me to Abraham, because I was already his before we married. . . . Now they say the same about Miriam! My daughter is a good girl! She has the blood of the little tailor in her! She couldn't do such things as they accuse her of! He

44

wouldn't allow it! He would raise all heaven against it! No, it isn't true!"

She reminded herself how beautiful and how pure Miriam had looked at the Siyum Hasepher, when she had come into the room with the silver tray, and had handed Reb Itzik, the scribe, of blessed memory, the mantle and the binding sash for the Sepher Torah that he had written in honor of the little tailor. She had looked like an angel, a true descendant of the little tailor.

And now? There was a shamelsss smile on her lips. There was a bold look in her eyes, and her cheeks glowed, not like a young girl's but like a married woman's rising from her marriage bed. She had become utterly changed.

Her thoughts turned to her husband. Perhaps he knew something of what was going on. A man saw things more quickly. That might be the reason why he was so silent and sad. He didn't speak to her about it because he didn't want to hurt her, wanted to spare her.

What was it she had heard people whispering in the town about Miriam? That she was going about with a Christian. . . . Was that why Miriam was always rushing out of the house after supper, and didn't return till late at night? Even Friday night and Saturday night. And all day Sunday. . . . And when she came back she went straight to her room, and shut herself up there. Avoided meeting her father and mother. . . .

Rachel pressed her hands to her forehead and wept. The next minute she scolded herself for believing such things about Miriam. It isn't true! It can't be true!

Joseph saw the tears in his mother's eyes, and his father grieving, silent and sad; and he knew it was because of him and because of his sister. He didn't know what he could possibly say to them—there was nothing that would comfort them. There was a complete revolution in the Jewish life of this town. The old beliefs and the old ways of life were being abandoned. And the little tailor's great-grandchildren had not escaped. He began to avoid his father, to avoid having to talk to him about it. He wouldn't be able to see it, as he, his son, saw it. It was not a wayward revolt by a few young people—it was a complete change on the part of the entire young generation, and it had very natural and irresistible causes. This thing that was happening in the town was not always and in all ways to his own liking. Many of the young people didn't understand the new ideas; they misinterpreted them. They were intoxicated by the new freedom, and it led them to excesses. He still thought that his great-grandfather, the little tailor, had been a fine man, a man of spiritual greatness, full of human love.

He wanted to understand his great-grandfather. He thought a lot about him, about the many stories and legends told about him. At bottom, it was the idea of the Jewish prophets, truth and justice and the love of our fellow men. It was not only Jewish. It was the striving of all decent people in all sections of the human race. They had all struggled—not only we Jews—to bring about a better world. Every idealistic movement strove toward it. But as soon as the ideals were accepted the performance fell away, and a degeneration set in. Each of these movements had adjusted itself to the time and the conditions had become debased.

Joseph thought of the Hasidic rebbe who had come so strangely to settle in the town, and how his Hasidism was a degeneration, a falling away from the high idealism of the original Hasidim. He thought of his parents, and of how they would suffer when they discovered the truth about his sister Miriam. He knew what she was doing, and he couldn't hold her back. He couldn't even blame her, though he thought differently about these things. But he understood how it had happened that she had fallen in love with a Christian, a poor peasant's son, who was now a workman in one of the big mills in the town. She was intoxicated by the ideas of Socialism and the brotherhood of man, of internationalism, of free thought. She knew little about the essence of Judaism—because Jewish girls were not taught, as the boys were, the Bible, the Talmud, and Jewish history, old and modern. She didn't know the Hebrew prophets, to realize that in essence the teachings of Socialism were already there in their teachings, were part of Judaism.

3

One of the buildings that had escaped the big fire was a little tumbledown house in which a Jew named Wolf Jonachek lived. The house had once belonged to his great-grandfather, Reb Mechel, who had been gabbai to the little tailor. It stood outside the town. The walls were crumbling, and Wolf Jonachek had propped them up with poles. The windows were tiny, and some of the panes were broken and the holes stuffed with rags.

Not because Wolf Jonachek hadn't enough money to put in new windows, but because the window frames were rotted, and he wasn't going to have new window frames made. He wanted to keep the house as it was, unchanged. Those windows which were in were black with dust and grime. The slate roof was overgrown with moss; it looked like a carpet of green velvet. The roof was so low, and kept sinking lower, that the neighbors' goats jumped up on the roof, nibbled at the moss, and went to sleep there. Little boys climbed up on the roof, and pulled the goats' beards and horns, and jumped down from the roof, just like the goats.

Superstitious women were afraid to pass the house at night. They said evil spirits haunted it. But by day it was a venerated relic of the former life of the town, as it had been in the old days. When the sun shone it made the grimy windows blaze with color.

There was a stagnant pool behind the house, covered with green slime. Wags called it the moat of the "castle."

Wolf Jonachek's neighbors were Christians, many of them ropemakers. They left their hemp and their finished ropes lying about with no fear of their neighbor, the most notorious thief in the entire area. They knew he would never steal from his neighbors. They left their pigsties open, and their goats and fowls wandering about freely. They had no use for locks and keys. They knew everything would be safe. And they were right. Nothing was ever taken. They lived at peace with their neighbor Wolf Jonachek. They frequented his home, drank tea with him, and sometimes something stronger; and when they needed it he helped them out with a loan. When one of these Christian neighbors spoke about Wolf Jonachek he said: "Good Jew! Nice fellow! Honest man!"

Wolf Jonachek kept no cow, but he had a goat and fowls. He let them run about outside with his neighbors' goats and fowls. And when he or his wife scattered corn for his goat and his fowls they didn't mind that the neighbors' goats and fowls also ate it. And if a fowl belonging to a neighbor laid an egg, and Wolf Jonachek found it, he took it to his neighbor, and said: "It's yours!"

"He's an honest Jew!" the neighbors said.

Wolf Jonachek's parents had both died when he was a small boy; he had been brought up by a grandfather who didn't want him to become an artisan, a worker with his hands. True, his father, Wolf's great-grandfather, had been a fence. But afterwards he had become the little tailor's gabbai. True, he himself, the gabbai's son, was a fence too, like his father in his early years. But he wanted the boy to be a scholar, a learned Jew. So he drove young Wolf to the Beth Hamedrash, sometimes with an angry word, sometimes with a box on the ears. "Go and study!"

But Wolf had no head for study. All that remained with him

from the Beth Hamedrash was his ability to read the Hebrew of the prayer book, and to translate a verse in the Pentateuch, word by word, without really grasping the sense of the whole verse, or its relation with the next verse. He was more interested to watch his grandfather doing a trade with a thief—sometimes a Jew, sometimes a Christian—examine the booty, and pay him his price.

When he was older and he needed money, he got a job with a carter. The work was hard, and he had to sleep in the stable, with the horses, and get up in the morning at dawn to feed them; and his master didn't spare his blows.

Then his grandfather died, and Wolf Jonachek left the carter and went to live in his grandfather's house. He persuaded one of the thieves who used to bring stolen goods to his grandfather to take him along with him on one of his burgling expeditions, and to teach him the trade. He became an expert thief. He was especially good at opening locks. There wasn't a lock anywhere around that he couldn't open.

By the time Wolf Jonachek married, he was known in the whole district as the most skilled and most successful thief anywhere around. There was nobody like him to steal a horse from under his owner's nose. He could walk into a big store and come out undetected with a valuable object in his pocket.

He had by this time worked out a very interesting moral code for himself, and he stuck to it.

He was tall and broad-shouldered, with a physique like a Samson, with fists like sledgehammers, his neck like an anvil, and his chest was massive. Later he grew an enormous beard, longer and broader than that of the most pious Jew in the town. He wore a long caftan, and a cap with a peak, such as all the pious Jews at that time wore. On the Sabbath he wore the same kind of Sabbath garb as the pious Jews wore, a fine caftan, with a broad woollen girdle round his middle, a silk scarf, and a velvet hat—like all the best people in the town.

In his own way he was a pious religious Jew. He went to the synagogue for the Sabbath service. He held that it was the duty of a Jew to keep Judaism. And by Judaism he meant

Jewish tradition, the old Jewish ways and customs; he didn't like the new ways that had come in since the factories had been built. He hated them as much as all the pious Jews did.

He had a big tallith, in which he wrapped himself from head to foot. He was a Cohen, and when he went up to the Ark to *duchan*, to recite the Blessing of the Priests, his voice was heard above all the others. He set great store on being called up to the Reading of the Law, and he paid more for the privilege than the richest man in the town.

Wolf Jonachek gave with a generous hand for the maintenance of Judaism in the town. He gave to the synagogue and the Beth Hamedrash, the Talmud Torah, the *Chevra Kadisha*, the Dowries for Brides Society, for everything that would strengthen Judaism.

The Beth Hamedrash was a particular object of his generosity, first, because it was the little tailor's Beth Hamedrash, and was named after him, and he considered that he had a special relationship with the little tailor and with his Beth Hamedrash, for his great-grandfather had been the little tailor's gabbai, and second, because he needed a rebbe.

So when the rebbe had settled in the town, Wolf Jonachek had been one of the first to become one of his Hasidim.

Wolf Jonachek was specially devoted to trying to save Jewish girls from becoming old maids. If a young woman was so ugly or so poor that the dowry from the Brides Society wasn't enough to tempt a man, they came to Wolf Jonachek, and he found an old bachelor or a widower in a neighboring town, or in one of the villages, gave him a hearty slap on the back, so that he nearly fell, and said:

"I want you to marry this girl! You'll get a dowry! You'll get a complete outfit for her and for you! You'll get furniture! And you'll have a lovely wedding—everything of the best!"

And there was no escape. The man knew that what Wolf Jonachek said was final. He must obey.

He never went to a man who was divorced, who had left his wife or his wife had left him. He felt that a man who wasn't good enough to keep his first wife, or she wasn't good enough and he couldn't mend her, was no man, was no use to any woman. A man's got to be a man, he said. He's got to earn money and he's got to keep his wife and his household; he must be a craftsman, or a carter, or a carrier; but never a thief, because a thief must marry only among his own kind.

He always told the newly married couple that they mustn't quarrel; and that if they were short of money they should come to him.

Even now, when the town had grown so big, Wolf Jonachek still played the part of the peacemaker, the conciliator, a kind of rabbi, a kind of judge. If husband and wife couldn't get on, but they didn't want a divorce, the woman would go to Wolf Jonachek and pour her heart out to him. Then he would send for her husband, or he would go to the husband, and he would talk to him, and he would put things right. The same if two Jews had a dispute. They generally went to Wolf Jonachek, instead of going to the rabbi for judgment. And they accepted Wolf's settlement of their dispute. Usually it was satisfactory to both parties. In any case, no one wanted to incur Wolf's anger.

Desecrating the Sabbath was a risky business if Wolf Jonachek was anywhere around. He would stop the man, swear at him, and make him promise that he wouldn't do it again. And if the man didn't listen to him he knocked him down. If he met a young man in the street, one of those new "free-thinkers," walking about on the Sabbath day with a cigarette in his mouth, he left fly at him. Such a man was not to be envied. Wolf Jonachek didn't like all this newfangled Socialism they were talking about. He knew about the Trade Union and Labor movement, and he wasn't quite sure if this was something to be allowed or not. On the one hand, they told him that all the workers wanted was better conditions; they were working too hard, too many hours, for too little pay. It was only justice to improve their lot. And Wolf Jonachek was always on the side of justice.

But on the other hand, people said that the Socialists wanted to turn the world upside down; they wanted a world where there would be no rich and no poor, where everybody would be equal. They wanted "freedom," to chuck the Czar off the throne, to take over the government, seize the factories, the banks, all the business concerns, all the shops. And that was something Wolf didn't hold with at all. He laughed at it. Fools! But he didn't do anything about it.

"There are plenty of police to deal with these mad folk," he said. "And if there are not enough police, there's the army to deal with them. Why should I worry?"

But when they told him that these people didn't believe in God, and that they made fun of Judaism, and of every form of religion, he flew into a fury.

More than anything else Wolf Jonachek hated an informer, a tale-bearer. And if he got hold of one of these, the man was lucky if he got away alive. And he hated the idea of a Jew going to the law courts against another Jew. Almost always, when a Jew committed an offence against the law, the police, from the inspector down to the lowest policeman, went to Wolf Jonachek, and told him that so and so had done this or the other. And then Wolf Jonachek dealt with him. The police left it to him.

If a policeman arrested a Jew and brought a charge against him, somebody was sure to tell Wolf Jonachek within minutes. And then Wolf would call the police inspector to his house, or he would go up to him in the street, when he was in full uniform, with his sword at his side, and his revolver in his holster, and he would slap his face, twice, left cheek and right cheek, with such force that his hat with the cockade on it flew off.

The inspector, who didn't want to lose the weekly wage he got from Wolf Jonachek, not much less than his weekly pay from the government, didn't say a word, and the Jew was immediately released.

If any one of Wolf's gang molested someone in the town, or stole from somebody in the town without Wolf knowing, that man was sure to spend the next month or two in bed, recovering from his blows. That didn't mean to say that Wolf didn't

53

send a doctor to treat the man immediately, and pay the doctor's fees, and send him good things to eat, till he was better. But before he got out of bed, Wolf came to see him and warned him not to do it again.

All the thieves in the town, Jewish and Christian, regarded Wolf Jonachek as their chief. The strongest among them went in fear of him, even those who used a knife or an iron bar, though Wolf never fought except with his bare fists. In a fight, all he did was to fling off his caftan, and every time his fist shot out somebody hit the ground.

He had a well-organized system for his thieving operations. He himself specialized on the stables of the nobility. He had a way with horses. Before anyone knew what had happened he had unlocked the stable door and ridden off with the horse.

He was an expert cracksman. No safe was too much for him.

And he dealt with the receivers himself. For every one of his gang. He told the members of his gang where to go, what to take. They had strict orders never to rob the poor. That was part of his moral code. Indeed, when he got to know of a family that was struggling hard to make a living, he would call one of his men and tell him to break into that house, and to leave money and goods on the table, that had been taken from some wealthy house. And though the victim knew who had taken his property and where it had gone he kept quiet—it wasn't healthy to complain. The police wouldn't do a thing where Wolf Jonachek was concerned.

If one of his men blundered, and stole from a house that wasn't really rich, the stolen goods were returned to the victim the same day. This was all part of Wolf Jonachek's moral code.

Wolf Jonachek's wife's name was Golda. When they had married she had been a good-looking, strapping wench. Just the right mate for him. The son she bore him nine months after their marriage was the image of his father. He grew up tall and broad-shouldered, like Wolf. They named him Jacob; but they called him Yankel, and later it became Yantek. He wore a short jacket and a blue cap with a glossy black peak. He had a fat face, which made him look dull. He had big yellow teeth, and big brown eyes, with the look of a simple soul in them. He went to heder, unwillingly, like his father before him; and he learned even less. But he had to say his prayers, and he knew that much Hebrew, and he had to keep the laws and customs of Judaism, and be dressed on the Sabbath like a Jew, with a long caftan and a velvet hat, and a sash round his middle. And go with his father to the service in the Beth Hamedrash.

But if you looked more closely at Yankel's fat face, you saw a certain gentleness there, a kind of slumbering intelligence, not yet awakened.

Against his father's wish Yankel became a thief. He stole at first without his father knowing. When his father found out he gave him a good hiding. It was the worst thing that could have happened to Jonachek, that his son should be a thief. He decided to take Yankel to the rebbe, to ask the rebbe to give him his blessing, so that he should be an honest man.

"Holy Rebbe!" Wolf Jonachek cried. "I'll give you any amount of money, so that my son . . ."

At that moment Sheba, the rebbe's youngest daughter came into the room, to ask her father something. She didn't stay more than a moment or two. But her face remained in Yankel's heart. From that moment, whatever Yankel was doing the thought of Sheba was in his mind. It obsessed him.

The rebbe promised Wolf Jonachek that God would listen to his prayer. He asked Wolf to come to his Sabbath table with Yankel.

Yankel had no desire now any more for the Christian peasant wench in one of the neighboring villages to whom he used to go. As for Zlatte, the Jewish maid-servant in the town, she had never really attracted him. He still saw the village wench because he was full of unrest, which drove him to her; and he still went thieving, though every Sabbath he went with his

55

father and the other Hasidim to the rebbe's table.

Till one day he said to himself: "This has got to stop! All that I've been doing till now has got to stop!"

His desire for the rebbe's daughter grew so strong that he couldn't do anything else but hang around the rebbe's house in the hope of seeing her. One night he walked all night round the rebbe's house, watching her window. He kept hoping that he would see her in the morning when she opened the shutters of her room. He imagined himself saying "Good morning!" to her when he saw her. Then he decided that he wouldn't say anything, but he would bow to her silently, as they bowed in the synagogue at prayer to God. That was how he would bow to Sheba when she appeared at her bedroom window.

He put on his best suit, for the occasion. Then his face clouded: "But Yankel, the suit you are wearing is stolen! You stole it from Shlomo Stern's shop!"

He determined to return all his stolen suits and everything else that he had stolen, everything to its owner: "This is yours! I stole it! I'm sorry! Please take it back!"

In this mood he even though that he would get up in the market place and call out aloud to everybody: "I'm no longer a thief! I've stopped being a thief! I'm a Jew now like all good decent Jews! An honest man! I'm going to be a religious observant Jew!"

His heart melted with happiness as he went out. There was a drizzling rain all that night, and Yankel got soaked through. He was wet and cold. There was a biting north wind. And it was pitch dark. Yankel walked all night up and down outside and round the rebbe's house, where the rebbe's young daughter Sheba was sleeping.

On his way to the rebbe's house Yankel had passed the Beth Hamedrash. There was a light there, and he had stopped to look through one of the windows. He saw several older Jews and a few young students sitting at a table studying. He made an effort to hear their Gemara chant, their sad, persistent, and finally triumphant song, as they sat there swaying all the time to the rhythm of their song. Their pale, melancholy faces shone. Yankel felt it was warm and good in there, and he wanted to go in and join them. But he didn't go in, because he suddenly remembered that he was a thief.

He went away from the Beth Hamedrash with bowed head, feeling ashamed of himself. And he walked about all night in the dark, up and down outside and round the rebbe's house.

The cocks were crowing. Yankel shivered, not only because he was cold and tired. The sky was beginning to turn gray. And through the gray he heard hard steady monotonous footsteps—big clumsy top boots—beating on the pavement and the roadway. Must be one of the night watchmen keeping guard that the shops shouldn't be burgled in the night. He thought the footsteps were coming toward him. Without thinking Yankel's hand moved toward the top of his boot where he kept his knife, ready. Meanwhile the rain had stopped. It was beginning again now, but very fine, like needles.

Yankel felt sorry now because he hadn't gone to heder when his father had sent him there. If I had gone to heder regularly, he reproached himself now, I would be a scholar, a rabbi. But he had preferred to play with the other boys, to play ball, to play horses. And most of all he had loved to go by himself into the forest outside the town, and catch birds. He always let them fly away afterwards. But once a little bird that he held in his hand had struggled violently to get away, and by the time he had opened his hand to let it go, the bird had died. He never again caught birds after that.

He had big heavy hands. And the rebbe's daughter Sheba was a little bird. . . . If she married him he would be very gentle with her. He wouldn't even touch her, not at all. . . .

He decided that when he saw her coming to open the shutters, he would step forward and open them for her, bow to her, and go away without saying a word. That would be the best way. He would go on doing that every day till she would one day speak to him. Ask him what brought him there so early in the morning.

The wind grew fiercer, howling and screaming. The rain

had stopped completely. The sky was growing more gray. The clouds scurried away before the wind and disappeared. It was day.

Now Yankel could see the houses in the street, which had not been visible before; one by one, gradually, bit by bit, all along the street, till he could see the whole street, and the side streets running off it. But everybody in the town was still asleep; the streets were empty. The doors of the houses and the shops were shut, locked, barred. All the shutters were closed. And there was a frost in the air.

He started slapping his big long arms across his chest to warm himself. Suddenly he stopped. He had seen a young man coming out of a narrow side street. It was Shlomo Chaye's Bujas, with whom he had gone to heder as a boy. They said that he was keeping company now with evil spirits, that a dybbuk had entered into him. The demons had got hold of him, because he had strayed from the straight path.

But Yankel wasn't thinking of that now. He was glad to see somebody he knew. There was a familiar warmth about Shlomo. They had gone to heder together when they were boys. They had played together. And he came to the rebbe's table now on the Sabbath, as he himself did, and his father, Wolf.

He watched Shlomo till he was out of sight. He knew that Shlomo was going to the Beth Hamedrash, to say his morning prayers and to study. Shlomo would become a rabbi, and he would marry the rebbe's daughter—if he wanted it.

A night watchman loomed up in front of him, with a lantern and a heavy oak stick in his hand.

"Whom did you clean out tonight, Yantek?" he asked. Yankel didn't answer him. He looked the man up and down, and the watchman walked away.

A Jew in a caftan and a skull cap came out of a house, and opened the shutters. It was the house next door to the rebbe's. The man's presence there annoyed Yankel. He was clenching his fists, when luckily the man went back into the house.

The sky brightened. Jews began coming out of their houses. In the factories the machines were already roaring. The shops in this street started opening. Jews with tallithim and tephilin bags under their arms hurried to the Beth Hamedrash for the morning prayers. This was the month of Tishri, which is full of the Holy Days, and allowed no work and no trading for almost a third of the month.

The shopkeepers stood in their doorways, looking out for customers. Their sour faces angered Yankel.

But now the shutters in the rebbe's house were being opened, and Yankel's eyes hung on the window of Sheba's room. He felt like calling up to her:

"Stay in bed, Sheba! It's frosty out here. Stay in bed, and keep warm. Stay in bed all day! I'll come in the morning to open the shutters. I'll come every morning!"

He smacked his thick lips with relish. "When she is my wife. . . ," he said to himself. And then scolded himself for daring to think such a thing: "I'm a thief! And my father is a thief. . . . And she is the daughter of a rebbe!"

He suddenly remembered the Christian wench in the village and it made him furious with himself.

"Yantek!" he growled. "Wolf Jonachek's son. . . ."

He wanted to go away from this street—as he had wanted to several times during the night. But he stayed. He couldn't move away. He couldn't take his eyes off Sheba's window. He was thinking again of Sheba as his wife . . . if she would agree to marry him. If she were his wife he would steal all the money in the Town Treasury, and give it to her! He would knock out the guard—even if there were two guards, even if they were soldiers with guns! He would bring her all that money. He would bring her cakes and wine and cherry brandy. He would feed her only on dainties. And he would bring her fat capons and geese and ducks from the villages. He would roast them himself, and bring them to her in bed, with hot rolls. In winter he would keep the stove going all day, so that the room would be warm, like a Turkish bath. He wouldn't touch her . . . not lay a finger on her. Except when

59

she asked him to. He would do anything for her, even cut his throat, or hang himself, drown himself, burn himself alive, for her sake, if she told him to.

Jews were coming back now from their prayers in the synagogue. The factory sirens were hooting and whistling, and Yankel was still being held by the closed shutters of Sheba's room. All the other shutters in the rebbe's house were open. The weather had changed. Blue sky and sunshine. And now again clouds and wind. Yankel's heart was like the changeable weather—sad, joyful, despairing, and then again hope and again despair. Till the shutter of her room opened, and Yankel's heart began to beat more than ever it did when he went to burgle a house.

Then Sheba showed herself at the window. She was wearing a dark blue dress, with a white knitted shawl over her shoulders. She looked like a child not yet fully wakened from her sleep. It frightened her seeing this big fellow staring at her. She knew who he was—the thief's son. His father was that giant of a man with the big red beard who came to her father's Sabbath table.

Yankel stook gawking at her.

When Yankel was at last able to move, he walked away dejectedly, in the direction of his home. His legs were like lead. He could hardly lift them. He had a bitter taste in his mouth. He spat. Spat blood. He remembered that when he had seen Sheba at the window he had wanted to call out to her, and had bitten his tongue to stop himself. He didn't really want to go home now. He didn't want to face his father. Nor his mother. How could he tell them where he had been all night. His father would say he had been out thieving, and would thrash him.

He heard someone call his name. It was Zlatte. The servant-maid. She was on her way back from the market, shopping for her mistress, carrying a heavy basket full of food.

"Yankel!" she called. "Yankel!"

Zlatte was a big strapping girl, with red cheeks and laughing eyes. She wore a red scarf with green leaves on it, draped over her shoulders, with the ends tied over her big bosom. She was madly in love with Yankel, and she couldn't understand why he was so cold to her. But it made no difference to her feelings for him. Yankel was so big, so strong! A giant! A hero! "Og, King of Bashan!" she called him in her mind.

She didn't like the idea that Yankel was a thief, but she accepted it. And she took the money he always gave her, and paid it in at once to the savings bank on her deposit book, and consoled herself with the thought that it was for both of them, that she was saving his money against the time when they would marry. There was quite a big sum there now. But every time she tried to tell him how much it was he refused to listen.

"I've joined the Party!" she told him excitedly. "We'll down the bourgeoisie! No more rich and poor! Justice and equality for all! My mistress will have to go out and do her own shopping. And her own cooking! And the master won't live on the profits that his workers earn for him! He'll have to go to work himself! Everybody will have to work! You too, Yankel! You'll have to learn to be a cobbler or a carpenter. We'll both work! We'll be honest proletarians!"

But Yankel stared at her dully, uncomprehendingly. Zlatte waited for him to speak, and when he still said nothing, she realized that he was looking absolutely exhausted, ready to drop.

"What's the matter?" she cried. "You look all in! As if you hadn't slept all night!"

Yankel looked at her dumbly, and then walked away.

When he got home Yankel lay down, in his clothes, in one of the big carts standing outside his house, and dropped off to sleep. He slept heavily, and was tormented all the time by dreams. He dreamt that he was running, and somebody was running after him. There were high fences in the way, barring the road. He jumped over them. He leaped over houses, over

61

hills. As he ran he flung away sacks of loot, all that he had stolen, silver and gold. He came to a river and plunged in, fully clothed, and swam. He was being dragged down! A woman had got hold of him, and was dragging him down. A naked woman, stark naked. . . . She looked like a pig, like a big fat pig. . . . Peasants were round him, beating him with cudgels and iron bars, and shouting. . . .Then an angel from heaven came, a blue angel with white wings, and took him by the hand, and flew away with him. . . .

When he woke, his father was standing over him, with a whip in his hand, shouting. Now he understood. . . . His father had been laying into him with his whip. Without saying a word, with clenched teeth, with angry eyes, Yankel climbed down from the cart, and went into the house. He didn't know, he didn't remember, and he didn't ask if it was night or day. He didn't see if it was light or dark. But he felt hungry, terribly hungry.

So he went to his mother, who was standing at the stove, and said:

"I want to eat!"

She dished out a big bowl of kasha soup with butter beans, and then some big chunks of meat, half a loaf of bread and a whole black radish. He ate, not saying a word to anyone. He didn't answer his mother nor his father when they flung questions at him. He undressed, got into bed, and went to sleep again. It was a bright day, the next morning, and Yankel was still fast asleep.

Wolf Jonachek rose early, as every day, let the fowls out, fed them corn, and watched them eat. He loved watching the birds peck.

The members of Wolf Jonachek's gang lived and ate in his house. As there wasn't enough room in the house, some slept in the lofts, and in the stables. They were all up now, and gathered in front of the house, big, well-fed fellows, with long quiffs and check riding breeches and highly polished top boots. They slouched about, with their hands in their trouser pockets.

Wolf Jonachek was in a vile temper:

"Why doesn't one of you go and feed the horses?"

The gang looked at each other, as though each one was telling the other: "You go!"

Wolf went back into the house.

"Is he still asleep?" he asked his wife, who was standing, half-dressed, at Yankel's bed.

Her gray hair straggled down from under her red kerchief. Her eyes flashed fire. She was ready to defend Yankel against his father's blows.

Yankel had been dreaming again in his sleep. He was in a forest, holding on to a tree, kissing it. . . . He was again a baby, lying in his cradle, and his mother, young again, beautiful, was bending over him.

Then suddenly his mother went away. He wanted her to stay, but he couldn't call out, and she walked away, further and further away. He stretched out his arms to her; and he woke.

He saw his mother, half-dressed, disheveled, looking angry, standing by his bed, facing his father, who was shouting: "Where was he all night?"

His father moved toward him, ready to hit him; but his mother barred the way. She flung herself down on top of Yankel; her big breasts lay over his face, and made it hard for him to breathe. She held on tight to the bed, so that his father couldn't get at him.

"Where was he all night?" his father kept shouting. "Whom did he steal from?"

"I didn't go stealing!" Yankel shouted back.

"Then where were you all night?" Wolf demanded. "With that wench of yours in the village?"

"No!" Yankel shot up violently in bed, and then lay back again on the pillow, with his hands under his head, his black hair tousled, and his naked chest exposed.

His father moved away. His mother too. Yankel lay silent, staring up at the ceiling. His mind was full of Sheba, the rebbe's daughter. He had fallen in love with her, and felt that he couldn't live without her. But he was a thief! And even if he stopped being a thief, would she want to marry someone like him?

Wolf Jonachek turned away, growling:

"Couldn't find a Jewish girl! Had to get a Christian wench!"

"I told you I wasn't with her!" Yankel burst out.

"I don't believe you! Don't tell us you're turning into a saint!"

"He's a good boy!" his mother kept saying. And bending over Yankel, she kissed him on the lips. "He's a good boy!"

Yankel stared at his father and mother, and felt that he hated them both. He felt he couldn't stay in this house any more with them! He must get away!

When Wolf Jonachek came out of the house he found his gang lined up, against each other, with knives in their hands. One had been stabbed and was bleeding. The horses, brought out of the stables, stood contemplating empty buckets. The fowls were scampering about the yard, frightened.

Wolf Jonachek raised his fist, and sent the nearest man sprawling. The rest hid their knives shamefacedly, picked up the buckets, and led the horses away to be fed.

"Couldn't you feed the horses first, and fight afterwards?" Wolf grumbled, helping up the man he had knocked down. The man rose to his feet and stole away.

That same moment Wolf Jonachek saw Reb Chaim Yossel approaching, with his tallith and tephilin under his arm.

"Good morning, Reb Chaim Yossel! Coming to see me?"

"Yes!"

"Did anything happen in your house last night? Anything missing?"

"No!" Reb Chaim Yossel answered, in a frightened, squeaky voice.

"Because if so," said Wolf, "I wouldn't give it back to you anyway. I respect you, Reb Chaim Yossel. They say you are the most learned man in the town. But I wouldn't know about that. I'm only Wolf Jonachek! But I do know that you're an honest man. That there are no stolen goods in your shop. And yet, if a thief has robbed you, I wouldn't give the stuff back to you! D'you know why? Because you're a rich man! That's why! It wouldn't hurt you a bit to have your shelves emptied—they groan under the weight of your stock. What are you going to do with so much money?"

Reb Chaim Yossel stood listening to Wolf Jonachek with a surprised look on his face. He screwed up his eyes, so that they became pinpoints of light. They were good, kind, friendly eyes, full of love for all and everyone. It was true that Reb Chaim Yossel was a very learned man. And a very pious and observant Jew. Everybody in the town loved him. Yet something had happened to him lately. He had become a puzzle to his closest friends.

He was a man in his fifties, who had always sat day and night studying the sacred books. Every morning before day-break he went to the ritual bath, no matter how great the frost. He never stepped into his business. His wife ran the shop, with no interference from him.

And now the talk was that this man had suddenly strayed from the straight path, had become a doubter and, skeptic, a heretic, a disbeliever.

Reb Chaim Yossel knew what people were saying about him. It surprised him.

"I haven't let a word escape my lips, because I am not yet sure what I feel about it—yes or no? Yet it is already common talk that I have said, God forbid, that there is no God! True, I don't go to the Beth Hamedrash as often as I used to. I don't study as much as I used to, not in the same way. But—I still say my prayers. Do they say that I've turned heretic because I go walking almost every day now outside the town, something I never did before? That isn't a sin!"

But Red Chaim Yossel knew that the talk in the town about him was not groundless. He was no longer what he had been all his life. Doubts had gradually crept into his mind, and were growing stronger every day, till he had really begun to question the Deity—was there a Divine Providence? He had reached no definite conclusion. But something had suddenly

65

begun to draw him to the forest and the fields, to the countryside outside the town. He felt that he could breathe more freely there, in the open air. He grew to love the trees. He had got into the habit of standing still in front of a tree or a rock, and enjoying the sight of it. A blade of grass could hold his whole attention. He loved watching the clouds, looking up at the sun, especially at sunset. A bird's song sent him into ecstasy. His hear jumped with joy when he saw a stream flowing past. He could stand still for hours in a field of corn. He grieved at the sight of the reapers with their scythes cutting down the grass, but he also inhaled happily the scent of the new-mown hay. It tickled his nostrils, and made him sneeze. It cleared his nasal passages. This was all quite new to him. He loved watching the peasant women pitchforking the hay on to the farm carts. And the cows being driven into the fields to graze, with their calves running at their side.

Walking through the town, too, he saw now and enjoyed sights that he had never noticed before—like the blacksmith's forge, and the blacksmith hammering the red-hot iron on his anvil, or the workers on their way to and from the factories, the droshkies driving through the streets, young people walking together. His eyes had always grappled with the pages of the Talmud or some other sacred tome. They had not risen beyond the walls of the Beth Hamedrash, or of his home, and of Jews like himself at prayer or poring over the holy books.

In the winter he had never been so aware as he was now of the beauty of wide stretches of virginal snow, of trees quite bare, stripped of their leaves, white snow-covered roofs, black crows, grey skies. All his life till now he had been like a blind man to these things. And he wanted to make up for it now.

So on his way to the Beth Hamedrash for morning prayers, he had seen this half-ruin of a house, with moss growing on the roof, and fowls scurrying about in the yard, and something had drawn him to go in; and Reb Wolf Jonachek had greeted him: "Good morning, Red Chaim Yossel!" That had brought him to a surprised, wondering stop.

Wolf Jonachek looked searchingly at his unexpected visitor. Then he said:

"And what brings you to me, Red Chaim Yossel?"

"I was on my way to the morning prayers . . ."

"Here?"

"In the Beth Hamedrash."

"This isn't the Beth Hamedrash, Reb Chaim Yossel."

"I strayed from the path . . ."

"I see," said Wolf Jonachek sarscastically. "You don't know your way from your home to the Beth Hamedrash. Every day for nearly fifty years, you've trodden the road to the Beth Hamedrash, every day, twice, three times a day, sometimes four times. And now you don't know the way. You've strayed from the path . . . Tell me, Reb Chaim Yossel, is it true what people say, that you have really strayed from the path, that you are no longer a believer, no longer a pious observant Jew? If it's a lie I'll bash the brains out of those who are saying these things about you! But if it's true, I'll send some of my gang to lighten the load on the shelves in your shop! Well now? Answer me! I know it's not very kind of me to pester you. But I'm going to ask you to give me a hundred roubles. That's the penalty for straying into my yard. It's not for me. It's for a poor widow with a dowerless daughter who's getting married. I'm going to give her half her dowry; and you will give the other half. Tell your wife that she's to let me have it. I know that you don't handle the money. She does that! But you tell her! I'd rather you told her than I should. Tell her to send me the money. Today! Because if she doesn't send it she'll have to pay double, ten times as much. I'll break into your shop one night, and I'll take away everything you've got! All your best cloth, your silks and your satins, your velvets and your cheviots, everything!"

Reb Chaim Yossel saw that Wolf Jonachek was angry, and he couldn't understand why. He looked at him wonderingly, and took a step back. Then he turned round and walked back to the town.

Yankel was still in bed. He lay there, looking up at the ceiling. Recalling the last dream with which he had wakened—his mother, young and beautiful—it was not his mother at all, it was the rebbe's daughter, bending over him, with tender loving eyes, comforting him, telling him that he would become good and pious, and he would become a rabbi, and she would marry him. . . .

It was that shouting outside that had wakened him from this beautiful dream. It infuriated him. He would gladly have killed everybody in the house, including his father and mother. He felt as though there was a great heavy mountain on top of him and he couldn't release himself from the crushing weight. He tried to sit up in bed, and—crash! He was lying on the floor, with his bedding. The bed had collapsed under him.

His mother was at the stove again, and when she heard the crash she turned round, stared, and started cursing and swearing:

"What's wrong with you, smashing up the house! Who the devil do you think you are!"

The stove was giving out a lot of heat. The pots on the boil sent out a cloud of steam. It made the room like a Turkish bath. The low ceiling—so low that a man of any height could touch it with his head—was full of stains and patches, yellow and brown, which took on all kinds of fantastic shapes as you looked at them. The walls were black and damp, and covered with cobwebs. The furniture was old and decrepit—legacies from Wolf Jonachek's grandfather and great-grandfather— holy relics to him.

Golda kept moving one pot from the fire and putting another in its place, adding water, stirring, tasting.

"You're not putting on your best suit again?"

Yankel didn't answer.

"Whom are you going to see today?"

Yankel, now fully dressed, didn't say a word. He stood staring at his broken bed, lying on the floor with the bedding.

"Wait till your father comes in! He'll give you what for! Nice son you are—to both of us! But the calf is like the ox! You think your father doesn't know that you cleared out Reb Israel Moshe's barn! If at least you'd given me the money, I would have put it by for you!"

Yankel grunted.

"What do you do with your money?"

"I give it away!"

"To whom?"

"To everybody!"

"You give it to Zlatte!"

"I give it to everybody!"

The steam grew denser. The room was full of the smell of food. Golda was boiling potatoes, frying onions in a large pan, and cooking a stew in an enormous pot. She had another pot with cabbage cooking. And another with milt and tripe and chunks of beef.

Yankel took his father's big prayer book and his tephilin, and began to say his prayers. His mother opened her eyes wide and stared at him with glad surprise.

"Ma Tovu . . . . How goodly are Thy tents. . ." he began. It was hard going for him, but it gave him a lot of satisfaction.

Suddenly the door was flung wide open, and Wolf Jonachek's gang, headed by Wolf himself, filed in, and sat round the table. Golda dished out big plates full of stew, and placed a huge bowl of steaming potatoes on the table, and an enormous loaf of bread, that must have weighed over fifteen pounds.

Each member of the gang cut his own bread with his own knife. They ate noisily. It sounded like a cooper fastening the iron hoops round his barrels. They ate like starving soldiers.

Wolf kept looking up from his plate at his son saying his prayers, and it did his heart good. It made him so happy that he told Golda to get out a bottle of brandy; and then he wanted to know why she wasn't sitting at the table, eating with the rest of them. So she took a seat at the end of one of the benches, took the glass of brandy her husband gave her, sipped, and couldn't catch her breath. She hadn't tasted such strong drink since she was a young girl.

She went back to the stove, and returned with the pot and served chunks of meat, milt, and tripe to each of them.

The sun shone in through the grimy windows. It was one of those rare beautiful autumn days that sometimes follow a night of biting wind and monotonous, depressing rain.

Yankel was still saying his prayers, seeking comfort and hope, not in the Hebrew words that he didn't understand, but in God, to whom he was pouring out his heart as never before in all his life. He felt sad, but the sun coming into the room brightened him up a bit. He began to feel sorry for his father, and for the other thieves. He began to love his mother again. Love and pity mingled, because he had suddenly remembered how his teacher in the heder had taught him and the rest of the class the passage in the Pentateuch that said that you must not suffer a witch to remain alive. It hurt him to remember how the boys had drawn pictures of a witch, and all the pictures looked like his mother. It meant that everybody knew that she was a witch, and so when she died she would go to hell. The thought made the tears come to his eyes. He prayed to God that He should have mercy on his mother and not punish her. He prayed to God that He should make the rebbe's daughter feel kindly toward him, and agree to marry him. And as he prayed, he remembered that this was Friday, so that the same evening, when the Sabbath began, he would go to the rebbe's house, to the rebbe's table, and again the next day, the Sabbath.

Wolf Jonachek and his gang having finished their meal and emptied the bottle of brandy, rose and went straight out again. But at the door Wolf turned round, took out a handful of money from his trouser pocket and gave it to his wife Golda:

"That's for your Sabbath shopping. Get a big pike or two; the bigger the better—ten or fifteen pounders—wrap them in paper and take them to the rebbe as a gift from us!"

When Wolf Jonachek got outside he decided that he would now go to see Reb Chaim Yossel's wife Freida in her shop, and collect the couple of hundred roubles for the dowry of the poor widow's daughter.

There was nobody in the shop when he got there. It was dark in there, very dark, though the sun was still shining outside. For a moment Wolf thought he had come to the wrong place. His eyes, trained by his trade to see in the dark, in shops and private houses, barns and stables, searched in every nook and corner. Yes, it was Freida's shop. But where was Freida?

"Freida!" he called aloud. Then he saw Freida, hiding in a corner. He realized that her husband must have told her that he would be coming for the money, and she had seen him walking along the street, and had tried to hide. Why was it so dark in the shop? She had pulled the blinds down, thinking he would not see her.

"You shouldn't have left the door open, Freida!" he called over to her banteringly. "When you pull the blinds down, you should lock the door as well. I could have walked off with your entire stock now, and you wouldn't even have seen me in the dark!"

Freida came forward, and greeted him: "Good evening, Reb Wolf Jonah!"

"Did you say, good evening? With the sun shining outside?"

"There's no sun shining for me! It's dark all round me!"

"Pull the blinds up and it won't be dark any more."

He walked over to the window and drew up the blinds himself.

"You see, it's quite bright now. Lovely shop you've got. All those rolls of cloth on your shelves. You must be doing a big trade! Making lots of money!"

Freida groaned. If she had dared she would have run to the door and screamed: "Help!" So that people should come from all sides to save her from this thief. But she didn't dare. She stood helpless, not knowing what to say to him:

"How about my giving you a present of a length of cloth for a coat, Reb Wolf Jonah?"

He looked her up and down, and didn't say a word.

71

"You're such a nice kind man, Reb Wolf Jonah! I know you won't do me any harm!"

"Go to blazes!" he suddenly exploded. Then he restrained himself and tried to speak more calmly:

"Don't you know what I've come for! Didn't your husband tell you to give me a couple of hundred roubles?"

"A couple of hundred roubles?"

"Three hundred!"

"What for?"

"There's a poor widow, who's got to get her daughter wed, and she has no dowry. I want your three hundred roubles toward it. I'm giving another three hundred. Now d'you know what for?"

Freida felt dazed, as if Wolf had knocked her over the head with a heavy stick.

Wolf Jonachek went to the door leading to the living rooms, and flung it wide open. Reb Chaim Yossel was pacing up and down the big room, with wild eyes. His lips kept muttering all the time. The table was heaped high with gemaras, all open, one on top of the other. The bookcases stood all wide open.

He stopped still when Wolf Jonachek came into the room. But only for a moment. Then he ran to the table and began turning the pages first of one book, then of another, and then a third. He read aloud a passage here, and passage there, very loudly, almost shouting. And then he sank back exhausted in a chair.

Wolf Jonachek stood in front of him, full of respect and deference, like a beggar at the door, looking at Reb Chaim Yossel, afraid to move, so as not to disturb him.

Freida recovered from her stupor, and ran her eyes over the shelves of cloth. She went to the till, took out the money, put in in a bag and hid it in her bosom. Then she followed Wolf Jonachek into the living room.

Seeing her reminded Wolf of what he had come here for. He would much rather have been left standing quietly listening to Reb Chaim Yossel repeating words from the holy books. He didn't understand any of it, but the melody, the chant, fascinated him.

Reb Chaim Yossel only now seemed to become aware of Wolf Jonachek's presence. And at first without even now recognizing him. He stared at him wildly. Then he remembered, and his face cleared, and he said quietly, gently:

"Good evening, Wolf Jonah!"

"So you find it dark too, Reb Chaim Yossel?"

Chaim Yossel looked at Wolf.

"What is the time?"

"If you haven't had your breakfast yet it's late. But if you're waiting for your midday meal it's early! I didn't mean to disturb you, Reb Chaim Yossel! I loved listening to you. It was your wife who disturbed us, coming in as she did!"

Freida burst out laughing. She laughed and laughed, and her whole fat body shook with laughter. Wolf Jonachek made a face of distaste.

Freida stopped laughing.

"Would you like a glass of tea with a piece of cake, Reb Wolf Jonah?" she asked him, trying to be conciliatory. "Or a glass of brandy?"

Wolf Jonachek went close up to Reb Chaim Yossel, and said to him:

"If I had a wife like that I'd strangle her! Just a big barrel of fat!"

Reb Chaim Yossel had forgotten completely what Wolf Jonachek had come for. He had forgotten that whole conversation with him earlier that morning. He had forgotten everything. He stared at him blankly.

"You see, Reb Chaim Yossel," said Wolf, "I've come for the money myself. I decided not to wait till your wife would bring it round to me. Of course, you told your wife about the money, didn't you?"

"Of course!" Chaim Yossel suddenly remembered. "I told her as soon as I came home!"

"Well?" Wolf demanded, looking fiercely at Freida.

Freida cowered in a corner, puzzled and frightened, trying to collect her wits. Three hundred roubles! What for? She would have to sell half her stock to get that money!

"I'll give you thirty roubles, Reb Wolf Jonah, toward the

73

poor widow's daughter's dowry. But three hundred! All from me! I haven't got it!"

"I said at least three hundred. If you haggle with me I'll want five hundred!"

"I haven't got it!"

Wolf Jonachek walked to the door, looked back, and said: "It'll cost you more than five hundred now!"

Freida ran up to him, and pleaded with him: "I'll give you a hundred roubles, Reb Wolf Jonah! You tell him, Chaim Yossel! He'll listen to you!"

A light came into Reb Chaim Yossel's eyes. The next moment they went dead again, and he turned to the books on the table, and became absorbed in them.

"I've got an idea, Reb Wolf Jonah!" Freida cried. "Tell the bride to come here, and I'll give her my wedding dress! I've worn it only once—on my wedding day! It's like new! And I'll give her all her underwear, and sheets, and pillow cases!"

But Wolf Jonachek was paying no attention. He kicked the door open, and walked out.

Freida ran after him:

"Please, Reb Wolf Jonah! I'll give you the three hundred!"

He stopped at the door, and she counted out the money and gave it to him. Three hundred roubles.

4

The rebbe had four daughters and two sons. Two of the daughters were married. They had married into good, rich families. One was sixteen and the other seventeen when they married—according to the Law, which says that one should marry before eighteen. The older of the two, when they told her she was to marry a rabbi's son, who later became himself a rabbi, didn't say a word against it. Her mother asked her what she thought of it only for the sake of appearances. She dropped her eyes, as is proper for a rebbe's daughter, and said: "As my father and mother please!"

Her mother kissed her on the forehead; and that was that.

It was a little different with the younger girl. She didn't wait for her mother to ask if she liked the young man, but as soon as she heard whom they had chosen, she said: "I won't marry him!" And she didn't. She kept picking and choosing, and finally she told her parents very firmly and categorically that she wasn't going to marry any son of a rabbi or a rebbe, and that she had no intention of becoming a rebbitzin.

Her mother screamed at her, and scolded her. Her father pleaded with her. It was no use. She insisted that she would marry only a man of the world, not a Yeshiva student. And she had her way. She married the son of a wealthy businessman, who worked in his father's business.

The third daughter—Eve was her name—was older than eighteen, and she still wouldn't hear of getting married at all. When her mother asked her how long she was going to wait, she said: "Till the right man comes along."

Her mother had avoided the subject of marriage with her after that. She'd been afraid of provoking a scene.

But Eve had confided to her youngest sister, Sheba, that she was already in love with somebody—somebody her parents wouldn't want her to marry. "The German teacher!"

"But he's a Christian!" Sheba was shocked.

"He's tall and handsome. And he's a gentleman!" said Eve. "He has such manners! And he's in love with me!"

She hugged her younger sister and kissed her. Sheba pushed her away. She warned her not to do this thing! "You're going to bring down shame upon us! Upon all of us! And you'll suffer for it in the end! He'll seduce you! And then he'll leave you!"

Eve laughed. "He won't leave me! He'll marry me!"

That frightened Sheba more than ever.

"You don't mean you're going to turn Christian to marry him!"

Eve laughed: "You're a very naive child, Sheba!"

After that, every night when Eve came home late, with flaming cheeks and burning lips, she stole into Sheba's room, and wanted to snuggle up to her in her bed, and tell her all her confidences.

"I don't want to listen to you!" Sheba cried. "Leave me alone! Let me sleep!"

But Eve snuggled up to her younger sister, and poured her heart out to her, told her all about her love and her lover.

"How can you do such things, Eve! Aren't you ashamed of yourself! If I were you I wouldn't dare to show my face! Get out of my room!"

"Please, let me stay!" Eve pleaded with her. "I've got such a lot to tell you!"

"No!" Sheba sat up in bed. "I don't want to talk to you! Go away!"

Sheba now kept the door of her room locked. She was three years younger than Eve, but she was more mature, a stronger character.

Sheba was under average height, slightly built, with a small delicate olive-skinned oval face, bright brown eyes, and a firm chin. Her lips were like her sister Eve's, full and red and passionate, but not so sensuous. She had a lot of vitality. Unlike Eve, who was like her mother, Sheba looked like her father.

Eve's hair was like glowing copper; her face was round, and her skin was fresh and rosy. She was a little over average height, and she was always chattering about love. Sheba got irritated by it, and said: "You're a little fool, Eve! You've got no sense!"

Sheba worried terribly, not only about Eve, but about her parents. She sensed that there was something wrong between them. Something was going on in their lives that she would never have believed possible.

Sheba had never, even as a child, loved her mother. She was aware of it; she didn't try to conceal the fact from herself. She had loved her father. But lately she had been wondering about him, shocked by some of his actions. She pitied him, because she felt that he was doing things against his will, because something was hurting him, because he was suffering.

The whole atmosphere of the house was getting on her nerves. She was growing to hate it. She began to detest the Hasidim who came to the house on Friday night and on the Sabbath day, and ate and drank, and packed every room. She hated the Hasidim, those who lived in the town and those who came from far places, to ask her father to bless them and help them.

But when her father expounded Torah to his Hasidim, she was spellbound. She stood in a corner and drank in every word.

Sheba had lately come to admire Reb Abraham's house—that house near by, which had those beautiful paintings and carvings on the front. She knew it was Reb Abraham's son, Joseph, who had done this painting and carving. She grew to admire Joseph. She had often seen him about; she had met his parents and she knew his sister. But the families were not friends, did not go visiting each other.

Sheba couldn't understand the reason. Because Reb Abraham, and his wife Rachel, were fine people, good religious people, and Rachel was the little tailor's grandchild.

Sheba decided that her best approach would be to become friends with Miriam, the daughter, Joseph's sister. She knew what she really wanted was to get to know Joseph. And she began to think it was forward of her. She feared that Miriam would realize what she really wanted. So she gave up trying to make friends with Miriam.

Then one day Sheba was looking out of her window, admiring the painted front of Reb Abraham's house, when Joseph came to his window. Sheba went red as fire, and turned away. For some days she didn't look out of the window. But she waited behind the curtains, till she saw Joseph look out; then she opened her window and she also looked out.

After that they both looked out of their windows every day, about the same time, as if they had arranged the time between them.

Then one morning she had come to her window and there was that big young fellow standing there looking up at her, that young fellow whom she had seen several times at her father's table with his father. She had felt a great pity for him. His face looked so gentle under his outer coarseness; it was the rough exterior that the intellectuals of the time imposed upon themselves, so that they could go among the peasants, working and teaching among the masses of the people. . . .

The big room where the rebbe had his table was packed so tight with Hasidim that it was impossible to move. Only the top people sat round the long table. The others stood around, not only in this room but in all the other rooms, whose doors were kept open so that they could pass in and out, if the crush allowed it. Not only the rebbe's Hasidim who lived in the town had come, but many who had arrived from various towns round about, and who were staying in the local inns.

And there was a crowd of women outside, looking in through the windows.

It was the rebbe's custom to say kiddush about an hour after the people had come back from the synagogue service, to allow them time to eat at home with wife and children, and yet reach his table in time for kiddush. He knew how his Hasidim wanted to be there when he said kiddush, how they hung on his words.

And though he shook and swayed to and fro, he knew how to balance skillfully the golden goblet so that not a drop of wine was spilt. He kept his eyes closed while he chanted the words, and the expression on his face changed with his movements, now mild and gentle and compassionate, now anguish stricken, pleading, supplicating, now radiant with joy. His voice, likewise, was soft and singing for "In love and favor Thou hast given us Thy holy Sabbath," sobbing for "In remembrance of the departure from Egypt," and prayerful for "Thy holy Sabbath as an inheritance."

It was the same in the hearts of the Hasidim—now they shook and trembled, now they rejoiced, now they soared up to heaven, now they were down again on the earth, now they were sorrowful, now radiantly happy.

The rebbitzin stood at the door leading from one of the side rooms to the big main room, her eyes piously closed, reverently listening. Her breathing rose and fell with the rise and fall in her husband's voice as he said kiddush. A girlish purity lay on her fine, delicately formed red lips. Her two daughters, Eve and Sheba, stood on either side of her. Eve, like her mother, kept her eyes closed and her lips half open, with an almost hidden smile playing over them. Sheba looked as though she were undergoing martyrdom.

The rebbe took a long time over his kiddush. Some of the Hasidim were in such a state of exaltation that they had lost all sense of time and place—they were in a trance. Not on this earth. There was nothing around them but light. The flames in the burning candles in the silver candlesticks on the table, in the two silver menorahs, in the chandeliers, and in the sconces on the walls had all merged into one great flame, one great light that had swallowed up the room, the table, the crystal carafes, the glasses of wine, the silver knives and forks, the plates—the very walls. Everything was a great light.

But from one corner two burning eyes were turned on the rebbitzin. They crept like serpents over her bosom, over her arms, and her face, and her closed eyes. She felt them burning with lust. She knew whose eyes they were. Her pale face went red with shame. But presently those lustful glances creeping about the room toward her got tangled with other glances, first from one corner and then from another, and from a third. Six eyes were all turned on the rebbitzin. And then they leaped from her to her elder daughter, Eve.

Eve grew soon aware of them, and she snuggled up against her mother. The two women looked beautiful standing there, the mother like her daughter's elder sister, all the light concentrated on her, flashing from the jewels she wore, the necklace, the brooch set with rubies, the diamond earrings, the rings on her fingers.

Then Sheba became aware of male eyes turned on her. They had licked round Eve, and now they were creeping towards her. She felt them burning on her face, her bosom, her tiny breasts. She knew whose the lustful glances were; that they came gliding off her mother's breasts and Eve's. Her small slim form contracted, grew smaller and slighter, shrank, as if wanting to melt away, to vanish. She would have liked best of all to slip through the door and to run out of this room. She drew her long fingers, as though they were knives, up to her throat, as though to defend herself. She flung a scornful look into the corner from which these hateful glances came. They were aimed at her. They were desirous, pleading, tremulous. And she stood there with those glances on her, till her father ended Kiddush with the words, "Who hallowest the Sabbath."

When the rebbe had sipped the wine from the goblet, he poured some into a big jug and handed the goblet with the rest of the wine to the shamash to pass to the rebbitzin and their two daughters. The gabbai poured more wine into the jug from the carafes, and then into goblets for the shamash to hand round among the Hasidim, first among the top people at the table. They sipped and passed the goblets further, till all the Hasidim, even in the other rooms, had sipped from the rebbe's kiddush wine.

People pushed and shoved, everybody wanting to sip the wine sanctified by the rebbe's blessing, just a drop, enough to feel on the lip, to taste on the tip of the tongue.

It was the same with the food that the rebbe tasted and let the rest be passed round.

Then, afterward, they sang table hymns, sweetly, with great fervor, and the singing was heard outside, all over the street.

Then the rebbe expounded Torah till midnight.

Wolf Jonachek and his son Yankel were there, among the Hasidim. But they stood in a corner, apart from the others. They loved it, all this that their eyes saw and their ears heard, though they hardly understood any of it. Full of wonderment and awe. At the most simple things. And for Yankel there was the additional joy and happiness of seeing Sheba there. He didn't take his eyes off her the whole evening.

On the Sabbath, after the morning prayers and a quick bite at home, Wolf Jonachek was the first arrival at the rebbe's house. He and his son Yankel.

"Good morning, rebbe! Good Sabbath, rebbe!" he cried in a ringing voice, holding out his hand in greeting.

There was something he wanted to say to the rebbe, something he had wanted to say to him for a long time but had never been able to put into words, though he had repeated them over and over again, learned them by heart, like the blessing when one is called up to the Torah. He stood for awhile, mute. Then he found his voice again:

"There's something I want to talk to you about, Rebbe. But it's the Sabbath day, and I can't talk about it on the holy day. I'll come to see you tomorrow, Rebbe, and then I'll tell you what it is!"

"Yes," said the rebbe. "After the Sabbath." And he looked at Wolf with great compassion. "This big strong man, and he shrinks when he has something to say to me!"

The effort of saying these few words to the rebbe had completely exhausted Wolf. He turned pale and seemed to totter; the rebbe, fearing that he might fall, pushed him down into a chair at his side.

"Sit down, Wolf Jonah!"

Wolf's head swam. There was a mist before his eyes. He couldn't see the rebbe, nor the table, nor the walls of the room.

The Hasidim started arriving. The important ones took their usual places at the table, staring hard at Wolf Jonachek and his son Yankel who were already sitting beside the Rebbe.

"The thief and his son! Thieves both of them!" they wondered. But, "if the rebbe, bless him, has seated them at his side . . . "

The shamash brought the basin for the rebbe to wash his hands, and say the blessing. Then the shamash served a huge dish of fish, giving a helping also to Wolf and to Yankel.

Wolf was stunned by this unexpected attention, and sat as if petrified. And the same with Yankel. Till the rebbe gave them a bit of the Sabbath loaf, to say the blessing, and said, "Eat!" Then they fell to.

As always, the Hasidim pushed and jostled to get the rebbe's leavings. Actually, he only just touched the food, most of which was passed round to be snatched by the Hasidim—the food the rebbe had touched. Then all joined in singing the table hymns. Next the shamash brought round kasha with a thick gravy. And after that kugel—pudding.

The kugel was brought in by the rebbitzin herself. The Hasidim greeted her with wild shouts: "Make way for the rebbitzin! Way for her kugel!"

As the shamash was busy clearing the table the gabbai went up to the rebbitzin to take the kugel from her and to serve it round. The rebbitzin wouldn't let him have it.

"I made this kugel! And I'll serve it!"

The Hasidim cheered her, backed her up:

"Good for the rebbitzin! She's right! She made the kugel! Let her serve it!"

Some of the Hasidim raised their voices in praise of the rebitzin and her kugel:

"A lovely kugel! The kugel that the rebbitzin herself made!"

Suddenly some of the Hasidim at the far end of the room were shouting: "Stop him! Don't let him!"

Hersh-Leib, the Gemara teacher, had darted out of a corner, as if he had been lurking in wait there, and before the rebbitzin was aware of him, he had seized the kugel from her, and left her standing confused, with empty hands. She dropped her eyes, abashed. For as he had taken the dish with the kugel from her his hand had touched hers, and an electric current had shot through her.

Hersh-Leib stood holding the kugel, triumphantly. And he ordered her, as if he were her husband: "Now let the rebbitzin bring in the other kugel!"

Hersh-Leib smiled at the rebbitzin, and the rebbitzin smiled back at him. And she confirmed to the Hasidim near her, that the Gemara teacher had been right. There was another kugel. She left the room to go and fetch it.

Hersh-Leib marched to the table like a victor with his kugel. He looked like a satyr, with his long beard, black as the night, his bronzed face, his eagle eyes, and his big eagle nose and wide nostrils. He set the kugel down on the table, looked at the rebbe, swept the room with his glance, and said to all and everyone, as if issuing an order: "Don't snatch!"

Some of the Hasidim at the table thought that the rebbe looked sad. Wolf Jonachek thought so too. He stared at Hersh-Leib, and wondered if there was something happening between the rebbe and the rebbitzin and Hersh-Leib. But he pushed the thought away, and reproached himself for it:

"Reb Hersh-Leib isn't Wolf Jonachek, and the rebbitzin . . ."

The Hasidim sang table hymns. The rebbe clapped his hands, threw back his head, rolled his eyes, and cried out aloud: "O, God in Heaven! Sweet Father! Dear Father!"

And he sang with the rest in chorus:

> *If you keep the Sabbath day,*
> *God will be your staff and stay.*

Then cries of joy were raised: "Here comes the other kugel. Make way for the kugel!"

This time it was not the rebbitzin who brought in the kugel, but her daughter Eve. She held the dish high over her head, so that it couldn't be taken out of her hands so easily. Yet she was soon screaming: "Mother! Help! They're taking away my kugel!"

One of the Hasidim was trying to get hold of the kugel.

"You won't get it! I won't give it to you!" Eve screamed. "I'll give it to nobody except my mother!"

At the same time, she liked the game, she liked this struggle with the Hasid, with a man, who now had several other Hasidim to help him in his effort to take the kugel away from her.

The rebbitzin was now making her way to her daughter's side: "Hold on to the kugel, Eve! Don't let them take it! I'm coming!"

Eve was putting up a fight. But before her mother arrived, Hersh-Leib was at her side, and she called to him: "I'll give it to you, Reb Hersh-Leib!"

The Hasidim struggling around Eve for the kugel didn't like the idea of the Gemara teacher capturing the second kugel as well, to carry it to the table in triumph like the first. But Hersh-Leib pushed his way through them, reached his long arms up, and took the kugel from Eve, and smiled as he did so to the rebbitzin and to Eve.

The rebbitzin looked annoyed. But nobody was watching her now, because new cries were being raised:

"Here comes a third kugel!"

This time it was Sheba who brought in the third kugel. Hersh-Leib was immediately at her side, anxious for his third victory. But Sheba looked at him contemptuously: "Don't you dare to touch!"

She handed the kugel to the nearest Hasid, and told him to take it to the table and to say: "Mendel the orchardist has sent Sabbath fruit!"

Sheba moved toward the door to leave the room, but her mother, the rebbitzin, put her arms round her and held her back. They stood together at the door, both with their painful thoughts, watching the rebbe rule the table.

The rebbe passed round the bits and pieces from the food served to him, which he only tasted. Those nearest to him helped themselves from his plate, which then went round and round, till nothing was left on it.

Sheba hated it all. She loathed this kind of scene that she saw being repeated over and over again—her father presiding at the table, tasting the food as it was served to him, and then all the Hasidim grabbing at it, scrambling for the bits. Yet she couldn't help loving her father and admiring him. But the more she admired him the more ashamed she felt of what he was doing.

She felt like running out of the room, but her mother had her arms around her and held her back. It made her hate her mother. She wanted to get away. But her mother, the rebbitzin, just kept on hugging her daughter, full of maternal love!

While waiting for the meat to be served the Hasidim continued singing *zemiroth*, table hymns, in joyful praise of God and His Sabbath day, and His bounty in food and drink. Their hearts swelled with gratitude. The chief singer was Hersh-

Leib. He had a strong and sweet voice, and sang with great feeling. "Keep holy," he sang, "the Sabbath day, God's Commandment we obey!" And every time he lifted his eyes as he sang and met the rebbitzin's gaze he felt a thrill go through him, like an electric current. She bit her lips and looked away, and held on to her daughter Sheba. But every time she met his glance a tremor passed through her. Sheba, too, was aware of the glances of two young men following her about all the time—Yankel, who was sitting beside her father, and Shlomo Chayele's Bujas, about whom there were strange stories going about.

Hersh-Leib loved singing. He knew he had a good voice and that he sang well, and he enjoyed it. He showed off with it. It made him vain and conceited. But the Hasidim were carried away by his flights of song. Their hearts were full of gladness because of God's goodness, because of His Sabbath day of rest, and because of the food and the fruit and the wine that went round and round, and their mouths were filled with praises. Their song lifted them to wordless ecstasy, and Hersh-Leib led their song. Their voices rose like waves, higher and higher, on wings, up into the heavens.

The rebbe pressed Hersh-Leib's hand. "Thank you, Hersh-Leib! More strength to you! You have excelled yourself today! Thank you, everybody!"

The shamash brought in two big dishes of meat, roast chicken, beef, veal, and tongue, and served it round. Afterwards the rebbe distributed bits, and the Hasidim fought for them, as they had done before with the kugel. The same with the fruit. The rebbe took a pear, and then all snatched at the fruit.

The rebbe put his hand to his forehead as the preliminary to his exposition of Holy Writ. The Hasidim at the table called: "Quiet, please! The rebbe is going to speak Torah!"

There was an immediate hush, first in the big room, then in the adjoining room, where those Hasidim stood who hadn't been able to get into the first. As though everybody were holding their breath. But the rebbe felt somehow unable to say now what he wanted. He took one verse after the other, and explained it, drawing a moral from each, trying to pass on the thoughts that were occupying his mind. Useless. Other thoughts kept getting in the way. This wasn't the first time it had happened to him, but he had always before subdued the rebellious thoughts, and brought out his ideas clearly. This time he couldn't conquer those other thoughts. Perhaps because he had lifted his eyes a little while before and had seen his wife, the rebbitzin, bring in the kugel, and Hersh-Leib snatch it with the plate from her hands. She was now standing at the door, with closed eyes, apparently intent on hearing his words of Torah. But there was another thought that tormented the rebbe—was she there to listen to his exposition, or. . . . Why was Hersh-Leib standing so near to her!

Sheba too was standing at the door, but not as previously at her mother's side. Yankel couldn't take his eyes off her. He kept muttering to himself:

"You're a thief, and your father is a thief! You stood all night under her window to tell her how much you love her, hoping at least to say good morning to her, and so get to know her. But you just stood there like an idiot. Because she is the rebbe's daughter, and an angel from heaven!"

He remembered his dream, a young mother with her infant in the cradle. He had immediately realized that it was Sheba, and that she was kissing him. That he was the infant!

He saw Shlomo Chaye's Bujas also staring intently at Sheba. He envied him. Because Shlomo was studying and was sure to become a rabbi, and then she would marry him.

The rebbe began again: "And the earth was unformed and void, and darkness was upon the deep." He spoke of the emptiness, the void that had been and that might still be. "Only there is God in Heaven, and the Holy Spirit, His Shechina, and the angels. The world of the spirit, the higher world, the eternal, the true world. Only man . . . "

The rebbe passed to another thought that he wanted to relate to the first, and he couldn't. "And the spirit of God hovered over the deep." He tried to explain the connection between spirit and hovering—when man divests himself of the gross, the material, and becomes spiritual, he rises above the deep, is saved from the abyss, from chaos that lies in wait for him—he hovers over it, and does not fall.

Then he proceeded to a third text, also in Genesis: "Let there be light!" But again profane thoughts got in his way and confused him. His face darkened, and showed how he was tormented. Then suddenly: "And God created man in His own image, in the image of God He created him, male and female He created them." He began to argue that it is only man whom God created in His own image; when it says God created him male and female, it means that every man has something feminine, is part woman. Else man would not be drawn to woman, as he is, because she is part of him, and the parts unite through holy marriage, the wedding canopy, by which they become "one flesh."

He pursued his thought on different lines. "In the second chapter of Genesis, verse 21, it says that God caused a deep sleep to fall upon Adam, and He took one of his ribs, and of the rib He made a woman, and Adam said, 'This is bone of my bones, and flesh of my flesh.' " The rebbe interpreted the passage to mean that woman is not something outside man, apart from him. She was in man, bone of his bones and flesh of his flesh; only God cut her out of man's body. "She was taken out of man." "It is not good that man should be alone. I will make her as a help-meet for man."

The rebbe expounded the word *help-meet*, which in the original Hebrew is *kenegdu*, and pointed out that the word *keneged* means "Against"; that brought him to the serpent— "And she, the serpent!" he cried.

His unhappy thoughts wound themselves round his brain, became coiled serpents, hissing and biting and filling him with venom. Till finally he cried out: "I can't speak Torah now!"

The Hasidim were dismayed. They had seen for a long time how the rebbe was engaged in combat with the evil powers, with the Against, the Adversary, Satan! Ashmadai, the Devil himself! The silence laid its fingers on them like a strangler. But the gabbai soon dispelled the gloom and fear. He whispered to the shamash to bring in the wine. And as soon as he placed the big basket of bottles on the table everybody was cheerful again. Two Hasidim started opening the bottles. The shamash brought glasses and goblets. Wolf Jonachek recognized the basket and the bottles—his! He had brought them as a gift to the rebbe for Simchat Torah. So he said to the two Hasidim: "I'll open the bottles!" He used a corkscrew, and in no time he had all the bottles opened. And every time he pulled out a cork and it went pop, he laughed like a schoolboy with a popgun.

The gabbai filled the glass for the rebbe, and the shamash for the Hasidim. When the rebbe held up his glass and said "*L'Chaim*" the whole room rang with the response, "*L'Chaim*, Rebbe!"

When the crowd was a bit tipsy—there wasn't enough wine to make them drunk—they formed a circle and started a round dance. "Round the table!" some of them called out. Several clapped their hands and stamped their feet to the rhythm of the song.

"Take the table out!" some of them shouted. The ring of dancers grew bigger and wider. Out went the table. Wolf Jonachek lifted it himself—that big heavy table—and dumped it in the next room. Then he got hold of Yankel, and danced with him into the ring. His big red beard flew all over the place. He lifted his feet higher and higher, dancing more and more wildly, holding on to Yankel on one side and Hersh-Leib on the other.

5

All *sorts of* rumors were going around about the rebbitzin and Eve. Those religious Jews who were not Hasidim spoke of them openly, even with some *schadenfreude*, though also with considerable anger and indignation. The Hasidim dismissed the rumors with a wave of the hand, or denied them hotly: "Evil tongues! Slanderers! How can people invent stories like that! The rebbitzin herself! And the rebbe's daughter!"

Nevertheless, a good many Hasidim were worried. They didn't like Hersh-Leib—he was arrogant; and he did treat the rebbitzin with undue familiarity. They even began to wonder about the rebbe himself. They couldn't forget that he had seated the thief Wolf Jonachek and his son, another thief, next to him at the table.

But some had an answer to that—hadn't the little tailor himself taken this same Wolf Jonachek's grandfather, a receiver of stolen goods, to be his gabbai?

Then suddenly the rumors died away. There was a new sensation in the town, and everything else was forgotten. A man had come from some distant place with his son, who had a dybbuk, for the rebbe to exorcise.

"You see, how our Rebbe is famous all over the world!"
"They say the man has come all the way from Austria! Brought his son with the dybbuk to our rebbe!" "I saw the young man with the dybbuk! I saw him myself! His father was taking him to the rebbe's house! Such wild eyes he had!"

A sound of singing came from the distance, a wild frolicking air! No Jew would go through the streets singing like that! It could only be the dybbuk! Panic fell upon the crowd. Then presently the singer appeared, nearer and nearer. It was Sender Bebeck, a poor ragpicker, a man in his sixties, and despite his poverty always jolly and cheerful. He carried a big black bread under one arm, and held his wife on the other, and as he sang he kept calling to his wife:

"Come on, Zippe! Come on, Dance!"

"What's got into you, Sender! What are you so happy about? What makes you sing like that!"

Sender laughed. He was happy because he had a whole loaf of bread! His deep-sunk gray eyes gleamed as though he had been drinking brandy.

People used to ask him in fun: "Who's better off, Sender, Rothschild, or you?" His answer was always: "Me! I haven't got Rothschild's worries!"

Sender and his wife lived in a cellar that had only a hole instead of a window out to the street. Their children were all grown up and married, and as poor as they were. An upturned barrel served as their table, two old boxes for chairs, and a broken iron bedstead held together with rope and wire, and a straw pallet, and small iron stove that always smoked horribly. This was all their furniture. The place was overrun by mice and rats. But Sender felt more confortable, he said, there than Rothschild in his palace. And that was what people chaffed him about. "I've got nothing," he said, "and I need nothing!" Or else, "God gives me all that I need!"

His wife, who was so tall that he had to look up to her, was the opposite of him—always unhappy, always angry. She worked hard, carrying water to rich houses, and washing their clothes there. They gave her food, and she always brought some of it home for her husband. In return he gave her every small coin he got for the rags, old iron and bones that he picked out of the rubbish heaps. And he was always singing. He refused all offers of charity. He had no need of help, he said. He kept looking at his loaf of bread, and told his wife to dance! "Go on, Zippe, dance! We've got a loaf of bread, and we're going to buy a herring! Dance!"

The stranger who had come to the town with his son who was possessed by a dybbuk stayed at Reb Ozie's inn. Many Jews from the town came there now who were normally rare visitors. Because of the dybbuk. They told stories of other people who had been possessed by a dybbuk, and how this rebbe or the other in one of the towns they knew, had exorcised it. They knew just how and under what circumstances a dybbuk seeking a human habitation can enter into one's body. They argued about which dybbuk was more dangerous—that of a virgin maid, or of a woman who had already known a man, one who had lived a life of sin or one who had been a woman of virtue. They had heated discussions about young maidens who had died and had hung about the home of the young man to whom they had been betrothed, waiting for the opportunity to enter into him, and about young men who had been so much in love that they could not depart from the presence of the beloved, and had visited her and finally possessed her.

They spoke of the different ways of exorcism, how the rebbe fasted and prayed, the prayers he said, his spells and incantations, and some repeated thoughts that had filtered down to them from the Cabala. They spoke of the transmigration of souls, and of wondering souls that came to occupy the bodies of beasts and birds.

Reb Ozie's inn did a roaring trade. He and his wife, his sons and daughters, were all kept busy serving beer and brandy and food. Not that Jews were really beer drinkers. They drank an occasional glass, and made a face at the bitter taste. They sat puffing at their pipes and their cigarettes, filling the room with thick smoke that hung from the ceiling and got inside the double windows that were stuffed between the outer glass and the inner glass with cotton wool to keep out the cold and the wind, and were decorated with colored paper and small toys. The air was dense with smoke and alcohol, pickled herrings and onions and vinegar, cooked meats and roast meats and fish and cakes. The door opened and shut all the time, with people coming and going. And groups stood in the street outside all the time, discussing and arguing. Those who felt the cold came into the inn and had a drink and a bite. Every time the door opened an icy blast blew in.

Reb Ozie, the innkeeper, was a plain, honest man who, before the big power factories had come to the town, had been a dealer in flax, and had made his living at it. But the power factories had put him out of business, so he had started the inn. He remained the same pious, honest Jew. Every evening he went to the Beth Hamedrash to join in the prayers. He could read and understand a learned work of pious literature. He was neither a Hasid nor a Mithnagid, one of the pious antagonists of the Hasidim. He liked the good in both of them. He didn't go to the rebbe, and knew little about him. So that when people asked him for his opinion about the rebbe he shrugged his shoulders and said nothing.

A crowd of arguing Jews stood round Reb Ozie, demanding that he should tell them what he thought about dybbukim and about exorcising them. He smiled good-naturedly and said there were different ways of looking at it. And when they pressed him to say something about the young man who had the dybbuk and was staying at his inn, he said that the father had told him the boy had immersed himself too deeply in Cabala.

"And through using a false Name! (Shem)," several broke in excitedly.

"Yes, through a Shem," Reb Ozie went on, calmly. "The young man wanted by using the Shem to establish contact with a great cabalist and wonder worker who had lived in his town and had died a few years before. He wanted to discover through him the date when Messiah would come and redeem the people of Israel from exile, and the whole world from sin and suffering. That wasn't all. He wanted to discover things that must remain secret, hidden, must not even be mentioned. Then suddenly the dead cabalist began to speak from his tongue. Only people were not sure if it was really the cabalist who spoke, or if it was a great sinner, a dreadful denier who had died in the same town, and had caused many Jewish boys and girls to stray from the Jewish path. More than a year now that the dybbuk speaks from the young man's tongue. That's what his father told me."

"Have you heard the dybbuk speak from the young man?"

"I have spoken to the young man," the speaker answered evasively.

"Then you have spoken to the dybbuk."

"I said I spoke to the young man!"

"You don't believe in the dybbuk?" several voices rose incredulously, menacingly.

"I believe in God, Blessed be His Name! And I believe in His Torah."

The people returned to their tables, arguing, disputing excitedly.

It went on like that almost the whole day. Till the people became aware of something happening outside. There was a noise there, running and shouting. Everybody ran to the door, rushed out. From all sides people were streaming toward Reb Ozie's inn, crowding round the side door that led to the rooms kept for guests. The story had got round that the stranger would be coming out any minute now, with his son who was possessed by the dybbuk, to take him to the rebbe's house. But the afternoon was already turning to dusk, and the stranger and his son had not appeared.

Some who were waiting outside the inn said the Mincha afternoon prayers out there in the open. Some didn't. By the time the gabbai and the shamash arrived it was quite dark. They looked grave and solemn. They mounted the four steps to the door and vanished inside. The few minutes till they reappeared at the same door with the stranger and his son seemed endless. A thrill ran through the crowd when they saw by the light of the electric lamp the thin young man with drawn face and long earlocks leaning like a sick person on his father's arm. The father, who had a very long beard, looked worried and depressed. The crowd parted to make room for the four, and then followed them to the rebbe's house, the gabbai in front, then the stranger with his son, and the shamash last. The crowd remained outside when they entered the house.

A feeling of awe fell on the crowd gathered outside the rebbe's house, hoping to catch a glimpse of the dybbuk being exorcised. This house, which was for so long familiar and friendly ground to them, their habitual meeting place on Friday nights and Saturdays and festivals, now cast dread upon them. The town hall stood near the rebbe's house, and the metal weathercock on the roof turned in the wind with a creaking, frightening noise. The people looked up at it, and began to imagine that the town hall was growing upward, lifting itself high into the air. The houses round about, the tall factory chimneys, and the cupolas of the church took on fantastic shapes, became huge black shadows reaching into the sky.

One man with tense eyes and pricked ears thought he heard the rebbe speak to the dybbuk.

"Can you hear it?" he whispered to his neighbors. And immediately everybody was sure that they could hear. Then came the blast of the shofar, and the rebbe ordering the dybbuk to depart from the young man's body.

"Dybbuk of Reb Gershon Markushov! I command you to leave the body of Zephania ben Baruch!"

But the dybbuk wouldn't go. Now the waiting crowd heard the rebbe command that the great shofar blast, *Tekiah Gedolah*, be sounded. They saw the black candles burning, and they heard the Tekiah Gedolah, loud and long, drawn out; it ended with a strange screech. There was a rushing in their ears. And a throbbing in their heads. The air grew oppressive, and they found it difficult to breathe. Then they heard the rebbe's voice, and the dybbuk answering him. There were two voices answering the rebbe—a weak, sick voice, that of the young man who was possessed, and a harsh, deep voice, the dybbuk in possession.

"Can you hear?" people whispered, awestruck, to each other.

"There is no world to come!" they heard a deep, scornful voice proclaim. "There is no God! There is no Heaven! Only this world! Hell and Paradise, angels and demons, Shechina and the Powers of Darkness, Ashmedai and the Great Father—they are all only in this world!"

They heard the rebbe shout and storm: "Silence, dybbuk! Be quiet! I command you to be quiet!"

But the dybbuk wouldn't be quiet. They heard the rebbe's voice rise louder:

"Dybbuk! You speak falsehoods! What you say is lies and nonsense! You are a soul gone astray!"

The dybbuk shouted back: "Lies! Lies! All I was taught is lies and nonsense! Torah, Talmud, all falsehood, lies and foolishness!"

The rebbe banged his stick on the floor.

"Quiet, you! You didn't understand what you were taught! You're a fool, and you're an ignoramus!"

Now the weak, sick voice was heard:

"Rebbe . . . Rebbe . . ." And the voice broke into sobbing. "Rebbe, I'm a liar and a fool! I have lost my faith in God, in the Holy One of Israel, who will redeem His people from Exile, and in the Messiah, who will establish truth and justice!"

Then the strange deep voice rose again: "I will create a new world, a new heaven and a new Torah! There will be no clouds in heaven! Paradise without hell! Angels without demons, Torah, the Law without the letter. Man will not need to learn and will know everything! He will do only good! He will not sin! He will only create, and he will not destroy! He will not believe in God, yet God will be within him! There will be man, not God!"

Only a few people standing right on top of the rebbe's house could hear all this. The others caught broken words, isolated words that made no sense, and they filled in the blanks each according to his own imagination, so that the next day all sorts of conflicting versions of what had been heard went round the town.

The winter transformed the town completely. The small houses in the narrow streets shrank and huddled together under the thick cover of snow on the roofs and on the ground below, into which they were stuck. The new big dwelling blocks and the massive factory buildings in the broad pavemented main streets had also lost their usual gay boisterousness, and now looked grim and sullen, though within their walls the rush and roar of industry and commerce went on just the same.

But to the outskirts of the town, to the fields and the forest and the great highway stretching into the distance, the winter brought peace and tranquility.

The Jews of this town, where the little tailor had once lived, and the Jews of the neighboring town, regarded the winter as the most favorable time of the year for marriages. Jonachek decided that this would be the right moment for the marriage of the poor widow's daughter for whom he had been collecting a dowry and wedding expenses. It must be a grand wedding, he told himself. He had got three hundred roubles from Fat Freida, and had added three hundred roubles from his own pocket, and he had given the whole six hundred to the widow, placed it in her hand. "Make it a grand wedding!" he had said to her. "No stinting! If you're short I'll let you have more! Everything of the best! Plenty to eat and plenty to drink. And ask everybody in the town to come! All the poor people! Leave nobody out! Get the best musicians and let the dancing go on all night. Let them enjoy themselves!"

The wedding was on a Tuesday, exactly a week after the rebbe had demonstrated his wonder-working powers by expelling the dybbuk from the strange young man. On the previous Sabbath there was a big party in the widow's house, as the custom was. Women and girls, poor but dressed in their

Sabbath and festival best, came there with true joy in their hearts, to share in the happiness of the bride and the bride's mother, thus adding to their happiness. The room had been freshly whitewashed, the floor scrubbed, the stove heated and spreading the heat through the room. The bride sat at the table in a new dress, the guests all round her. They cracked nuts, chewed sweets and chocolate, and drank cherry brandy, fruit juice, and tea, with cakes and biscuits, and wished the bride happiness. This went on till late at night.

On the Monday, the day before the wedding, the widow and several other women took the bride to the ritual bath. They had cake and cherry brandy, and drank to the bride's health. Afterwards, in the house, the women spoke with piously veiled allusions about the love that a woman must give her husband, and offered her womanly advice on how to conduct herself.

On her wedding day the bride rose very early, put on her white dress, and said the morning prayers.

"This is your Judgment Day, daughter," her mother said to her, "the day on which your whole future life is being determined. Today you must stand before God with a broken and contrite heart, praying to Him to forgive and pardon all the sins which you have committed all through your life. This day is your Yom Kippur. And as on Yom Kippur, it is for you a day of fasting!"

The bride wept bitterly. She said the "Al Chait" prayer, "For all these sins, O God of forgiveness, forgive us, grant us pardon, grant us atonement."

Then she went with her mother to the cemetery, to her father's grave, to invite him to her wedding. She prayed all day to God to forgive her sins and to grant her and her husband a happy life together and good children.

The first wedding guests, the bride's closest girl friends, arrived around three o'clock. They hugged her and kissed her, and wept with her. Then they all helped her on with the white wedding dress and the veil, and stood admiring her: "You look lovely! Beautiful! Like a princess!"

Next the girls prepared the bridal chair. They set a chair at the top of the room, with blocks of wood under the legs to make the chair higher, like a throne, and other blocks of wood in front as steps for the throne, and draped it all with a sheet. The bride was seated on her throne, with two small tables on either side, one with polished brass candlesticks with lighted candles, the other with vases of flowers. Two of the bride's best girl friends stood on each side of the throne as her attendants.

The guests were now arriving in streams, girls and young women, all in their best clothes, so that even the poorest looked well dressed.

They all admired the bride. The girls and women kissed her. "You look really beautiful!" "What a wonderful throne!" "Just like a real throne with a real queen!" "A bride on her wedding day is a queen!"

The musicians started playing—waltzes, polkas, mazurkas, and the guests danced.

Wolf Jonachek was busy with the wedding from early morning, as though he were the bride's father or uncle. He engaged the town shamash to go to special houses to invite the guests he particularly wanted. None of them were rich or persons of quality. They were ordinary poor people, but such who in Wolf Jonachek's opinion observed Judaism properly. He invited nobody who had a reputation in the town of being "enlightened," a disbeliever, a heretic. And he sent the shamash to the rebbe to ask him to come and perform the ceremony. When the shamash suggested that this was the prerogative of the rav, Wolf Jonachek glared at him, so that the shamash was scared:

"When I say the rebbe I mean the rebbe! If the rav has a prerogative, and there's a fee to be paid to him I'll pay it. But the wedding ceremony must be performed by the rebbe."

The night was falling now. Several guests came running to the bride with the news that the bridegroom had already arrived in the town.

"He's just arrived! Five sleighs with bells!"

The bride blushed, dropped her eyes, and smiled happily.

"Is he handsome?" some of the younger girls wanted to know, thinking ahead to the day when they would themselves be brides, waiting for their bridegroom to arrive.

"We didn't wait to see," those who had brought the news answered.

A big jolly man with a heavy fur raised his voice to ask why the musicians hadn't gone to meet the bridegroom and play him into the town. Immediately the musicians broke off playing, and went with their instruments to receive the bridegroom with musical honors. The girls and young women who had been dancing stood around, waiting. And presently the musicians were heard coming back, playing a cheerful march, and the girls and young women ran out to see the bridegroom.

There were indeed five sleighs. The bridegroom was in the first, with several young men, his friends. His parents were in the second sleigh with his brothers and sisters and other members of the family. And in the other three sleighs were the guests on the bridegroom's side, people from his own town. And the sleighs not only had bells, but flaming torches as well. So the sleighs came with a rush and a clatter, their little bells tinkling, and drove at full speed three times round the town hall. The bridegroom's party had been drinking. They had several bottles of brandy with them, and they were in a merry mood, shouting and singing.

The girls who had come out to see the bridegroom rushed back to the bride:

"We've seen him! He *is* handsome!"

The sleighs stopped outside Reb Ozie's inn. Wolf Jonachek had made arrangements for the bridegroom to stay there. He had himself selected the best room, and said:

"See that there's plenty of beer and brandy! And lots of food! I'll pay!"

Young men and older established householders and businessmen settled in the town came to welcome the bridegroom. A lot of tables had been arranged in the room, all with white tablecloths, and cigarettes everywhere, the best brand—provided by Wolf Jonachek. All the men were smoking. Even some who had never smoked before.

The musicians were playing in a circle round the bride. The girls and young women didn't want to stop dancing. The tables in the women's part of the room were also loaded with food and drink, but they were mostly sweet drinks, liqueurs, and there were cakes and sweets and fruit flans. The mothers of the bride and bridegroom both went round with trays, pressing the guests to have something, not to break off to go to the loaded tables. The girls and young women were too much taken up with their dancing even to bother to help themselves from the trays. Of course there was no mixed dancing. The women and girls danced only with each other.

This continued till it was time to "cover" the bride. The playing and dancing stopped. The bride's best friends undid her plaits, so that her hair hung loose. All the other girls stood round, admiring her hair that tomorrow would be cut off. More candles were lighted, and a hush fell on the room. The "badchan," the jester, had taken his place beside the bride. "Dear bride," he sang, "remember what this day to you will betide."

When you go with your bridegroom under the wedding canopy
    as his bride,
It means that on this day
You must confess your sins to God, and pray
That He may forgive whatever you may have done.
As a father forgives his own child, his own.

The bride sobbed bitterly, and all the women and girls sobbed and kept wiping their eyes.

At the end of each line of the badchan's song the musicians came in with a flourish, the fiddles and the trumpet and loudest of all the drum.

The badchan was now declaiming a long rhymed harangue, which all might hear but which was addressed primarily to the bride, full of hints and allegories, pointing the moral about human life, brief and full of trouble, like a bit of wood tossed on the waves. And the bride had a good cry.

Mordecai, the first fiddle, was also the conductor. And when the badchan finished, Mordecai struck up the Kol Nidrei. He closed his eyes and put on a very serious face, and his fiddle sobbed and moaned. He played well, with great feeling, and all the wedding guests were in tears. They loved it. It was so solemn, so full of pious memories—the synagogue on the holiest night of the Jewish year, the congregation hushed and awestricken for the great Day of Judgment.

There was a sudden cry: "The Bride has fainted!"

Mordecai stopped playing. He woke as if out of another world. For a minute or two his orchestra was silent. Then off he went with a merry tune that set all feet dancing. The bride recovered, and smiled. Everybody was happy.

Then the badchan started again. Now he was calling the bride's dead father to her wedding, to give her his blessing when she stood under the canopy. The women drew back to make way for the dead soul. Two candles were lighted specially for him. The bride bent her head. Some of the women guests went pale, feeling the presence of the dead soul.

The badchan spoke about the bride's dead father, who had died young, had not lived to see his daughter grow up and be a bride. That made the bride howl. "My dear father!" she cried out. And fainted again. Women dashed water in her face, and revived her. Then the chazan sang the *El Mole Rachmim*, the Memorial Prayer—"O God, full of mercy!"

With the last note of the Memorial Prayer joyful cries rose—"The bridegroom is coming!" The fiddlers played a merry tune, and the shamash moved right up to the front of the crowd—"Make way for the bridegroom!"

The bridegroom approached, and placed the headcloth on the bride's head. The women pelted him with hops, and the girls with confetti. Then his companions led him away again.

Colored candles, all colors, were passed round. Each woman and each girl was given a candle; she lighted it, and took her place, each with a burning candle in her hand, in the procession that now formed behind the bride. Her escorts made sure that when they came to the threshold the bride should cross it right foot first. The musicians went in front, playing. The bridegroom already stood under the canopy, waiting, and her escorts led the bride round him seven times.

But the rebbe, who was to perform the ceremony, had not yet arrived. Then the shamash came rushing in, to say the rebbe couldn't come.

Wolf Jonachek went white. An old pious Jew performed the marriage ceremony instead. The bridegroom repeated word for word the "Harei At," "Behold, thou are consecrated unto me. . . ." The bridegroom and then the bride sipped wine from the consecration glass, which was then placed on the floor, and he set his right foot on it and crushed it.

Then the marriage certificate was read, and everybody wished the newly wed pair happiness and good fortune, Mazel Tov.

Back to the widow's home the bridegroom walked with the bride on his arm; the musicians went in front, playing a jolly tune. An old woman danced toward them with a big loaf of bread. When they reached the house they were taken to a separate room and left alone. The old woman stood by the door to see that nobody should come near. Soon the door opened, and husband and wife came out. They were seated at the top of the table, and they now had their first food after a whole day's fasting. The guests drank their health. There were two waiters who served at the tables.

It was a jolly wedding. Everybody ate and drank and was merry. Especially the old woman, who when she was offered a glass of brandy, men's brandy, took it, and then took another, without turning a hair.

Wolf Jonachek thought the waiters were too slow; so he tied a big apron round his middle and helped them. He served double portions to the poorest—"Eat!" he kept calling out to them. "East as much as you want!"

Some slipped cakes and rolls and chunks of meat into their pockets for afterwards.

The badchan improvised rhymed verses for the chief

guests. He started with the bride and bridegroom, poking quiet fun at them, nothing that would hurt, yet made everybody laugh. Then he sang a verse for Wolf Jonachek, satirizing him as an honest man, who never touched anything belonging to someone else. But he also sang his praises, as an upholder of Jewishness, a friend of the poor, a man who couldn't stand an injustice, who always took the part of those who were wronged and aggrieved. Most of the guests applauded. But Wolf Jonachek wouldn't have it. "It isn't true!" he cried. "Tell them the truth about me! I'm a thief! Why hide it! Everybody knows!"

Then the badchan made up a song about the rich—that nobody got rich by working with his own two hands—they lived on the work of others, exploiting the workers, making profits out of them. The same with the merchants, who grew rich by getting the better of those they dealt with, outwitting them.

Wolf Jonachek's wife Golda liked that.

"You're right there!" she shouted. "Absolutely true! Here's a whole rouble for you!"

Wolf Jonachek was puzzled—it didn't seem right. He didn't see it that way. So he stood up and he said so: "I don't agree! There's nothing wrong with becoming rich through business and industry. It's the Bolsheviks who don't like rich people. We'll deal with the Bolsheviks afterwards. They cause all the trouble here—strikes and fights and undermining Judaism! All the same, you sing well, and you make up clever rhymes. Here's three roubles for you!"

It was not a rich crowd, but there were three plates on the big table into which everybody put a coin or two, with a sign in each plate, "Bride's Dowry Fund," "Help for the Sick Fund," "Aid for the Old People's Fund."

The badchan then got up on a chair and announced the presents. "On the bridegroom's side Reb Aaron and his wife a pair of 'gold' candlesticks—no carat mark, but they shine like gold!" "From the bridegroom's older brother, Reb Isaac and his wife six small 'silver' spoons and forks and knives, for the newlyweds' children to use. . . ."

The bride blushed, and all the girls giggled.

"On the bride's side," the badchan continued, stating each present, and whom it came from. He inflated everything, exaggerated the value and importance, made it look big, "gold" and "silver"; and a rouble was announced with a flourish as if it were a hundred. And everybody was Reb Somebody, and everybody was "respected" and "renowned" and "honored" and "esteemed."

Some of the guests had clubbed together, and one group presented a table, another a bed, a third sheets, a fourth a tablecloth, or cups and saucers or a pot and a pan. Most of the presents, especially the household necessities really came from Wolf Jonachek, only he had arranged to have them announced in the names of different guests, not his own name.

When all the presents had been announced the musicians started playing again, and the guests danced and talked and laughed and enjoyed themselves. Then the badchan announced: "Now we will join the bride in the mitzvah dance!"

A young woman took off her silk scarf, and this was held out to keep the sexes from touching. First the bridegroom danced with the bride. Each held one end of the scarf, and turned three times from right to left. The music played, and everybody clapped.

Then the shamash called by name the next man privileged to dance the mitzvah dance with the bride. It was Wolf Jonachek, and his wife. Others followed. And after a time, the bride disappeared. The old woman said that she wanted to dance a waltz, and she wanted a young girl to partner her. All the young girls volunteered, but she chose the youngest and prettiest girl to dance with. The musicians played slowly, because she was an old woman, and they thought she wouldn't be able to take quick steps. But she protested loudly. "Faster! Faster!" she kept calling.

The young girl with whom she was dancing couldn't keep up the pace and dropped out. "Young girls nowadays!" the old lady scoffed. "Go and sit down, my child, and rest your poor feet!"

Then she turned to an old man, about her own age, and

said: "You come and dance with me, Itze! Play, musicians, play!" And keeping their proper distance, the silk scarf between them, the two old folk danced as fast as the music played, singing the words to the tune:

> *Don't look at me with anger,*
> *Because I said that and this!*
> *Put a meal on the table,*
> *And I'll give you a kiss!*

Then the two old folk, widow and widower, kissed. Before the winter was out they were married.

Next everybody formed a circle with the bridegroom, and the musicians played a round dance, fast and faster, till suddenly in the midst of the dance the bridegroom disappeared as the bride had disappeared before.

It was now getting late, and the orchestra struck up the final song, in which the remaining guests joined:

> *Home, home, home!*
> *Now we must all go home!*
> *We've danced and had a jolly time,*
> *And now must all go home!*

6

Though Joseph had got more or less accustomed to the new ways of life that had come to the town with industrialization, he was not altogether at ease in his mind about them. How long is it, he kept saying to himself, since this was a small town. And it is after all still a small town. Many of the old houses that escaped the fire are still standing, and all the old narrow streets are here, and the market place is just the same as it was—whole parts of the town hadn't changed. Even the old small-town way of life had persisted.

Joseph began to look under the surface; he became a passionate seeker for beginnings and sources—how things had happened and why. From the time he had started reading profane literature, worldly books, it had been clear to him that the flames that had seized hold of the old ways and customs had really been smoldering underneath for a long time before. The sparks had been there—the new thoughts. Not only in this town but in most towns of the same character round about. The sparks had been kindled in every Beth Hamedrash, though most of those who had adopted the new ideas had at first kept silent, fearing that they would be persecuted if it became known. But some couldn't keep silent. And

107

the heavy hand of religious orthodoxy had fallen on them and crushed them. But the smoldering continued, and then at last it had all flared up into a great blaze, into a conflagration that had swept into the quiet pious home of his parents, Reb Abraham and his wife Rachel, and had overwhelmed the little tailor's seed.

Joseph saw how the catastrophe affected both sides—the young people who had plunged into the broad stream of Socialism, and the older folk, who clung to their religious beliefs, and had tried to revive the old Hasidic fervor round the table of the wonder-working dybbuk-exorcising rebbes.

Fireworks, he called it, compared to the rich glow of the old Hasidism, which had started with the Baal Shem and had ended with his own great-grandfather, the little tailor. Fireworks was the name he also gave the opposition movement, the new Socialism that had invaded the town, and preached a cheap freethinking and a cheap free love; compared to true Socialism it was demagogy.

Joseph spoke to the rabbi of the town, who had become his guide and adviser. The rabbi urged him to go to Warsaw and take up systematic study. He gave him the address of a friend of his in Warsaw, a man of learning, he said, who could assist him. Joseph jumped at the idea. Though the town had grown tremendously it was still provincial at the side of a city like Warsaw. It was not the place where he could find the education he wanted. He was anxious to get away also for another reason—not to have his parents see what he was doing, not to hurt them. He knew how upset they were seeing him reading "Goyish" books instead of studying the Gemara. He stopped drawing and painting and carving. He fought down this passion of his as he had fought down too his love for Sheba, which had still not progressed to the stage of their becoming acquainted. It was largely due to the natural shyness of a young man who had been brought up in the Beth Hamedrash; but he had also held back because of the rumors in the town about her older sister Eve. It all added to his desire to get away—to Warsaw.

Joseph came to Warsaw a naive provincial. He had never been in such a big place before. And he had the idea that everybody in such a city was wise and learned and even the poorest lived better than the people in the provincial towns. He expected to find himself plunged into a sea of knowledge. He came eager to drink of the fountain of wisdom.

He set out on his journey to Warsaw soon after Passover. He stared out through the window of his train, and everything seemed wonderful—the fields, the meadows, the forests, the rivers, the wide expanses. At first it seemed to him that the whole countryside was rolling past him, and he was stationary. He recalled the lessons in astronomy that the rabbi had given him, and how it was the earth that moved around the sun, while it seemed to us that we stood still and the sun moved around the earth.

He sat in the train thinking of his parents, and of his sister Miriam, and of Sheba. He decided to forget Sheba. But the further away the train took him the stronger his love for her grew. He could see her now as though she were standing in front of him. Then suddenly the train stopped, and he was in Warsaw.

The rush and roar in the station and in the street outside the station absolutely bewildered him. He felt lost in the whir and whirl of the city's traffic, the droskys and tramcars and the streams of people hurrying past. He was overwhelmed by the height of the tenement blocks; so many windows and so little sky. He felt a stranger there, in a different world.

He walked through the streets, carrying his valise, not knowing, not thinking even where he was going. Why were all these people in such a hurry? All these people rushing past!

Suddenly he stopped. Where am I going? he asked himself. He took out his notebook from his pocket and ran his eye down the list of addresses. There was a cousin of his father's, there was a timber merchant with whom his father did business, and there was the rabbi's friend. He decided that he would pay his first visit to his father's cousin—his own flesh and blood.

He tried to ask several people how to get to the Mila Street, where the cousin lived; but nobody would stop to listen to his question. They had no time. One barked at him: "Get a drosky!"

There was a beggar standing in a gateway. Joseph gave him a few small coins and asked him how to get to the Mila Street. "Take that tramcar!" said the beggar. So Joseph jumped on, only to find that he was going in the opposite direction. A man who was getting off the tram put him on the right side and told him what stop to get off at. At last Joseph arrived there, at his relative's home.

Joseph was tired and wanted desperately to sit down, but his relative, a little shriveled man with an untidy beard, didn't offer him a seat. He looked at Joseph suspiciously. "Who are you? What do you want?" he said to Joseph. That puzzled Joseph, because he had said who he was as soon as he came into the room. But finally it struck him that the man was deaf. So he went close up to him, and shouted into his ear. Still the old man hadn't heard.

The old man called to someone outside. Joseph began to wonder whether he hadn't better make some excuse and go. He looked round the room, and his heart sank.

It was a dark damp cellar, and it stank. It had hardly any furniture in it, but against all the four walls stood iron beds covered with dirty blankets, and valises and trunks under each bed. There was a table and a pail. Only one small window in the whole room. A rat ran by and disappeared down a hole.

Joseph felt homesick for his father's clean comfortable house with its fine furniture.

An old woman came in, in answer to the old man's call.

"What d'you want?" she asked Joseph.

He told her.

"He's a relative! Abraham's son!"

"Abraham's son! Shalom Aleichem!" said the old man, brightening. He brought over a chair and asked Joseph to sit down.

"How's your father? And your mother?" And he started telling the old woman how rich and kind Joseph's father, his cousin Abraham was.

"You never told me you've got a rich cousin!" the old woman complained, still not very friendly to Joseph. Till the old man reminded her of a number of occasions when Joseph's father had sent him money when he had written to him that things were hard. The old woman thawed.

"What brings you to Warsaw?"

"I've come to study. . . ," he stammered.

"Have you said your Mincha and Maariv prayers?" she wanted to know.

Joseph flushed. In the confusion of his arrival in Warsaw he had forgotten to say his prayers.

"I know them, these small town provincials!" the old woman grumbled. "As soon as they leave home they forget to say their prayers!"

Joseph said the Mincha and Maariv prayers and then she put a dirty cloth on the table, the heel of a loaf, a salt cellar, a knife and a tin fork and spoon. And when he had washed his hands, and her husband too, she served the meal, a kind of stew, in tin bowls. Joseph couldn't eat it. It was horrible stuff. He couldn't get it down his throat. But he didn't want to offend, so he tried to swallow it. He left more than half. He left the bit of boiled meat she had put in his bowl.

After they had said grace and the two old folk began to discuss where their visitor should sleep. They decided to put him in the same bed as the carpenter who hadn't paid his rent for the second month.

Joseph couldn't get to sleep in that narrow iron bed, though he was terribly tired. The blanket was heavy and torn and saturated with the sweat of many previous sleepers. The sheet was stained. The pillow was hard. And it smelt. His eyes were

111

like lead, but the weight of the blanket and the dirt and the smell kept him awake. Then he jumped. Something had bitten him. The bed was full of vermin. Joseph scratched like mad.

The two old folk lay in one of the beds partitioned off from the rest by a sheet that could be drawn aside by a cord. They too couldn't sleep, though they were inured to the vermin and the other discomforts of these beds. Joseph heard the old woman grumbling: "They're not in yet! Nice bunch of lodgers we've got!"

The lodgers who came in very late were all workmen who had come to Warsaw from the provinces. Some were married. Some were single. There had been no work for them in their own small towns. They were tailors, shoemakers, cabinet-makers, bakers. There were some, too, who had no trained occupation, unskilled workers.

The lodgers started to arrive in ones and twos and threes. And though it was late they didn't go to bed, but sat around by their beds, smoking and talking, very quietly, whispering, among the shadows which the glow of their cigarettes cast in the dark.

Joseph lay wide awake. He kept his ears pricked, to make out what they were saying. They spoke of Socialism, of a strike that "the Committee" had ordered. One said "Peretz is with us! Absolutely! Have you read his poem 'The Night Watchmen'? How he digs at those pious frauds!"

He began to quote:

It's a beautiful night, folk! Time to retire.
But guard against fire! Guard against fire!
No light in your minds, in your pious hearts not a spark!

Be quiet, leave everything dark!
Now sleep soundly in your beds!
We are the night watchmen! Don't trouble your heads!

The old man and the old woman had fallen asleep and were snoring. Some of the lodgers, too, had got into bed and complained that the whispering kept them awake. One by one all the others went to bed. The man who climbed into the bed where Joseph had been put was annoyed to find somebody there already.

"What are you doing in my bed?"

"I was given this bed!"

"Get out! It's my bed! There's no room here for two!"

The noise wakened the old woman, and she called across from the other side of the sheet:

"If you don't like it you can have your money back and get a room at the Hotel Bristol!"

Joseph felt uncomfortable and wanted to get out of bed. But the other wouldn't let him. "Stay where you are! We'll manage!"

They both had a very bad night, twisting and turning and finding no comfort. But in the end they dropped off to sleep, first the carpenter and then Joseph. The last thing he remembered before he fell asleep was the name Peretz.

All the lodgers had gone when Joseph woke. The old man told him where the privy was—out in the yard. Then he showed him the tap where to wash. The cold water refreshed him for a while. But it wasn't long before he was feeling like a man with a hangover.

He was hungry, and he opened the valise where his mother had packed some food for him. His tephilin bag lay on top, and reminded him that he still had to say his morning prayers first. He put on his tephillin and said his prayers. He ate a roll and butter and a beigel and a hard-boiled egg. He gave the rest of the food that he had brought in the valise to the old woman. That pleased her, and she gave him a glass of hot tea.

He asked her the way to the Leszno Street, and she gave him the directions. "It's quite near."

Leszno Street was where the rabbi's learned friend lived. Joseph mounted the stairs to the third floor. There was the name on a brass plate, in Russian, Polish, and Hebrew: "Zvi Perlman, Private Teacher in Hebrew, Russian, and Mathematics, and writer of official Petitions."

Holding the rabbi's letter in his hand Joseph timidly knocked at the door.

"Who is it?" came a woman's voice from the other side of the door.

Joseph explained through the door that he had a letter to Mr. Perlman from his friend the rabbi in his town. The woman undid the bolt and let him in. She was plump, with blond graying hair, and she wore a blue flowered kimono. She took the letter from him, went off with it to her husband, and returned to conduct him to the learned man.

Joseph found himself in a large room with two curtained windows, bookcases crammed with books, a big table, a couch, some chairs and an armchair, in which Pan Perlman sat.

Joseph was very deferential, but Pan Perlman was frigid and aloof. He held out two fingers condescendingly, and said, "And how is Reb Israel Sapiro, the rav in your town?"

Pan Perlman was a stocky man with a neatly trimmed little gray beard, a high forehead, dark glasses, and a gold watch chain over his paunch.

"And what can I do for you?", he went on. "My friend writes that you studied in the Beth Hamedrash and you know a little Gemara—and that's all you know. You've read a few books. What about the Bible—the Prophets and the Chronicles?"

"I know them."

"What about Hebrew? Grammar?"

"Not enough."

"Russian grammar?"

"Not enough."

"Polish?"

"Even less."

"So it means the only language you know well is Jargon. Listen to me, young man. I'm going to write down for you some books you've got to buy—and you must buy them in this bookshop, at this address. I'll give you four lessons a week. That'll cost you twenty roubles a month. I charge thirty to anyone else. But as you've been sent by my friend . . . "

Joseph walked down the three flights of stairs slowly, hesitatingly, one step at a time, as though trying to recall something he had forgotten. He didn't remember what it was till he had got down to the bottom. He had meant to ask the learned teacher where he could get a room. The man's attitude had put him off, and it had gone out of his head. He didn't care for this Zvi Perlman.

Joseph was feeling very depressed. He didn't like Warsaw. It was an unfriendly place.

As it happened it was a beautiful sunny Spring day, and the Leszno Street was a broad bright road with a wide expanse of blue sky, not like the narrow little streets round Mila, where he had been wandering before, and where he had spent the night. He was still bewildered by the rush of traffic and the endless stream of pedestrians, and deafened by the shouting of the street traders. Warsaw seemed to him an inferno.

He stopped at the first corner and took out his notebook to look up the address of the timber merchant to whom his father had given him an introduction. He might help him to find a room; he couldn't spend another night like last night.

He asked a man how he could get to the Jerusalemska Avenue.

"Take that tram. It goes right through Jerusalemska Avenue."

When Joseph got off the tram his mood had changed completely. The Jerusalemska Avenue was quite a different Warsaw. Like another world. None of the rush and roar of those narrow little streets, no shouting and no ringing of bells, no market traders. The air was fresh and clean. The houses were tall and handsome. And there were trees on both sides of the Avenue. This was where he would like to live!

The porter at the gate asked whom he wanted to see. And when Joseph said, "Pan Goldstein" the porter looked at him with respect.

"Pan Goldstein lives on the first floor."

Joseph admired the marble staircase and the red carpet. A maid wearing a white apron opened the door to his ring, and asked him to wait in the hall. Pan Goldstein came out immediately. He was an elegant, dignified-looking gentleman, and he treated Joseph as a very welcome guest. He invited him in and presented him to his wife.

"This is Joseph Sherman. His father, Reb Abraham, supplies most of my timber."

Joseph couldn't believe it—this young woman Pan Goldstein's wife! She looked like his daughter. But then he realized that it was the way she dressed and her makeup that gave her this youthful appearance. She thought Joseph was a nice boy, and she liked him. In the fashion of the Polish gentility she extended her hand for Joseph to kiss, but he was ignorant of this polite custom, and she was peeved when he ignored it. But the smile didn't leave her face. She asked him the name of his town—was it a big town? Where was it?

It was clear to her husband that she was putting the young man in his place, making him feel by her questions that he was a little provincial who didn't know his manners. He didn't think he would realize what she was doing. All the same, in case he did, he tried to put things right.

"My dear," he began, "this young man's great-grandfather was a saint in Israel, a famous rebbe to whom Jews went on pilgrimage, not only poor Jews but men of wealth, even a non-Jewish landowner whom he had helped. His name rang in those parts. His son was an expert on forests and timber. He built up a big timber business. He had one child, an only daughter, this young man's mother. You met her about two years ago when she was in Warsaw with his father. We had them to dinner here. Remember?"

"I remember. She was a very beautiful woman. So this is her son!

"I remember your mother!" she went on, turning to Joseph. "You should be proud of your beautiful mother. D'you know, you look very much like her!"

Then remembering what her husband had said of the young man's saintly great-grandfather, she went on:

116

"I also come of a pious Jewish family. My bobbe, my mother's mother, is still very orthodox, scrupulously observant. But she is also a very elegant, highly cultured lady."

She said that because in her eagerness to put the young man at his ease she had overdone the emphasis, had even thrown in a Yiddish word, bobbe, instead of using the Polish word for grandmother. Yet she was glad, too, that she had made this concession to him, to make him feel more at home in her house.

Joseph felt that he must return the compliment, say something nice and flattering. But he had no flair for that sort of thing. He had no experience at being a cavalier. So he blurted out this very trite remark—"When I came here I thought you were Pan Goldstein's daughter."

It made Joseph feel very embarrassed when Pan Goldstein growled good-humoredly: "Do I look so old?"

"You don't! You look quite young!"

"Then I must look like a child," Madame Goldstein said with a laugh, kissing her husband on the cheek and calling him "Daddy!"

Joseph saw that he had blundered. But Madame Goldstein came to his rescue. "You're not the first to make this mistake. Lots of people think we're father and daughter. Now let's see what you make of our real daughter! Tanichka!" she called.

"Yes, mummy?" and a young girl came in who might have been Madame Goldstein's younger sister.

Joseph stood up and bowed, and committed another blunder. He put out his hand to shake hands, and when the girl put out her hand he didn't kiss it in the Polish fashion, the same mistake that he had made with her mother.

Madame Goldstein again saved the situation: "Doesn't she look like my sister?"

Joseph blushed. "I wouldn't know which was which! Like twin sisters!"

Joseph had been completely captivated by Tanichka's appearance. For a moment Sheba's face swam before him, but it soon disappeared, as though she didn't want to stand in his way.

Pan Goldstein asked Joseph how long he would be staying in Warsaw, and when Joseph said he had come to study, and might stay a long time, he invited him to come and live with them. "You'll find it better than going into lodgings and having to eat out in restaurants."

Joseph hesitated, afraid to say yes. Madame Goldstein added her invitation. It would help him in his studies, she told him. They had a big library in the house that he could use, and Tanichka was also studying; they could study together. It would be helpful to both of them.

Joseph said yes.

Pan Goldstein and Madame Goldstein treated Joseph as if he were their own son. They grew to be very fond of him. The servants behaved as though he were the young master.

"I tell you he's going to marry Tanichka," said the pretty maid Jadzia, who had opened the door when Joseph called the first time. She was speaking to the cook, Wiechcza, in the kitchen. "I went into the parlor a few minutes ago, and there they were, kissing! I swear it by the Holy Mother! Take my word for it, he'll marry her!"

"I'm sure you're right," the cook nodded her head vigorously. "A girl like Tanichka wouldn't let a young man kiss her is she wasn't going to marry him. She's a fine girl! I've known her all her life. I've seen her grow up since she was a baby!"

"Yes, there's no doubt about it," said Jadzia.

Joseph had changed out of all recognition. He had discarded his Jewish caftan and his Jewish peaked cap that made him look like a provincial from some small Jewish town. He was now dressed like a European gentleman. And there was just as great an inward change in him. In this assimilationist Polish home he had begun to revise even those advanced views about Judaism and Jews which he had adopted under the influence of the rabbi of his town and the books he had given him to read. In the Goldstein home the whole atmosphere was one of Polish romanticism, with a very small admixture of Judaism.

Both Pan Goldstein and his wife came from good Jewish homes. His father, a rich property owner, had been a very pious Jew and a Jewish scholar. Her father who had owned a glass factory, had been more "European" than his father, but he had not concealed his Jewishness. Pan Goldstein's mother tongue had been Yiddish, and when he was alone with Joseph he spoke Yiddish. Her mother tongue was Polish, and she spoke French just as well, but she had also heard Yiddish spoken at home, by her parents, not so much, and by her grandparents always. So that when she wanted to be playful, she peppered her conversation with Joseph with Yiddish words, often quaintly mispronounced, though in her heart she despised Yiddish and Jewishness.

But what irritated Joseph most was the wealth and luxury in which the Goldsteins lived, something he had never known in his father's house, not even when business was at its richest. Perhaps, too, because in his hometown he had never struck against such stark poverty as in Warsaw. He couldn't forget the cellar home of his father's relative, and the young workers who lodged there.

Joseph's chief interest now was study. He had gradually discovered that his first impression of the teacher to whom his rabbi had sent him had been wrong. The man was a good teacher, and worked hard to give Joseph the benefit of all he knew. Joseph grew not only to respect but to like him. And the teacher, for his part, was delighted with Joseph's passion for study. He promised him that he would pass his university entrance examination with flying colors.

Joseph read a great deal also outside the actual reading that he had to do for his studies. Now he was glad that he had come to Warsaw. He told himself that the rabbi had done excellently when he had advised him to go to Warsaw. He

119

laughed now when he recollected the naive picture of Warsaw he had painted for himself on his first arrival.

But he realized too that his time in the Beth Hamedrash had not been wasted either. His study there had sharpened his mind, had trained him to think, had disciplined his brain. He came to respect the spirit of the Jewish teaching, the nobility of Jewish religious thought, the greatness of the Jewish sacred books.

He also read newspapers and periodicals in Hebrew, Polish, and Russian, as well as in Yiddish. And he again met the name Peretz, which he had first heard from the workers lodging in his relative's cellar. He was excited by Peretz's Hasidic stories, "The Cabbalists," "Jochanan the Water Carrier." He was happy that his descent from the little tailor had linked him in his own person with the great world of Hasidism, and that his upbringing in that small town where the little tailor had lived and worked had given him some understanding of the Hasidic outlook and way of life.

But his teacher, who was a Litvak, a Mithnagid, a rationalist, laughed and scoffed when he tried to talk to him about Peretz and about Hasidism. "Pity you should lose time from your studies on such nonsense," he said, "such worthless writers! Hasidism is a fraud, to deceive the ignorant masses who believe in wonders and miracles."

Joseph saw that he had again blundered in expecting a Mithnagid to discuss Hasidism with him. But he felt a strong desire to discuss it with somebody, to share his thoughts and emotions. And one day he tried it with Pan Goldstein. He remembered that when he had first come to the house Pan Goldstein had in introducing him to his wife spoken of his great-grandfather, the little tailor, as someone to value.

But Pan Goldstein, though he was the son of a Hasid, knew nothing of Hasidism, and he too dismissed Peretz: "I don't know a thing about Yiddish literature. I've never heard of this Pan Peretz."

It was Tanichka who surprised her parents by saying, with a fond look at Joseph, "I have read Peretz. I like him. I read his story 'The Rose.' In the Polish translation. It's a lovely story!"

Her parents looked at each other in surprise. But the surprise soon gave way to pleasure. They were glad that their daughter and Joseph had found something in common, had come together like this. It was what they had hoped.

When Joseph got up in the morning he found himself again thinking of Peretz, and the lines he had heard the workmen quote from "The Night Watchmen" kept going through his mind. Here he was, living comfortably in the Goldstein's rich home. But he hadn't forgotten his father's poor relatives and their cellar doss-house. He visited them as often as he could. Not so much because of his relations as because he was interested in the workmen who lodged there, in the talk about Socialism that he had overheard that first night in the cellar. It linked on to his sister's talks with him about Socialism when he was still at home. The problem was worrying him.

The young carpenter with whom he had shared a bed that night was a sort of leader among the workers; he was a very intelligent young man, and Joseph got to like him. He was known as Comrade Shimmele, which is a diminutive for Simon; his surname was Nussbaum. He had become a carpenter, but his family was a good religious family, and he had himself studied in the Beth Hamedrash. "I wasn't a very bright student," he told Joseph. "I couldn't work up any enthusiasm for Gemara."

But he let himself be drawn into a discussion about Hasidism. He didn't agree with Joseph that this great religious mass movement among Jews had rendered important services also in connection with Socialism. He did, however, concede that Hasidism in its original form, before its decline, before the establishment of rich dynasties of Hasidic rebbes, before it had become Clericalism, had been a popular movement, a democratic folk movement, a social revolt against the rabbinical hierarchy. As for Peretz's Hasidic tales, they were sentimental romanticism. He was in agreement with his comrades who said that Peretz, in taking up this kind of writing, was deserting the cause of the workers. "It's always like that!"

he sighed. "These great men come to us when they start, full of high hopes for the good of mankind; but then they get infected with romantic ideas about the old ways, and they leave us. Poets are no good for disciplined work in the organizations. They have their heads in the clouds. They have no patience with strikes, more pay to buy bread, better housing, better working conditions. They can't be bothered with these things. They are humdrum matters, not lofty enough for their poetic fantasy.

"But we are grateful to our poets," he went on, "for the beautiful things they write, for inspiring us, for making us see where beauty lies, for giving us strength for our struggle for liberation from wage slavery and oppression and exploitation by the bourgeoisie."

The Jewish labor movement was, like the general non-Jewish labor movement, sternly conspiratorial. But it had conducted several strikes in Warsaw, in the baking and shoemaking and other industries, much to the surprise of both the working class and the rich employers, though there had been no really important gains. The trouble was that the workers were split and divided among several parties, though they all had the same ultimate aim—Socialism. But each party had a different program. And the only union between Jewish and gentile workers was in the parties of the extreme left. In the parties on the right there was only a partial union, because the Jewish workers insisted on Jewish national autonomy. On the extreme left of the movement there were the Anarchists, whose very name put fear into people, conjuring pictures of bombs and political assassinations, a world without governments, where everyone did as he pleased, worked only when he felt like it, and lived in free love.

The parties were known by their initials, P.P.S., S.R., S.D. The secrecy that surrounded them and their talk of a bloody revolution that must come throughout the country and all over the world struck fear into people's hearts.

The workers looked very different now; they were no longer humble and fearful, but proud and defiant. There was much talk of arrests, that Comrade so-and-so was in prison for organizing strikes or conducting Socialist agitation. Somebody had been taken out of his bed at night; it meant the end of a secret printing press. Illegal proclamations were distributed in the streets. Pickets stood outside factories and workshops where there were strikes. There were cafes that were meeting places for the organized workers. News came from Russia of strikes in Rostov, Baku, Donbasin, Tiflis, in the factories and plants, in the coalmines, the steel works, the oilfields. Most of the strikes were not for economic betterment but political in character. The same kind of political strikes soon spread to Poland—in the weaving mills in Lodz, and the coalmines of Sosnowice and Dombrowa. The flames of revolution were catching hold.

Joseph was drawn into the movement. He went to the workers' meetings. Comrade Shimmele had taken him there and had vouched for him. And soon Joseph was accepted as one of their inside men, though he did not actually become a member. He was considered reliable and trustworthy, even if they thought him rather naive in regard to party maneuvering and party slogans, and the rivalries and conflicts between the different Socialist parties. He said they were all working for the same end, so they should all work together as a united movement. He said that at one of the meetings; the Comrades just laughed at him—why, the P.P.S. and the Bund and even the S.D. were traitors to the working class!

Once Joseph went even further. Not only should all workers unite, as Karl Marx had told them to, but all people should unite—all the parts of a nation together make up, he said, the complete body of the nation, and all the nations make one humanity. Not only the workers must unite, but all mankind, all classes, rich and poor, all nations into one world.

They laughed at him. Not disrespectfully, not without regard for the sincerity of his views and his belief in the goodness of men, but—impossible! That's what they said. Society is divided into exploiters and exploited, with the class war as a result; you can't live at peace with those with whom you are at war!

He wouldn't have it. He spoke of the human spirit, of the good of the world, and of Socialism as the unifying force to bring the classes and the nations together. One of the comrades called him a sentimental romanticist, and said he didn't believe in Joseph's "spirit of man." He was a Marxist, he said, and he read Joseph a lecture on historical materialism. The spirit of man, if there was such a thing, he said, lay in his stomach. The moving force for a man's actions was hunger, his physical needs.

Almost everybody there sided with Joseph's opponent. They were all materialists. Joseph's friend Shimmele too. They dismissed the idea of spirit as part of the whole conception of God and heaven and hell and submission to the will of the priest and the rabbi in order to keep the workers enslaved. Everything, they insisted, came from material causes.

Joseph didn't give up. If only material causes, hunger and other physical needs, he said, drive men to do things, not the spirit, why had Karl Marx and Engels and others who were not oppressed and hungry workers thrown in their lot with the workers, to help to build Socialism? They had been driven by the spirit of man, by the desire of the human soul for justice and righteousness. The material was not everything. What was liberty? And brotherhood? And friendship? Love? Self-sacrifice? How could they say these were material? They were all idealist, part of man's desire to improve himself and improve the world. Something much more than the need to stuff one's belly. The struggle of the poor against the rich was based simply on the desire of the poor to be like the rich— selfish and egoistic. And how in that regard were the poor better than the rich? But rich and poor could unite to fight together to make the world a better place for everybody.

Joseph felt that he had done well in coming to Warsaw. He was improving his education in a way he could never have done at home. And he was in contact here with the ideas and movements of the day, right at their center.

But he was worried by the letters he was getting from home. His mother's letters pleading with him not to forget his Jewish observances, and always concluding with the same six words: "Miriam sends you her best greetings." These six words filled him with anxiety and foreboding. They were his mother's way of saying—"Miriam is lost to us! She has broken my heart and your father's heart! Don't you forsake us! Be a Jew, Joseph!"

His father's letters were sad. They were usually long letters, not like his mother's. She kept her letters short. Joseph felt that his father had a need to talk to him, to get something heavy and burdensome off his chest. Yet his father never came to the point. He only hinted at what was troubling him. He always stopped at the edge—Joseph felt how close to the edge his father stood.

Joseph didn't reply explicitly to what was not explicit in the letters; but he was pretty sure of what was happening. He had talked to Miriam enough to know where she was going. So in return for the hints that he got from his father and his mother he answered also with hints. He felt the whole atmosphere of anguish and despair that was now filling his home and bowing down his father and mother with sorrow.

He began to toy with the idea of going back home, to be with them, to comfort them in their grief.

Thinking of his sister's love affair with a young Christian mill worker, the Socialist son of a peasant, led Joseph to thinking about love generally. Mixed marriage, marriage between Jew and Christian was something he had never actually encountered. He had read about such things happening. His own feeling was that people could not possibly be happy together if their background and upbringing were so completely different as that of a Jew and a Christian, especially when the Jew came from such a religious Jewish home as his sister, and the Christian from such a solid Catholic village home as her Christian lover. There were centuries of mutual hostility between them, persecution and bloodshed by the powerful Church against the Jews, a small minority, helpless and at the mercy of the rulers of the country and the masses of the people. The minds of Jew and Christian had been differently fashioned; each had inherited a different tradition and had age-long memories. After the first passion of love was spent those differences must make life together impossible.

Then Joseph thought of his own love affairs. He had been sure that he was in love with Sheba; yet no sooner had he come to Warsaw than he was in love with Tanichka. Had he really loved Sheba? How could one be in love with somebody one has never spoken a word to? How did he know that she ever gave him a moment's thought? What did he know about her? She was the rebbe's daughter! But how did he know that she was like her father? She might be like her mother, about whom and about her other daughter Eve such nasty stories had gone round the town.

What attracted Joseph to Tanichka was not only her beautiful face and figure and the gentle gracious air with which she bore herself, but her intelligence and her qualities of heart and mind, which had won his respect and admiration. He had never spoken to Sheba, but he had discussed things often with Tanichka, and he had formed a high opinion of her knowledge and her ability to reason.

Joseph began to make comparisons between Sheba and Tanichka. Most of all he concentrated on their eyes, those mirrors of the soul, to discover what qualities lay hidden in their hearts. To his great astonishment he came to the conclusion that Sheba was inwardly like his mother. While Tanichka remained to him an enigma; he couldn't penetrate to her depths—the deeper he went the more mystery she became. And that was her magnetic pull over him. It was an invisible net that had descended over him and enveloped him, and he could not free himself from it.

These were his thoughts late at night, while he was undressing to get into bed. He looked round the room. The Goldsteins' room. . . . He was there because they wanted him there. He felt the net round him, he felt it tightening. Tanichka had captivated him, and her parents held him prisoner. He was trapped.

He thought back to the first time he had come to this house, and how wonderfully Pan Goldstein and his wife and Tanichka had received him, had made him feel at home there, had asked him to make it his home—and that was what he had done. They were wonderfully kind people; he ought to be grateful to them. This mad idea that he had got into his head that they had maneuvered him into dependence on them, so that he would be at their mercy—no escape! Whenever they wanted him, there he was! Down would come a firm hand: "Got you, son-in-law!"

He shook himself angrily: "It's all nonsense! I'm imagining things! Why should the Goldsteins, important people in Warsaw, rich and cultured people, want to trap me into becoming their son-in-law, as if Tanichka were not one of the most beautiful and charming girls I've ever seen, and one of the cleverest, with a first-class education? They could have the pick of Warsaw for their one and only daughter! I'm mad! They're only being kind to me!"

His eyes swept round the room again and fell on Tanichka's photograph on the wall. He wondered again, as he had done the first time they had shown him into this room and told him it would be his, if the photograph had always hung there, or had been put up specially for him. Wasn't it unusual to have a picture of the daughter of the house hanging in the guest room?

But he couldn't take his eyes off her picture. And when he lay in bed and had switched off the electric light her picture was still in front of him. Even in the dark.

He had a terrible night. Tanichka's picture wouldn't leave him. She tormented him all night. He had never desired a woman in that way all his life, and he woke terribly ashamed of himself. It was so utterly alien to his whole upbringing and his puritanical ideas.

At breakfast he was ashamed to look at her and her mother,

and her father too. As though he were guilty of a crime against her and against them. When they spoke to him he didn't hear, and when they repeated it he looked confused and mumbled something they couldn't make out. They thought he had received bad news from home and was upset about it. But as he didn't tell them what it was they did not try to question him. Tanichka might have asked him what was wrong, but she got no chance to see him alone. He avoided her. Immediately after breakfast he left the house. He decided that he would move out.

But Joseph did not move out. He didn't know how to face the Goldsteins and tell them that he no longer wanted their hospitality. He hadn't the courage to tell them the true reason. Yet he really did not want to live there any longer. It made him miserable being in the same house with Tanichka. Since that night something had happened to his picture of her that tarnished it. She was like a marvelous robe that shone and shimmered, and had then slipped off and fallen into a muck-heap, and now it smelled and was full of dirty stains— pah! He couldn't bear to look at it any more.

Tanichka sensed the change in him immediately. But as she didn't know the reason for the change, she had no idea what to do.

Joseph started thinking again about Sheba. He felt like going back to his home town, to see her, to be near to her. He felt uncomfortable in the Goldstein home. The rich household infuriated him. The idea of Socialism had taken hold of him, and he resented his indebtedness to these well-to-do people. He wanted to talk about Socialism, and he couldn't do it here. It was as though they had muzzled him.

He had also become interested in Jewish nationalism, which had been growing in the Jewish labor movement, because together with the increasing strength of the Polish Socialist movement there was also an intensification of antisemitism within the ranks of the workers. That made many Jewish Socialists look to Jewish nationalism and Zionism; it had brought into existence a powerful Socialist

Zionist organization. Joseph tried to talk about Jewish nationalism to Pan Goldstein, only to find him unwilling to discuss anything Jewish. He was a humanist, he said. His conception went beyond nation and creed to a broader humanity. He always tried to turn the conversation to a safer subject, books or theater. His wife didn't even attempt to hide the fact that she was bored by it. And when Joseph persisted she suddenly rounded on him with a fierce attack on the Jews, such as might have come from an antisemite—everything was the fault of the Jews, because they insisted on living apart from the rest of the people, separately, with their own religion and their own ways and their own speech, a kind of jargon German. They were uncultured, uncultivated people, who didn't know how to behave. They were still Orientals, and didn't fit in to European society.

Tanichka felt bad about her mother's outburst. She sided with her father when he rebuked his wife for saying such things, the very same things that the anti-Semites were saying. Whatever the rights and wrongs about the poor backward fanatical Jews, he argued, every humanitarian must condemn anti-Semitism.

It made Joseph feel more uncomfortable than ever in this house. He made up his mind that he would definitely go back home.

Joseph found his parents' house, which he had painted and decorated with such loving care, terribly neglected. His paintings were hardly recognizable. A great sadness hung over everything. The garden was in a fearful state. Nobody had been tending it.

He felt something was wrong as soon as he entered the door. Without knowing why he cried out: "Who is ill?"

"Your father," his mother answered in a feeble voice. She took him into the room where his father lay ill in bed.

He looked a very sick man.

129

"Father!" Joseph cried, and took his father's pale hand lying on the counterpane. It was cold. He looked into his father's eyes. They were dead. He bent over his father and kissed him, kissed his lips, made them wet with his tears. He felt his father's hand in his grow warm and try to return his affectionate pressure. Suddenly his father was weeping. That set his mother off weeping too. Tears of grief because of her sick husband, tears of joy because of her son's return, and tears of hope that seeing Joseph again might give him new strength and help him to recover.

Joseph sat thinking with a heavy heart that his father's condition was hopeless. He had been up all night with him, insisting that his mother should go to bed and rest. It was already day now, but the house was still dark—because the shutters were closed.

His father was paralyzed—couldn't make any movement; he had to be fed like a child. He couldn't utter a word.

Joseph picked up the book he had brought from Warsaw, that he had several times tried to read; he turned the pages and put it down again.

His head throbbed. He went to the window, opened the shutter and leaned out, inhaling the fresh cold air. In the dull gray of early morning he could see all the houses right along the street, and the workers on their way to the factories.

He closed the shutter again, switched off the light, and sat in the dark thinking of his mother, how much she suffered over his father's illness—the man she had loved all her life—and because of his sister, who was becoming a renegade, a traitor to Judaism, and because of him, who she could see was also departing from the Jewish ways of his forebears. She can see that I am no longer saying my prayers, he told himself.

He wondered why he hadn't seen any of the people of the town in the house, his father's friends. "Isn't it a Jewish custom to visit the sick?" he asked his mother.

"They can't look us in the face," she answered simply. "It isn't just our misfortune. It is a calamity to the whole town."

Joseph realized that his mother was now talking not of his

130

father's illness, but of his sister's defection. What his sister Miriam was doing was indeed a calamity, a blow to the whole town, to all the Jews in the town. How did a tree feel when one of its branches broke off? Miriam was no longer part of the Jewish tree. She no longer belonged to them—not to his father, nor to his mother, nor to him. Her place now was outside. The time for all peoples to be brothers had not come yet. It would not come for a long time. When Isaiah had prophesied that it would come he had said it would be "at the end of days." Miriam was before her time.

His mother hadn't been out in the street for a long time. She hadn't been able to face the people of the town, to meet their gaze. She had prayed and pleaded with God that Miriam should not forsake her people and her faith.

"Perhaps I am wrong too," Joseph reflected, "in discarding the old Jewish piety. I didn't realize how much strength and tenacity there is in this so-called Jewish 'fanaticism,' how much it has done to preserve my people."

He went to the door of Miriam's room and listened. There was no sound there. Miriam was still asleep. He returned to his own room, and sat down again, thinking of his father who lay ill.

Suddenly he heard his mother's desperate cry, "Abraham!"

He rushed into the room. His father was dead.

Miriam came running in.

His mother was weeping and wringing her hands:

"I wish I had died!" she cried.

Miriam disappeared immediately after the funeral. She did not come back to the house.

Joseph sat with his mother the seven days of mourning. At the end of this time he went to look for Miriam.

He found her in the old mill, the home of a Christian factory worker named Jan Swider, who was the leader of the Polish Socialist Party in the town. He was a tall man, with broad shoulders and blue eyes and a big quiff, over which he wore his hat at an angle.

Swider was not at home when Joseph came. He had been called out of town on party business. Miriam was there alone. She was only half-dressed, feeding the iron stove with wood. She liked the room warm.

She didn't answer her brother's greeting. She eyed him angrily, because she didn't want her old life to follow her into the new world she had chosen. And yet she was fond of Joseph. She also had a guilty conscience, because she had left her mother in the midst of her mourning.

"Have you had breakfast?" she asked her brother. He didn't answer, and she took that to mean he hadn't.

"Come to the table," she said. And then, with an embarrassed laugh: "If you will eat treif. I suppose you still keep kosher."

"I don't want any breakfast," Joseph said. "That isn't what I came here for. I want to talk to you. You're my sister, and there's a great deal I want to say to you. You've been evading me ever since I came back from Warsaw. We've hardly spoken to each other."

"Best to leave it like that, Joseph! I'd rather not speak about these things. Not with you. We have different ideas about the world and about life. Leave it alone!"

"No, Miriam! I can't leave it alone! You're my sister. There are strong bonds between us. And I can't let things go like this. It isn't only my father who's died. He was also your father. Only his body died. His soul, his spirit, is still in us, in you as well as in me. His life and his ideas and his beliefs are part of us. They are in our blood. They will live in us as long as we live.

"You decided to leave us, Miriam. You are no longer our father's daughter. No longer our mother's child. No longer my sister. I have watched you since I have returned. You were like a stranger in the house, the house where you were born, the house where you were a child, where you grew up, where your parents loved you and had high hopes for you. You have turned your back on us. Can you really kill your father and your mother who are in you? Can you take them out of your blood? Can you take them out of your heart? If you can, you have no blood and no heart, but ice-water for blood and a stone, not a heart."

"You're the same soft sentimental fool you always were!"

"Am I? What about you? Aren't you a sentimentalist? What has driven you to do what you have done if not your sentimental romantic dream about Socialism, your ideals about a brotherhood of man, your belief in the emancipation of the world—these dreams and these ideals have come to be more to you than your father and your mother and your brother, more than your people, whom you have deserted!"

"You're worse than you were before you went away! You've become a narrow Jewish nationalist!"

"Miriam," said Joseph, trying to speak calmly. "There are truths which are eternal. No weapons, steel or fire, will prevail against them. And nationalism, as I understand it, is one of them. Every nation has its own distinctive character. Every nation lives according to its own specific way of life."

"I don't want to listen to you! You're a bigoted nationalist! It isn't true that people are different! There are no nationalities. It's a trick of the capitalist class to keep the people divided. The poor feel the same hunger, whether they are Jew or Christian! We're all the same!"

"Miriam! Let's not forget that we are brother and sister. We're not strangers discussing cold abstract theories. We are talking about our own lives, about our own dead father, about our mother. Let us understand what this Socialism is that you think is more important than all our lives. Originally, the struggle against the rich was part of the struggle against injustice, the struggle for justice and righteousness. Socialism was only a part of that greater struggle, and therefore it is something smaller and less. Socialism wants to abolish exploitation, to take away the wealth of the rich and to establish a system by which the government will own the means of production and distribution. Then there will be no rich and no poor; all will be equal.

"Will they? How equal? There is nothing in life that is

equal, not really. Two leaves on the same tree are not equal. Two children of the same father and mother are not equal. What we are aiming at is not equality, but justice, the abolition of injustice, the establishment of righteousness. And that is what our Jewish faith has been teaching, what our Jewish Prophets have been proclaiming long before there was such a word as Socialism."

"You're talking religion to me! I don't want to listen! You're not a Socialist at all! You're a bigoted little Jew! Read Marx!"

"I've read Marx. Not every word of his. But I tried, as far as I could, to understand his theory. Have you read Marx?"

"Not much. I couldn't understand it. But I have felt what Marx said, and I know that he is right!"

Joseph saw it was hopeless. His sister had simply found a new religion, and she was as fanatically unreasonable about it as any fundamentalist about his faith.

"It's impossible to discuss these things with you, Miriam! You're like a child, thinking that everything began yesterday. The world goes back thousands of years, and the struggle that you imagine Marx started was being fought thousands of years before he was born. Isaiah cried, 'What mean you that grind the faces of the poor!' It was Isaiah who foretold the day when many people will join together and go one way. But that day is not yet. There is still fierce antisemitism in the world. How can we say we are all the same when the others say we are not the same? And for that dream you have forsaken your people! What you are doing, Miriam, is not to join all the nations together. You're simply leaving your own flock and going to another. You are deserting your own people to be with strangers! You want us to give up our faith, our synagogues and our Beth Medrashim, and our distinctive Jewish ways. Tell me, are the others giving up their Churches and their cross and their Christian ways? That is not a meeting of all the nations together! You are running away from your own and joining the others!"

"You are wrong!" Miriam cried. "We are the pioneers of the new world, the forerunners of the future. We are the first, who are laying the foundations of the brotherhood of man!"

"That isn't Marxism, Miriam! You ought to know that according to Marx individuals can't make revolutions, not even a strike. Individuals can only prepare the masses. But the masses must do these things. And where do you see the signs of brotherhood among the masses, the signs of brotherhood toward the Jews?

"Think of your mother, Miriam!" Joseph cried passionately. "Think how hard it was for me to say Kaddish after what happened at the gate of the cemetery!"

An angry flame lit up in Miriam's eyes.

"They wouldn't let me into the cemetery, those fanatical Jews! I would have profaned their cemetery."

Joseph dropped his eyes. "I felt ashamed!" he said. "But think what your mother felt at that moment! I have come to ask you to go home, Miriam. Go back to her!"

"No! Not even for my mother! I will not go back! Never! Why should I? I'm not going back on what I have done, on what I believe! Will mother do what I want her to do? Will she give up her religion?"

"I'm disappointed in you, Miriam! You're as hard and cold as the most bigoted fanatic you denounce! I've nothing more to say to you!"

"I'm sorry, Joseph! I can't say anything else! This is my life now! Next week, when Comrade Jan returns, I shall leave the mill and I shall go to live with my lover. Of course, I'm not going to get baptised. You can tell mother that!"

Joseph came home worn out, starved, (broken), dispirited. His mother was not there, the rooms looked empty and neglected, and they seemed filled with brooding sadness and grief—even the walls. He sank into a chair in the room, where his father had died a week before. How long he sat—eyes closed, head sunk—he did not know. At first he struggled to recall what Miriam had said to him. This effort led him to feel virtually collapsed, and he fell asleep in the chair. When he opened his eyes again, it seemed to him that he had had a long dream, which he tried to recapture. He had conducted a long conversation with someone. With whom? Was it Pan Goldstein from Warsaw? But he had not given any thought to him or to anyone in that city. It must have been the rabbi who had advised him to go to Warsaw. He should go and see him!

His eyes closed again. When he reopened them, it had become altogether dark. Was it nighttime already? He walked into the adjoining room, and his mother came toward him. She seemed to him like a ghost. As soon as he opened the door, she demanded to know: "Where is she?" Joseph was unable to answer. The shadowy figure with eyes like empty sockets in a twisted face waited in silent stubbornness for an answer. The eyes continued to stare at Joseph: "*Where is she?*" In agony Joseph growled, "She will never come back!!" "WHERE IS SHE?" "At the mill. . . ." As though in a gust of wind the shadowy figure disappeared, racing toward the mill—not aware of the fierce cold, although wearing only a dress.

The mother stopped outside of town, in front of the old, half-ruined mill, from which a feeling of terror was flowing all around. The mill property, along with its barn and storage sheds, was enclosed on three sides by a wooden fence, the fourth side being accessible to the pond that supplied the water for the mill wheel. The night was heavy with blackness—no stars—clouds enshrouding everything, no ripples on the mill pond. And then came an icy wind, foretelling snow. The surface of the water barely stirred; it was almost frozen, despite its depth. But from the dam spillway came a roaring noise. Black night of dread; wind whistling and rippling.

Rachel's outcry for her daughter could hardly be heard. She resembled a wraith at the millpond's edge. She screamed, "Miriam!" Out of the darkness the wind seemed to answer her with a long screeching "M...i...i...ri...am...am...." Rachel imagined that she could hear in the swirling wind the sound of devils laughing, mocking her, as she called for her daughter.

The mother screamed a second time . . . a third. Each time the wind echoed with the same shrill laugh. The decaying mill gave off an aura of fear.

"My child!" wailed the mother. "M...y...y...ch...i...i...ld," threw back the scornful voice of the storm.

Joseph did not know that his mother had run to the mill to reclaim her daughter, did not know where his mother had disappeared. All he knew was that she had run out, wearing only a dress.

He began to look for her. He sped from one neighbor's house to another, only to find out that each of them had already gone to sleep. Everywhere was darkness; no ray of light came through any of the closed shutters. He went to the house of friends of his parents, but there, too, nothing but darkness.

All night long Joseph ran around, searching for his mother. Finally, having been snapped at by barking dogs, and his face in pain from the cutting wind, he reached the old, decayed mill. He sought his mother all along the fence, all around the mill, along the pond, up one side, down the other, back and forth, maybe ten times. He peered into the water, plunged his arm in repeatedly. Nothing.

At last Joseph went home, thinking that his mother might have returned before him. She was not there. He went up to her bed, and as if he didn't trust his eyes, drew his hands over the pillows, looking for her. He looked for her in the bed, under the bed, in every room, in every corner. His heart hammered ever more, his hands trembled, his feet almost refused to move. Now he was sure that some evil had befallen his mother. Again he looked for her in the bed, under the bed, in every room, in every corner. He looked in closets, among dresses, in drawers, as though she were a piece of goods instead of a full-grown adult. She was nowhere. Cold sweat covered him, his head was splitting, his mouth was dry like leather. He seated himself at the table, his mind in a frenzy. He did not hear the wind banging the shutters. He was awake, but in a kind of faint, a sort of trance. . . .

Another day came, Joseph could not bear to sit still any

longer and ran again into the street, from alley to alley. There was no wind now. Snow had fallen during the night. The streets and the roofs were white, the sky clear like glass—an icy sky as blue as bottle glass, with a pink flush already evident in the east. The weather was freezing.

The town was beginning to come alive. Workers were hurrying on their way to the factories. Baker boys carried baskets with fresh bread and rolls. Women, warmly dressed and wrapped in heavy shawls around their heads, sold milk from big churns; in their baskets were bushels of apples, killed geese, and baked goods.

Joseph scrutinized each woman's face. The streets were growing animated. Jews were going to the Beth-Hamedrash for the morning prayers. The shops were opening.

Joseph ran on. Over there, a group of people, whispering. He ran to them. At his approach, they all fell silent. . . .

"My mother!. . ." No one answered, all too agitated, eyes full of panic, unable to speak. He shrieked wildly, "Drowned?"

"No," replied an ancient Jewess. "An old peasant, on his way to town, found a woman, no coat, just a dress and a gray scarf, frozen to death, not far from the mill. He recognized her, because he used to come to your father's house to deliver wood and collect money. So this peasant notified the police. They have already brought her into town. She is lying in the entrance room of the synagogue of her grandfather, the little tailor . . . ."

Joseph fled. The old woman shook her head. "He can't bring her back to life. Rachel is gone! Now there was a saintly one—the holy tailor's granddaughter!" The other women added their sighs: "What a pity! What a shame! See what has happened to such a pious and rich house, and in such a short time!. . ."

Before long a lot of Jews gathered at the mill, some with sticks. Women were there, too, among them the group that Joseph had questioned.

They all raged in a frenzy, "That great holy man, Reb

Feivel. . . ." "That baptized bitch. . . ." The ancient Jewess joined in at the top of her voice: ". . .to think she was the great grandchild of that beloved saint. . . ." Someone shouted: "What're you standing around for? Come on, Jews! Kill her! Let's go get her!"

The Jews in front who had sticks started advancing on the mill, screaming and howling. Those who had no sticks raised their fists. The women followed behind the men, all making a tremendous noise . . . until the door of the mill opened, and a burly (Christian) youth with two big dogs appeared, and behind him Miriam, pale and trembling. All the crowd turned and ran away.

After his mother's funeral Joseph was in despair. In one week he had lost his father and his mother—and his sister. He was utterly alone now. He had not been to see any of his old friends and acquaintances in the town. He felt that he had lost all contact with them. He stayed all alone in that big house. How different from the house he had left when he went to Warsaw! When his father and mother were alive and his sister Miriam was there with them. . . .

As the days passed he began to think that he must get down to winding up his father's business affairs, sell what was left—wood felling rights in the forests, pay out what was owing, collect outstanding debts. He felt he needed somebody's advice. He decided to go to the rabbi.

The rabbi tried to comfort him on the loss of his parents— he put his hand on his shoulder and said:

"Everything on this earth is transient, everything changes and passes, birth, growth, life and death. They are all changes, developments, and development alters us, and we pass out of contact with some of those who were part of our existence. The wrench is great. The pain is intense."

But Joseph was in no mood for philosophical discussions. The rabbi saw that he was not really listening. So he changed the subject. He asked Joseph about Warsaw, and about his friend the teacher in Warsaw to whom he had sent him. But again he had the feeling that Joseph wasn't listening.

"He has grown different in Warsaw," the rabbi thought to himself. They established no contact. Joseph went away without even mentioning what he had come for.

Joseph experienced the same inability to establish contact with a number of young men in the town with whom he had previously been friendly. He wondered at first if he had gone too far away in Warsaw on the road of enlightenment. But he found that in the matter of religious observance the others were no less advanced than he was. The old orthodoxy had lost its hold on them.

He realized that it was not because he had gone further than they did in his ideas about Judaism, because he interpreted Moses Mendelssohn and Krochmal differently, nor because he had become a Jewish nationalist, a Zionist or a Territorialist or a Folkist. No, it was because the rabbi and his former friends had sensed his Socialism. He hadn't gone as far with his Socialism as his sister Miriam, but he had gone quite a way.

It made him smile—the first time he smiled since his return from Warsaw. He decided that the only way to find himself was to go further along the road to Socialism, to become a whole man in this regard, like Comrade Shimmele, like his sister Miriam. He decided that he would join the Party.

With that decision his sense of loss grew less. Now he had lost only those who were dead—his father and mother. But his sister who was alive had been won back, regained.

Emotionally excited he paced up and down the room. And as he did so he glanced out of the window, and there at the window of her room was Sheba.

He hadn't seen her since he had come back, neither at her window nor anywhere else. His heart began to beat fast.

140

7

While Joseph was away in Warsaw a great many things had been happening in the town.

After the rebbe had exorcised the dybbuk, the pious Jews, especially among his own Hasidim, had kept quiet for a time. Nobody repeated the rumors about the rebbe's wife and the Gemara teacher Hersh-Leib, and his elder daughter Eve and the German teacher. Then it all started over again. And this time the rav took a clear stand against the rebbe:

"Those who exorcise dybbukim are sorcerers," he said. "He will soon be bringing the Messiah or proclaiming himself the Messiah."

Somebody thought up a song, and almost everybody in the town sang it:

> *The Rebbetzin made a Kugel of Lokshen,*
> *And the oxen—*
> *Bim, bim, bim . . .*
> *Reb Hersh-Leib teaches young boys Gemara,*
> *And gets the Kaporah—Bam, bam, bam."*

Old and young hummed it, especially the heretics, the scoffers, the rebbe's opponents, and the Socialists. Girls and young women sang it, and blushed. And the heder boys, Reb Hersh-Leib's own pupils, repeated it, and leered at their teacher behind his back.

Reb Hersh-Leib had a reputation for hitting his boys. He had his own way of inflicting corporal punishment. He didn't use the cane or the lash, only his bare hand. Not round the ear or on the shoulder, but always on the bare bottom. He would slowly and solemnly unbutton the culprit's trousers, made him lift his shirt to the navel, and then with his eyes lighting up sadistically and his black beard quivering, he flung the boy over his knee and brought the flat of his hand down on his naked backside, slowly at first, then gradually faster and faster. Till the boy in his pain bit the teacher's wrists. Then Reb Hersh-Leib would spring away, and let the boy fall to the floor.

The boys never told their parents about the way their teacher hit them. They were afraid their parents would say they must have done something to deserve it; that a teacher must keep discipline. Their fathers might even have added a few whacks of their own.

Some boys loved the teacher hitting them the way he did. It gave them a certain satisfaction, and some offended deliberately to get him to take their trousers down and hit their bare bottom.

A few Hasidim still put all their trust in the rebbe, refusing to listen to the murmurings against him that were growing among the majority of his followers. They said the rumors going round the town about his wife, the rebbitzin, and his daughter Eve, were part of the suffering inflicted on him by Heaven because of the sins of the town, which he had prayed to take upon himself. If he hadn't done that the town would have been punished: there would have been another big fire in the town, or another epidemic. The town ought to be grateful to him because the rebbe had saved it from punishment.

These Hasidim warned the others, the doubters, not to believe the slanders being spread against the rebbe and the rebbitzin and their daughter.

A zaddik is like fire, they said. Who can understand the mystery of his sanctity, and the actions of those who are privileged to be his womenfolk and his seed? If one looks hard at the sun, one imagines one sees blemishes there—but that is all imagination, they said. They threatened that if the slanderers persisted they would not hesitate to use violence against them—and behind them stood the strongarm men, the carters and the carriers and the butchers—and Wolf Jonachek.

It did not silence the rebbe's detractors. One of the leaders of these was Samuel Zeinvel, a stubborn man, with a tangled beard and big horse-teeth, who stood up in the market place and shouted:

"He's no rebbe, but a sorcerer! A charlatan, a swindler! He fools the people, to get their money out of them. If he can drive out a dybbuk why doesn't he drive the dybbuk out of his own daughter—the German Goy who possesses her? And the dybbuk from his wife—Hersh-Leib? You can see what rebbe he is if Wolf Jonachek is his Hasid!"

Someone went and told Samuel Zeinvel's wife that he was standing in the market place cursing the rebbe. She came running out in a panic, and dragged him away.

"Keep your mouth shut! You never know what punishment the rebbe can bring down on you!"

But he struggled free from her grip, and screamed:

"What are you scared of? That they may kill me? If they do you can marry one of the holy rebbe's Hasidim!"

They told that to Wolf Jonachek. And on the Sabbath, in the synagogue, the following happened.

Wolf Jonachek was standing in his place, as always, wrapped in his long big tallith. But he kept his eyes on Samuel Zeinvel. People saw it, and were expecting trouble. Round Wolf Jonachek stood the carters and carriers and butchers. No scholars, no rich householders. And some of his gang of thieves and cut-throats.

They had finished Shachris, and were now up to the Reading of the Torah.

143

Suddenly there was a disturbance, and people looked toward the Almemor. The rebbe had been called up for Shishi. But he did not go up. People started whispering. The whispering grew louder, an angry muttering:

"Give that sorcerer Shishi? No!"

Wolf Jonachek paled. He sprang towards the offender. And stopped. He remembered that this was a House of Prayer, in the middle of divine worship, with the Holy Torah lying open on the reading desk. Everybody was watching him. The carters and butchers were waiting for a sign from him. But Wolf Jonachek pulled his tallith over his eyes, and kept his clenched fists under it.

The silence didn't last long; but it seemed hours till the rebbe approached the rav, and said:

"You are the rav of this town. Shishi belongs to you."

The gabbai then called up the rav, who mounted the few steps of the Almemor. He said the blessing, and the Baal Korah read the portion. The rav said the second blessing and descended the steps.

They concluded the Reading of the Law, they ended Musaf, and nothing had happened. Yet everyone felt that something was going to happen. And immediately the cantor had said the last words the congregation dispersed without even saying "Good Sabbath."

Not many minutes after, one heard a big row somewhere outside. Jews ran out of the synagogue and the Beth Hamedrash carrying their tallith bags under their arms, women with fat prayer books, and young people, boys and girls, who no longer went to prayers.

Everybody asked everybody else what was going on, and nobody knew. People came pouring out from every street and side street into the market place, where they could see the rebbe's house, full of Sabbath-garbed Jews and their wives in silk and satin, with wigs and head-scarves. What might have happened before in the synagogue was happening here now.

"Served them right!" people said, "they deserve a good hiding, those unbelievers, after the things they dared to say! The cheek of them!"

A policeman appeared, in full uniform, the peak of his cap shining glossily, and the cockade in a straight line with his nose. He looked very serious. His hand was on the hilt of the sword hanging by his side. His pistol was in the holster, on his right. If he were not in uniform, with brass buttons and a cockade and a sword and a pistol, if he wore a caftan like a Jew, with a velvet hat and a tallith bag under his arm, and a black beard, coming from the Synagogue, he might with his features and his nose have been a Jew. But he wasn't. He was a true Russian.

The Jews moved aside when they saw him coming, making way for the guardian of the law. But they did not scatter, except a few women and a couple of cowards. On the contrary, the Hasidim raised their voices louder than ever:

"They asked for it! The blasphemers! Unbelievers and scoffers! The things they dared to say about our holy rebbe! Ought to be killed stone dead, they ought!"

And when they saw behind the policeman Reb Chaim David, the rich man of the town, who was hand in glove with the authorities, they guessed that he had sent the policeman, and they determined to show him that they were not afraid, not of him and not of his policeman and not of anybody! Not when they had to defend their rebbe against his detractors!

"Kill them!" they shouted. "Suffer not the wicked to live!"

"The wicked," taking courage from the presence of the policeman, and even more of Reb Chaim David, who was said to be a personal friend of the governor himself, answered back, and for their cheek got knocked about by the Hasidim.

The policeman was in a fix. He was between two fires. He was afraid of Reb Chaim David, who could have him kicked out of the force, but he was even more afraid of Wolf Jonachek, who could murder him before he could draw his pistol.

Reb Chaim David gave him an order, as though he were his superior officer: "Write down the names of all these people, and that you saw them hitting these others!"

The policeman straightened himself, as though on parade in front of the governor himself, as though Reb Chaim David were the governor, and brought out the notebook from his pocket. With the notebook in his hand he ordered the crowd: "Disperse!"

But nobody moved. Not till the policeman drew his sword; then the Jews with their tallith bags, and the women with their fat prayer books, disappeared.

Moshe the barber-surgeon had his surgery in the same large room where he carried on his barbering. He had two barbers' chairs there, and two young assistants with cheeky eyes, who cut hair and shaved. He treated scabies and boils, cupped and bled with leeches, gave enemas, set bones, pushed back ruptures, pulled teeth, and did many other things, more than a doctor would. He considered himself, and the town generally considered him, much more important than the doctor who had set up his practice there when the factories went up. Moshe did surgery too, and when they brought in a dozen or so Jews who had been bashed about and were bruised and bleeding, he told his assistants to shave all their heads. Then his wife—she was the town midwife and had delivered the children of all the Jewish women in the town, and afterwards their daughters and daughters-in-law—produced silk thread, needles, carbolic, iodine, cotton wool, and gauze. He put on his white coat, rolled up his sleeves, got out his surgical instruments from the case, lancets, scissors, and forceps, and set to work. He liked his work. And he had acquired a certain skill.

The only one who needed more attention was Samuel Zeinvel, the obstinate fool, who had started the trouble in the synagogue. Moshe had him taken to the hospital.

Wolf Jonachek's anger had cooled during the Musaf service. So he remembered in his calmer mood, and afterwards too, that it was the Sabbath, and that it was not right and proper to brawl and fight on the holy Sabbath. So he left the fighting to his gang, and only watched. He wasn't pleased with the way they had gone about it. He didn't like bloodshed. When he hit a man it was always with his bare fists. He never used a weapon, not iron bars nor wooden cudgels, and certainly never a knife; no cuts, no slashings. Sometimes he drew blood when he knocked somebody's teeth out, but that was all.

So when he saw his son Yankel pull out a knife and slash somebody—and on the Sabbath—he sent him straight home, and there he gave him a good thrashing. He boxed the ears, too, of some of his gang whom he had seen using knives.

"No real fighter needs a weapon," he said. "Bare fists are enough. If a man must have a weapon, it shows that he can't stand up for himself."

Yankel took his father's blows without a murmur. When his father decided he had had enough, and told him to get up from the floor, where he had knocked him down, Yankel said: "He won't call Sheba nasty names any more!"

"Whom?" his father asked. "Is that why you stabbed him? Not because he insulted the rebbe?"

He looked at his son queerly and grunted.

His wife Golda, who hadn't interfered all the time, was triumphant now.

"You're a good son," she cried, and kissed him. "You see, Wolf," she said, "where his mind is! He'll be a respectable man yet, and we'll be proud of him."

Wolf Jonachek was surprised and pleased.

"I understand how you feel, Yankel," he told his son. "But you shouldn't have stabbed him. Don't ever again use a knife, not on anybody. Besides, you misheard what the man said. He didn't call young Sheba any names. It was her elder sister, Eve, he was talking about. I have heard him talk. I don't know the truth about it. Perhaps there is something in it. But it isn't my business. She is the rebbe's daughter, and the rebbe will know how to deal with her."

He smiled into his red beard. He was pleased, too, because

his son had taken his blows without a murmur, and had stood up now without complaining. But most of all he was delighted over the discovery that his son was in love with the rebbe's youngest daughter.

He was so happy that he called his whole gang back into the house, and gave them the best there was in the house—a real Sabbath feast—huge chunks of gelfilte fish, with thick slices of Sabbath loaf, big plates of fried onions in goose fat, sholent, soup with kasha, stuffed tripe, enormous helpings of meat, tzimmes, kugel, and shtrudel with raisins.

But Yankel didn't touch the food. He sat brooding all the time, grieving because of what he had done to that obstinate fool, Samuel Zeinvel, when he had drawn his knife on him. He was worried, because Zeinvel was badly wounded, and was in hospital.

Wolf Jonachek was furious with himself. He liked things and people in their proper place. "A horse belongs in the stable," he used to say, "and a thief when he's caught in prison. So what am I, a thief, doing at the rebbe's table?"

Yet something drew him to the rebbe, against his own understanding and reasoning. He had always been attracted to a pious Jew. A rabbi had always fascinated him. Even before the rebbe had settled in the town, and he had become his follower, he had felt a special reverence for the rabbi, the rav of the town. He used to stop still in the street when he saw him, his knees trembling and his mind confused. He would have loved to go up to him and greet him, say a word to him. But he hadn't the courage. The older he drew the more he admired a pious, observant, devout, and learned Jew.

"I'm not a man!" he swore at himself. "I'm a bit of putty! I can't control myself! I can't master myself in the way I can master a horse! I always said straight out what I am—a thief! A cutthroat! A ruffian! So what am I doing hanging round the rebbe and those namby-pamby goody-goodies! I must be soft in the head!"

Wolf had a special reason for being annoyed with himself now. When Yankel had confessed that he loved the rebbe's youngest daughter Sheba he had suddenly grown soft as wax.

148

He had lost his hardness and had grown sentimental, had started spinning dreams about Yankel marrying Sheba, and he and the rebbe standing together under the wedding canopy, with their children.

He soon came back to his senses.

"Fool!" he stormed at himself. "You're a thief, and your father and your grandfather and your great-grandfather were thieves! So what's this idea you've got into your head? What rebbe is going to marry his daughter to your son? Especially when your son is himself a thief, and he's just stabbed a man, and the man is in hospital!"

He could kick himself for having let his dream run away with him. Both his wife Golda and his son Yankel got the rough edge of his tongue when they ventured to say a word to him.

Then one day two policemen and a sergeant came to the house. The sergeant saluted, and said:

"Excuse me, Gospodin Lerner! I have received an order from the Chief of the District Police to arrest you as the ringleader of a fight in the street in which one man was stabbed and a lot of others were badly injured."

"Right!" said Wolf Jonachek. "You've got an order to arrest me! I'm ready to go with you! Have a drink with me first, and then you can put the bracelets on me!"

So Wolf Jonachek went to prison. Before long the rabbi and the other opponents of the rebbe who had laid information against Wolf Jonachek and got him arrested, began to worry about what would happen to them when Wolf Jonachek served his time and came back to the town. The rebbe's Hasidim added to their fear by the way they went about gloating:

"You've got it coming to you! Wolf Jonachek won't stay in prison for ever! He'll pay you when he comes out!"

They began to think that it might help if they put in a word for Wolf, and let him know that he owed his early release to them. Reb Chaim David, who had a lot of influence with the authorities, put out feelers.

But just then something terrible happened to Reb Chaim

David, and it frightened all the rebbe's opponents out of their wits. Reb Chaim David's eldest son, a married man with children fell ill and died. As he lay dying, Reb Chaim David, the rich man of the town, the man of authority, the friend of the governor, ran to the rebbe in his stockinged feet, and begged him for forgiveness.

"I have sinned against the holy rebbe!" he cried. "I confess I did wrong! I was blind! I did not see that the rebbe has the ear of Heaven! Please, Rebbe, please forgive me for the sins I have committed against you!"

But while he was still with the rebbe his wife came running to tell him it was too late. Their son had died.

Dread fell on the whole town. All the opposition to the rebbe suddenly stopped. Now the town was divided in two separate camps, the believing Jews, who were now all followers of the rebbe, and the disbelievers, the heretics and the freethinkers, who were most of them found among the organized workers, the Socialists.

The rav, the rabbi of the town, who was an enlightened man with a modern education, was scared by both—by the religious fanatics and by the irreligious fanatics. He no longer dared to express his doubts about the rebbe. Some of the young students in the Beth Hamedrash, secret doubters, largely under the rav's modernistic influence, wondered what had happened to the rav that he was silent now.

Shlomo Chaye's Bujas, the sharpest intellect among them, the rav's star pupil and most devoted admirer, suddenly lost all his respect for the rav, and accused him of being dishonest.

"Why do you keep silent?" he asked him bluntly. "It's your duty as the rabbi of this town to open the eyes of the people. You must explain to them that the rebbe had nothing to do with the death of Reb Chaim David's son. You must tell them there are no miracles! That it's all nonsense about him being a wonder-rabbi, a miracle-worker!"

"It wouldn't help!" said the rav.

"But it's the truth!" Shlomo persisted.

"There are times," said the rav, "when the truth must be

silent. The desire to proclaim the truth always, under any circumstances, without regard to the consequences, is dictated not so much by the love of truth as pride, vanity, cocksureness, wanting to justify oneself over the others, to show them how much better one understands things, and how backward and foolish the others are. When you are climbing upward to the great eternal light on a black stormy night, and the wind may blow out the tiny light in the lantern in your hand, you will do well to hide the light under your coat for a while, to prevent it being blown out by the wind."

Shlomo understood that. He didn't try to argue with the rabbi. But he stopped coming to him. He fell into a melancholy. And he stopped going to the rebbe's table, to see Sheba. He stifled his love for her. He stopped speaking even to his best friends in the Beth Hamedrash. He became a solitary, withdrawn into himself. He did nothing else but study Gemara and Cabala.

Wolf Jonachek didn't stay long in prison. They set him free for three reasons—Samuel Zeinvel recovered and was discharged from hospital; Wolf hadn't stabbed him, had not indeed taken any part himself that Sabbath in the fighting; and the police inspector in the town had drawn up the charge against Wolf in such a way that the judge took a lenient view, and thought that justice had been sufficiently served by the period Wolf had spent in prison awaiting trial. But there was also a fourth reason, which was even more important—all the witnesses, all those who had been knocked about in the fighting and would have to be called for the prosecution, all those who had previously murmured against the rebbe, would not give evidence now against one of the rebbe's staunchest champions.

Wolf Jonachek came out of prison a changed man. He had decided in prison that he would stop being a softie, that he would be what he was, a thief and a rogue, cruel and hard, without pity. His eyes had taken on a grim look. He had hard lines round his mouth.

It was Hanukkah when he came out, when even pious Jews who never touch a card all the year round play cards—part of the Hanukkah routine. So they were busy, of course, playing cards in Wolf Jonachek's house. There was the whole gang sitting round the table. Two bottles of brandy had been opened, and there was a huge dish of steaming potatoes in jackets on the table, and another dish of sliced salt herring in vinegar with onions. Afterwards Golda served roast goose.

But Yankel was missing from the table.

They also played cards at Hersh-Leib's, the Gemara teacher's. He had several of his friends round the table, with a bottle of 96-proof vodka, and a dish of latkes.

One of the card players at Hersh-Leib's was Red Beinish, whom the Hasidim called the "politician," because he was always talking politics, what was going on in the big world, news about the Japanese war. "Oho! How these little Japs made our Emperor whistle! First they pretended as though they had only a few antiquated weapons and a couple of broken-down ships, and then they told him what they had to say in Japanese. They walloped him on his backside, if you will pardon the expression, so that he couldn't sit down and he couldn't stand up. But the knockout he got at Port Arthur! The biggest ship, the one that Kuropotkin himself commanded, is lost. Gone! Nobody knows where it's got to!"

"So his game was lost! Lost!" they all chimed in, looking hard at their cards.

"And the way he's lost!"

"Pique nine!"

"Let's have a drink first!"

"Sure!"

They put the cards aside again, and took hold of the bottle. "Your good health!"

They dipped the fresh bread-rolls in the fat, fished out bits of roast goose from the pan, and raised their voices in song, jolly songs and sad songs.

There were Hasidim there each of whom could down a good measure of the strongest aquavit, and accompany it with a whole goose. Yet all the sorrow of the world stared from their eyes. There were other Hasidim full of fire and always jolly, even when there wasn't a bite of bread in the house, and even when their hearts writhed in torment and their souls comprehended the woe of the whole world.

And when one of these began to hum something his neighbor joined in, and then a third and a fourth. Till the singing grew louder, more fervent, fiery, and very soon they were going round and round in a dance.

The whole time, while everybody in the town was talking about the Rabbi's wife and Hersh Leib, his friends only laughed and spoke their opinion.

"Oh, you dull workaday people, you poor things, you dried-up paragraph-sticking souls, what do you understand of such matters? Hersh Leib has cast an eye on the Rabbi's wife? So what? Mustn't a man look at a woman? Mustn't a woman look at a man? Fools! What is a woman? Why has God given her a different appearance than a man? Beauty and charm? If not for a man to look at her and marvel at the grandeur of the Creator of the world, who has placed so much beauty in the world? Why has He given a man eyes and the lust for beauty? The whole world is all beauty, all music. And God created man in His own image, so that he can marvel at the wonder of His Work. God is sad when a man doesn't see the beauty of His creation. The Tanna Reb Jacob sinned when he said: 'He who is walking by the way and studying, and breaks off his study and says, "How fine is that tree, how fine is that field, him the Talmud regards as if he had forfeited his life."' The Tanna Reb Jacob did not love the Creator of the world enough. For sweet are the sounds that fill the whole world. One must say a benediction for the beauty of the world!"

A Hasid who had already taken the cards in his hand, wanting to deal, flung them on the table and stood up. He put his hand on Hersh Leib's shoulder, and called out: "Hersh Leib! They say that you look upon the Rabbi's wife differently than one may. I answer them: 'How else? There is nothing written about the way one may look upon a woman.' And then: Only the body of the woman belongs to the husband whom she married. But her beauty God created for all!"

"That's right! Very true!" the Hasidim clamored.

Hersh-Leib's wife standing at the stove, frying another lot of latkes, heard this and looked at her husband with silent suspicion. Beinish caught her gaze, and returned to the subject.

"That's what I said! I told them that the woman belongs to the man she married. But her beauty is for everyone to admire!"

"True! True!" clamored the others at the table, except Hersh-Leib, who kept silent. He didn't like the way the conversation was going. He smiled into his black beard.

Red Beinish was already humming another Hasidic tune. The others took it up, and soon they were all dancing again, as before. As he came round where his wife stood at the stove, Hersh-Leib held out his hand and drew her into the dancing circle, beside him. Beinish took her other hand, and the circle danced round and round.

The dancers dropped one by one into their chairs; the hostess took the latkes off the stove and served them hot.

Another drink. "L'Chaim!" Then another drink. Then Red Beinish began:

"The rebbitzin and both her daughters, and the women who stand outside, behind the window every Sabbath, to listen to the rebbe's table hymns—we ought to take them into the circle with us when we dance at the rebbe's; we should dance with them! Like you did now, Hersh-Leib! The holy tailor used to say that we must share our joy with all living creatures! With our womenfolk too!"

"That's true! That's very true!" they all agreed. And went back to card-playing.

They were playing cards that night in every Jewish house, as the custom was at Hanukkah. All year round, no Jewish woman would let her husband take a card in his hand, but during Hanukkah it was considered almost meritorious to play cards. They filled the lamps to the brim with paraffin, to last the night. They fried latkes and pressed them on the guests who came to play cards.

Lessons in heder ended early, and the boys ran off to the slide. Each child got a *dreidel*, and Hanukkah money, so that they could play with their *dreidel* for money stakes, as their elders did at cards. The white snow gave the town a holiday appearance. The light of the Hanukkah candles shone out from the windows of every Jewish house, through the frosted fern-encrusted panes. It fell on the roadway and set the snow aglow. Sanctified with blessings and the singing of Moaz Tzur, the burning candles told the great world outside about the heroism of the Jew Matatthias and his sons, the Maccabees, and the miracle that was wrought by them, about a mysterious eternal fire that will always burn, and can never be quenched, by anybody, ever!

On the highways there was the merry tinkling sound of sleigh bells. Boys and girls of the Zionist movement met in their clubs and sang Hebrew songs. They were practicing for the big Zionist evening there was to be on Saturday night. They put most of their fervor into singing the Zionist anthem "Hatikvah." "Ode lo ovdu!" they sang, full of hope and yearning.

It was Thursday evening—only one more day to the great Sabbath Hanukkah, for which both the Zionists and the rebbe's Hasidim were preparing.

Wolf Jonachek was taking no part in the preparations. He had decided in prison that in future he would keep his place—he would be a thief, and not try to be a Hasid. So he was now out with two of his best men on a job.

He had stood at the railway station with his companions, waiting for the train, with a strange foreboding that something was going to happen, something very unpleasant for him.

He had a superstitious habit, and he tried it now, several times—he lighted a match, and held it between two fingers till it burned down to the end. But each time the match broke and fell away before it came to the end. To him that meant a sure sign that this present enterprise must fail.

He muttered an oath under his breath, and tried to reassure himself—"I don't believe in it!"

He took his two companions to the bar, and ordered three big glasses of vodka. And they drank to their success. Wolf Jonachek ordered another round, and put his hand in his trouser pocket, and brought out a fistful of silver to pay. A rouble slipped down on the floor. He wanted to let it lie, but one of the others bent down, and handed it back to him. It made him mad. He looked daggers at the culprit, and ordered another round, and another, and another.

They got on the train when it arrived, and the whole way, more than an hour's journey, the three didn't exchange a word. When they got to their station they proceeded along the high road to the noble estate where they were going to steal horses. There was a wood near by, where they sat down to wait till it was time.

It didn't take long and Jonachek grew impatient. "I can't sit around like this!" he grumbled. "Let's go to the inn near by and have a drink!"

The other two followed him silently, thinking, "The old man's lost his nerve! He's looking for Dutch courage! We're in for trouble!"

"There'll be no trouble tonight," said Wolf to them, as though sensing their thoughts. "The Vistula is frozen. Hard as iron. We'll lead the horses away without any trouble!"

It was freezing. The sky was black like pitch. The stars were pinpoints. But for the white snow Wolf wouldn't have known his way, though he knew the district, like all the other districts in which he operated and which were recognized as his province, where other thieves were not allowed.

They reached the inn and had several drinks. Then Wolf Jonachek said: "Time! Time to go! Come on!"

A hundred paces or so from the stables Wolf told his companions to stop where they were and wait for him. He preferred to do the actual horse stealing himself.

Despite their fears everything went off well. Soon they heard a lot of heavy muffled footsteps, and the next moment they had swung themselves into the saddles, and before long they were across the frozen river. On the other side they removed the rags that Wolf Jonachek had bound round the horses' hooves, so that their horseshoes shouldn't be heard. They turned into the wood, and found the path, and before dawn they were home.

It was late on Friday, near the time for lighting the Sabbath candles, when Wolf Jonachek stood in the stable with the three newly stolen horses, debating with himself whether to go to the rebbe's table or not. Hadn't he decided when he was in prison, no more Hasid, no more rebbe—plain thief! Yet the rebbe's table drew him. Especially this Sabbath Hanukkah.

He was furious with himself. "You're like your son, who's in love with the rebbe's daughter! You're in love with the rebbe's table!"

That reminded him that Yankel had not yet come back; not since he had disappeared that Sabbath, soon after the fight.

Wolf Jonachek slapped one of the horses on the behind, and the horse turned its head to see what it was all about. So did the other two, curious about their new owner. What were they doing in this new place? Wolf Jonachek thought the horses were sneering at him. Let them! All the better! Showed that they were superior animals! Would fetch a good price when he got to selling them. Good animals! He stroked them; and they nuzzled him.

That put him in a better mood, and he smiled and decided that he would after all go to the rebbe's table.

He stroked the horses fondly. He loved horses. He loved

fondling them, talking to them; he imagined that he could talk to them better than with most people. He certainly could tell a horse everything there was on his mind without it being repeated. And horses listened so intelligently.

He roused himself. "Time to go to the synagogue!" he told himself. He went into the house. Golda had already lighted the Sabbath candles. He changed, and went to the synagogue.

But he did not go to the rebbe's table. He felt that, having just returned from a stealing expedition, he couldn't go immediately and mingle with the pious Hasidim visiting the rebbe for the Sabbath, as though he were an honest Jew. There was a story he had heard when he came out of prison that might too have contributed to his decision—some of the Hasidim had been worried because in a complaint that a rich man had lodged with him against a poor man the rebbe had judged the rich man right. It had angered even Wolf Jonachek. No rich man could be right! And when they told him it wasn't the rebbe's fault, that his wife, the rebbitzin, had made him do it, that made it only worse—what good was a rebbe who let his wife tell him what to do!

So Wolf Jonachek gave up being a Hasid, and stopped going to the rebbe's table, and a good many Jews in the town whom he had spared before, because they too were Hasidim, now found themselves robbed of valuable goods, and they didn't dare to say a word.

Sheba suffered intensely because she had at an early age developed an aversion to her mother, and the aversion had grown till it had become hatred. It had started when she was very young. It came from the fact that her mother had never shown her any love or even interest. The rebbitzin had not wanted her youngest child. She had resented her birth; and Sheba soon felt her mother's coldness to her, and she had shrunk from her. By the time Sheba was grown up mother and daughter couldn't stand the sight of each other.

The two older daughters and the son had been much older than Sheba, and had already been going about with friends when Sheba was still a child. Then they had married and left home. Only Eve was near her own age. And Eve and she had never got along. They were different temperaments. And when Eve had told her about her affair with the Christian German teacher, Sheba had begun to avoid her.

It was not long after Joseph's return to the town and the death of his father and mother that the rebbe had shocked Wolf Jonachek and many others among his Hasidim by giving judgment for the rich man against the poor man. The rich man was Reb Isser, a moneylender, hated by the whole town. He was one of the rebbe's Hasidim. The poor man was also one of the Rebbe's Hasidim, Reb Moshe Jonah, a small shopkeeper, with a crowd of children and a heap of debts. He had borrowed money from Reb Isser at a high rate of interest, and he argued that he had repaid the debt and more than the debt. But the rebbe found for the moneylender, saying that he had repaid only the interest and the debt was still owing. Now the moneylender was going to seize the poor man's shop, and leave him without his means of livelihood.

Sheba was in the terrible position of feeling ashamed of being her father's daughter, of hating both her parents. The only person to whom she could turn, she felt, was Joseph. She had been interested in him even before he had gone to Warsaw, and they had opened their windows of a morning, and had greeted each other without words, each too shy to speak.

Sheba found it hard to overcome her girlish reluctance and make the first advance—to call on Joseph. But this was not an ordinary situation, in which she would be calling on a young man out of the blue. This young man was a neighbor, who was in mourning for his parents who had both died tragically the same week. It was only right that she, like other neighbors, should call on him to offer her sympathy and condolences.

8

Joseph's sister Miriam, Reb Abraham's daughter, Reb Melech's granddaughter, and the great-granddaughter of the little tailor, was now living with her Christian lover in a poor workman's cottage near the mill where he was employed. His name was Andrei, and he was the son of a peasant, and he worked as an ordinary mill-worker. His grandfather had been a serf on the estate of a nobleman in one of the villages near the town. When the serfs were freed, and the land divided among them, he had received a small plot, which had afterwards gone to his son, Andrei's father. Their family name was Victor.

There were several other children. The family was very poor. Andrei was the only one who could read and write. He was largely self-taught. The work on the small farm was done mostly by the mother, for the father and the older sons hired themselves out as laborers on bigger farms.

Andrei had gone to the town and become a proletarian. He had been a good son, and before he had left the land while he was still quite young, he had helped his mother with the farm work. Every time his mother knelt before the image of the Virgin and crossed herself in prayer she thanked her for such a good son.

ndrei was very different from her other children and
the villagers generally. He was a dreamy lad. Always
dreaming of distant places. His great dream was to become a
soldier and travel the world by train and ship, to see the big
cities of the vast Russian Empire. He pictured himself in
uniform, with brass buttons and a belt and a cap with a cockade. He hoped they would put him in the cavalry, and he
would wear spurs, and wear a sword, and ride a fine horse,
not like that tired nag which they used for the plough, and
that he often rode but could never get to gallop.

One day something strange happened to Andrei. He passed
the White Castle outside the town—an empty ruin, where the
local lord had lived many years before Andrei was born. The
villagers told frightening stories about the ruin. They said
ghosts lived there. That the old lord still held court there.
Andrei, greatly daring, scared yet inquisitive, entered the
ruin. In his imagination he saw the old lord sitting on a golden
throne like a king, with a face like thunder, and terribly long
moustaches. He had called Andrei to come nearer. But Andrei had taken fright, and ran home. But he went back again.
This time he thought he saw the lord with a young woman on
his knee, kissing her and beating her. It seemed to Andrei
that the young woman looked as his mother would have
looked when she was young.

He told his mother about it. And she laughed at him. Because when she was a young girl the lord had been dead a long
time. But it was possible, she said, that the lord had held his
great-grandmother on his knee, and kissed her and beat her.
Because when his great-grandmother was a girl the local lord
had insisted on Droit du Seigneur, the first night, if the girl
was pretty enough. Then he had beaten her and chased her
out of the place.

From that time Andrei had borne a great hate against all
lords and all rich people. When he grew up, and had to hire
himself out like his father and his brothers to bigger farmers as
a farm laborer, he began to think of the problem of rich and
poor.

He felt cramped in the village. It was too small for him. He wanted to get out of it, away to far places. Nothing came of his dream of soldiering in distant places. The local quota of army conscripts was filled before his turn came, so he wasn't called on.

So Andrei Victor had gone to the town and got a job in a factory.

He wasn't happy. The huge machines terrified him. And he hated getting up in winter before dawn to walk in the dark all the way from the village to the factory in the town, and then walk back.

He made friends with some of the workers in the factory; they told him about the Labor and Socialist movement, which was trying to abolish the long working hours, and in course of time to abolish masters and employers, and establish Socialism, which would make the workers the masters.

He liked that. The idea pleased him. He wanted to know more about this movement. He found one workman in the factory who was a leader of the local Socialist group.

"I think I can trust you, Andrei!" he said. "I have watched you and have made inquiries about you. You have a strong character and a quick mind. You can read and write, and you're honest. So I shall guarantee for you. I'll sign your application to be a member of the Party. The Socialist Party. But remember—it's a conspiratorial organization, a secret, illegal organization. The police know about us—about our organization of workers and peasants. But they don't know who the members are. Should they find out we would all be arrested and put in prison or sent to Siberia. So you must be careful, Andrei!"

Miriam had met Andrei at the Party meeting.

The peasants in the village where Andrei Victor was born and where his parents lived, and his great-grandparents had lived, were terribly poor; they hadn't enough land, and they hadn't enough cattle. And they had a lot of children—many mouths to feed. They were fanatically religious and very superstitious. They were scandalized because Andrei Victor, Stanislav Victor's son, was living with a Jewess. He lived with her in the town, but he also brought her to the village, only occasionally at first, on a Sunday; then almost every Sunday. Sometimes they stayed together for days in the village, with his parents.

They had a purpose in staying in the village—to spread Socialism among the peasants. It was Miriam's idea, to get a few peasants together, and talk to them, and try to organize them. She thought she could win them over by showing interest in their personal life, helping the mothers by taking the children off their hands for a while, or even helping them with the housework. She was anxious to gain their good will.

But the peasants had always looked on Andrei as somebody not quite their own. There was something strange about him. He had different ways, seemed to belong to another world— not a peasant, but one of the lords who had ordered them about, like an outsider among them, who had wandered in by mistake.

Andrei's father, Stanislav Victor, was one of them. They knew him and they understood him. He spoke their language and he thought as they did. So it puzzled them how he came to have a son like Andrei. Now, on top of all his other strange ways, Andrei had brought a Jewess to the village! That was more than they could stand!

They were stopped from anything they meant to do about Miriam by an old peasant woman in the village who warmed them that if they hurt the Jewess it would be displeasing to their Lord Jesus. There was nothing he liked better than to have a Jew or a Jewess come to him and turn Christian. Andrei, she said, had done a great thing by bringing the Jewess to the village, to make her one of themselves.

After that the peasants were particularly kind to Andrei and to Miriam. Miriam soon won their hearts. She gave herself completely to them. She listened to their tales of woe, she advised them, the comforted them, she showed real personal interest in them. She gave the children lessons, taught them to read and write; she helped them to make up when they quarreled. And if she had a few coins to spare she gave them to the poorest among them.

She planted the seed of Socialism in them. She spoke to them and opened their eyes to the differences between rich and poor, the way the rich live and the way the poor live. She made them see that there was a big movement among the workers and the peasants to overthrow the rich master class, and to distribute the good things of the earth more justly, among the poor. Gradually the villagers began to accept her ideas. A new fire came into their eyes, a new bearing in their whole attitude.

Then one Sunday the priest, from the altar in the Church, thundered against the villagers for allowing such a sin in their village—to let Stanislav Victor's son live there with an unbeliever, an unbaptized Jewess, and unmarried. Hell waited to consume them both, and all those in the village who tolerated such things.

That started the trouble. What! She hasn't been baptized? They're not married! Living in sin, like a dog and a bitch! We're not going to stand for that!

Then one villager said: "I saw her in Church last Sunday, many Sundays!" Another swore that she had been to Holy Communion! Of course, she was baptized!

But others were not so easily satisfied. There was one young village woman who had hoped to marry Andrei, who called "the Jewess" a whore and a witch. It gradually sunk in. Many of the villagers turned against Miriam. Even some who had benefited most from her and had said she was an angel. They were afraid that the others would denounce them as her friends. They were afraid of the word *witch*. Suppose she was a witch? It must have been by witchcraft that she had won them and made them her friends! The villagers began to avoid Stanislav's house.

Yet there were also a few villagers who had absorbed the Socialist idea. These stood firmly by Miriam.

Andrei didn't know what to do with all this talk against Miriam, his wife, whom he had not married.

"It would be better if you did become baptized," he said, "and we got married in Church. . . ."

He saw Miriam's eyes flash fire, and he stopped.

"Will you say that again?" said Miriam.

Andrei was a Socialist and a freethinker, and to him Miriam was his wife, though they were not married. The Church and the Catholic religion and the marriage institution were weapons used by the Czarist government to subjugate the masses of the people.

Yet he had in his heart remained a Catholic, and his instincts rebelled against the idea that he was living with a Jewess, without a proper Church marriage. At the same time he loved Miriam and respected her. The two feelings clashed and put his mind in a whirl.

"I mean," he began very lamely, "I mean it would be easier to win the villagers if they had more trust in us. If they didn't always have to think of you as the Jewess. If we were properly married in the Church. As it is, we're being ostracized. They even avoid my father. They won't come near our house. My father is upset about it. And he puts the blame on us. I don't like my father and mother suffering because of us!"

Miriam went very white. She thought of her own parents whom she had deserted for this Christian villager. She thought of her own mother pleading with her, mourning because of her. She remembered her father pleading with her on his death bed: "Remain a Jewess, Miriam!" These last words of her father's came to the top of her mind now, as on the waves of a flood. Even if she had not been a Socialist, which meant denying religion, Jewish or Christian, she still wouldn't have agreed to be baptized, because she had given her promise to her father that she never would! She meant to keep her word! Even—yes, even if it meant leaving her lover. . . .

"Marisha! Marisha!" Andrei cried, pleading with her. He went down on his knees to her.

"Don't be angry with me, Marisha! Forgive me!" He took her hands and kissed them: "Please forgive me, Miriam! The villagers are so bound to their religion, and they hate the Jews!"

"I am a Jewess!"

"You needn't be! Maria, I understand how the villagers feel! I know!"

"You know how the villagers feel!" Miriam burst out. "Because you feel as they feel! You hate the Jews too! And I'm a Jewess!"

Andrei was beside himself. "Dear Jesus!" he kept repeating. "Maria, my dear Marisha! I don't hate Jews! It isn't true! If I did it was before I became a Socialist! I know that all people are equal, that all proletarians are the same, that all workers are exploited, and that we must all fight together against the capitalist class—we are all brothers in the struggle for freedom and Socialism! Forgive me, Marisha, my dear Marisha! But it would be better for our cause if you became a Christian. The villagers would listen to us differently. The priest would stop inciting them against you in the Church. You would be one of us!"

Miriam bit her lip. She loved Andrei. She loved him because he was a man of the soil, with a healthy mother-earth feel about him; she loved him because he was a big, broad-shouldered, handsome man. Her anger left her. She rested in his arms, she fondled his hair. He held her tight.

"Andrei!" she murmured, "Don't ever say such things to me again! Jew and Christian! There's no such thing! We're Socialists! We know no differences of race and religion!"

"Yes, I know! All people are the same! All equal!"

"Those things you said before, Andrei, are wrong! I'm not Jewish, any more than you are Christian! We don't believe in any religion. So this talk of my becoming a Christian is meaningless. These people who want me to become a Christian, and you, too, when you say you understand them, are showing how deep the poison of anti-Semitism has sunk! It's a relic of the bad old days, when the rich landlords and the nobles, in

166

r kasha or rice or beans. Most of the Christi
cabbage with pork—cheap and satisfying. As
ent to bed very soon after the meal, because the
tired, and they had to be up again at six in th
wash, have a quick bite, and go back to the fac

were some who in spite of their weariness
went out to a meeting, or if there was no meeting
d Socialist literature, history, popular science,
lles lettres. The fact that their reading was il-
spiratorial was refreshing and made them feel

ferent levels, even among workers all suffering
ty. Compared with the factory workers, re-
s beside their machines, the artisans were
had at least the satisfaction of joy in their

ailoring workshop the apprentice boys and
g at their work, talking, telling jokes, laugh-
elf loved telling a funny story, sometimes so
ys and girls blushed.

e girls and women who worked for him les
men and boys. He explained the reason i
though he were reading it from the Pen

n. So Holy Script tells us. Eve was only
rib—therefore she gets less."

Eve?" he went on, going up to one of th
as Eve, and tickling her under the armpi
e?"

ing her needle, and didn't answer. Nott
wered for her. And his answer made th
before. And he got a slap across his nec

order to keep the people in servitude, made them believe that their poverty and all their troubles were due not to them, but to the Jews! I love you, Andrei! I love your parents. And I love these village folk, even though they are making me suffer so much. I want to stay here with them, and work among them!"

"It isn't their fault!" she went on. "I don't blame them. It's this poison that was instilled in them! Because they're not educated! Because they were given no schooling. Because they can't think for themselves. Because the Czar and the rich and the nobility wanted the people to stay ignorant, so that they would remain enslaved."

"We mustn't think badly of them, Andrei!" she continued. "We must love the poor, all the poor, Jews and Christians. The only people we have to hate are the rich, the exploiters, the oppressors! Wait till the people have their eyes opened to the truth! Then they will rise against those who are keeping them down! It won't take long now! You'll see!"

Her eyes flamed with the light of hope and conviction—her belief in the redemption of the world through revolution, through Socialism.

"And don't call me Marisha! Don't call me Maria! My name is Miriam! Say it! Mir-yam!"

He repeated it: "Mir-yam!" and he laughed.

They sat together, reconciled, their quarrel ended, happy.

Then Andrei began to tell Miriam the story of his strange experience in the ruined castle, what he had sensed and seemed to see on the two occasions when he had entered it; the lord sitting on his throne with a young woman on his knee, who might have been his great-grandmother, so his mother said.

"It might very well have been! Quite likely!" said Miriam. "That custom of Jus Primae Noctis was very much practiced in those days. Many of the peasants, as a result, have noble blood in their veins. A peasant in those days was the property of his lord; his wife and children were chattel, like cattle. Every young girl belonged to the noble master. No peasant could be sure if the oldest child was his or the lord's."

Andrei jumped up, in a rage:

"It means that I may have the blood of one of the oppressors in me! I'll murder them! I'll kill the lot of them! Down with the lords! Down with the dirty dogs!"

Miriam didn't know what to say. It seemed very likely to her that Andrei was descended from the lord of the castle through his great-grandmother. But it wasn't the kind of conversation she wanted to pursue. She tried to change the subject.

"We've got those proclamations still to distribute, Andrei!"

"Yes, Marisha!"

"Marisha?"

"Miriam," he said with a smile.

"Now," she said, "we'll continue reading the history of the French Revolution, Andrei."

for it from Velvel, the cutter, so that his pressing iron almost dropped from his hand.

Velvel considered himself one of the advanced school, enlightened and emancipated. He was a member of the illegal Jewish Socialist Party Bund. And he was in love with Eve. That is why he had put Notte in his place.

"How many times have I told you," he said to Notte, but addressing himself to everybody in the workshop, including Beirach, the boss, "that I'll have no coarse talk here, especially when there are women in the room! It's bad enough that people call us tailor-boys, meaning by that that we're lowlifes, gross and vulgar in our talk, and loose in our behavior. How can you laugh at the boss's dirty jokes, the man who exploits you, and insults his women workers with his smutty talk!"

Beirach, the master tailor, pretended not to hear what Velvel was saying. He knew his cutter was a Socialist, a member of the Party, and that he could easily have a strike called in his workshop. So instead he went for Notte:

"Haven't I told you to watch your tongue! I won't have any dirty jokes in my workshop! You may think you're very clever, but not here—in this workshop you're an apprentice, and no more! And if you don't pay more attention to your work you'll never be anything more than an apprentice! Be a gentleman, and ask Eve's pardon."

Velvel clenched his teeth to keep himself from going up to his boss and slapping his face. The other workers, who had laughed before, now looked very glum.

Beirach changed the mood, by suddenly calling out:

"Come along, all of you! You're asleep! There's a lot of work to be done! Get on with it!"

The sewing machines rattled. The girls plied their needles industriously. Notte was pressing the seams of a pair of trousers, and burst into song:

The Golden Peacock has come flying
From a distant land,
From a distant land.

171

The others all took up the chorus:

> *And she lost the golden feather,*
> *Why, I cannot understand!*

When that song was ended, David, a cheerful, handsome fellow with a shrill voice, started another:

> *Tell me, pretty maiden,*
> *What will you do in a land far away?*

And the answer came:

> *I'll go through all the streets, and call:*
> *Any washing? I'll do it all!*
> *There's nothing that I wouldn't do,*
> *As long as I may stay with you!*

Eve and Malka repeated: "*As long as I may stay with you!*"
That annoyed Velvel, because the response in which Eve joined was to David's question. It worried him. Was Eve in love with David?

Velvel was also annoyed because these workers were singing Jewish folk songs instead of Socialist revolutionary songs.

One of the other girls, Rachel, started another folk song:

> *I lay my little head*
> *On my mother's bed.*

Velvel couldn't stand any more of it, so he burst out, drowning Rachel's voice:

> *How long, how long will you still be slaves,*
> *And wear the chains of shame?*
> *How long will you work to make others rich,*
> *And let them rob you just the same?*

Some of the younger workers, Socialists like Velvel, also members of the Party, repeated:

How long will you work to make others rich?

A few of the older men, religious, non-Socialists, started chanting one of the Psalms from the liturgy:

The heavens are the Lord's,
But the earth is for the sons of man.

Velvel's powerful voice rose against them:

How long, how long will you stand with bent backs,
And wear the chains of shame?

His Party comrades, though scared of what they were doing, felt it was their duty to back him. Velvel was the shop steward here. So they struck up with:

Awake! The day is dawning!
See how strong you are!

At the same time they were all working faster, both to make the boss see that their singing didn't slow down the work, and because the quicker tempo of the machines helped the rhythm of the song.

Raisel was the button-hole hand in the workshop. She took real pride in the button-holes she made. They had to be perfect. Many of the other workers also were interested in the garments they made. They could slacken the pace of their work, or quicken it, they could talk or they could sing. It made things easier. And when they went home at the end of the day they were not so tired out as the workers in the factory. And after their supper those who belonged to the Party could go off to the secret meeting, which was held each time in a different home, and this time was to be in the house of the old cobbler, Reb Jacob.

173

Reb Jacob was a big tall man, getting on in years, with small eyes that shone with simple goodness. His high forehead and long white beard gave him the appearance of a scholar, and he got more deference on that account, though he was only a poor patching cobbler.

When he was younger he had also made new shoes, to order, but now people brought only repairs to him. Many pious folk thought he was a saint, perhaps one of the secret thirty-six. Everybody addressed him as Reb Jacob. And people not only respected but loved him.

Reb Jacob spoke slowly and meditatively, carefully weighing his words. Not everybody quite understood what he was saying because he spoke so simply that they expected some hidden meaning to be concealed there.

He charged less for his repairs than any other cobbler in the town. And if someone asked him why, he explained: "If I make a pair of new shoes or a pair of high books, I'm creating something; it's a piece of craftsmanship. Every craftsman puts something of himself into his work, his individuality. Every man is different from every other man, so what he produces is also different. I have a right therefore to charge more for work into which I have put myself. But what merit is there in putting a patch on an old shoe?"

He charged so little for the work that he had to put in more hours in the day. But he loved his work. He considered it a way of serving his fellow man, making unusable footwear usable. He felt as happy doing this as in saying his prayers three times a day, or reading Psalms, or Isaiah or Amos, his favorite Prophets, or getting absorbed in Proverbs or Ecclesiastes or in the study of the Midrash. Gemara had less attraction for him. He had tried it, but he hadn't been able to get the sense of it. He was not a pious man, but he was no disbeliever. He read profane literature—in Yiddish, because it was the only language he knew except the old Hebrew of the rabbinic books—with the same piety as he read the sacred writings. He employed no hired labor, not even when he was up to his neck in work, because he refused to profit by another man's

174

toil. He had thought of getting a man to work with him and share his earnings equally with him. But he had rejected the idea because he knew he liked talking to his customers, about all sorts of things, forgetting that he had work to do, forgetting that he was a cobbler, sitting on a three-legged stool at his bench, with a shoe or a top boot on his knee, which he was mending.

"What fair shares would there be," he said to himself, "if I sit and talk and he does all the work?"

Reb Jacob wrote down with his heavy cobbler's hand every tale he heard told about the little tailor, every legend that had grown up around him, every wise saying, every profound thought that had been attributed to him, had in all these years passed from mouth to mouth and had been preserved in the folk memory. He guarded this written record like a treasure. He spoke to nobody about it, yet everybody in the town knew that Reb Jacob was making a collection of everything known and said about the little tailor.

Joseph heard about it, and paid Reb Jacob a visit, wondering if he would be able to tell him more about his great-grandfather, give him a better picture.

"Yes," said Reb Jacob, "I have a very high regard for your great-grandfather. I'm no Hasid, but there is a great deal in what he said and did that has value for us all today. I find a lot of beauty and wisdom in it. And you, who are so much more learned, will understand it better than I can."

Joseph became a frequent visitor to Reb Jacob. He liked talking to the old man, most of all about Socialism and Hasidism, the two ideas that had at that time completely captured his mind and his heart, even more than in Warsaw when he had first come in contact with the Socialists.

"Times change," said Reb Jacob. "Each period has its own form of Hasidism. Today it is Socialism, which means justice, resisting the rich and the powerful, as at all times. That is our Jewishness. That is the way Abraham began. He stood out in opposition to the makers of idols. Moses fought against slavery. All our Prophets after him denounced the rich and the

175

mighty, they all took up the cause of the poor and the oppressed. Isaiah prophesied that the day will come when justice will prevail over the whole earth, and there will be no more war. That is Socialism. Things can't stay as they are, that those who work and produce everything haven't enough to eat and no decent home where to live, and those who don't work wallow in riches, and whenever the rulers feel like it they make war on each other, and the common people have to go as soldiers and are killed."

Joseph thought that Reb Jacob was talking as naively about Socialism as he himself had done in those first days in Warsaw. But he liked it. It was open and simple-hearted, and full of trust in the honesty and goodness of man. It was the eternal truth that lies at the bottom of Socialism and of every movement inspired by the desire to improve the lot of man. Reb Jacob's simple faith touched Joseph, and wakened in him again his old belief in the mission of Socialism; it made him decide to rejoin the Party, and work with it. His old enthusiasm returned.

It was Joseph who afterwards told Reb Jacob of the difficulty the Party had to find places to meet. The police knew all their rendezvous. Also most of the homes in which their members lived were poky little places that couldn't hold enough people—one room that served as kitchen, bedroom, and living room. They couldn't hire a room especially for their meetings because nobody would let a room to them for that purpose.

"Tell them to hold their meetings here," Reb Jacob said. "Look what a big room I've got! With a small side room and a kitchen besides. It was different when my wife was alive, and our children lived here. Now they're all married and gone away. I did think of giving it all up and moving into a smaller place. But I've lived here so long that I've grown attached to it. I know and I love every inch of it—every floorboard. I couldn't leave it. It isn't right to expect me to fit in to a new home at my age. Yet it's more than I need—it's too big for me. It's just what you want for your meetings."

Joseph told Boris, the leader of his local group; and that is how they came to hold their meeting in Reb Jacob's room.

The group decided to pay Reb Jacob for the use of his room. But he wouldn't hear of it. "What for? Are you going to live here? Work here? Sleep here? No! I'm going to live here and work here and sleep here just the same as before. You're only coming here to hold a meeting. So why should I charge you rent for it? I've managed to pay my way till now. I don't owe the landlord any rent. I can manage the same way as I did till now. I can still earn my living with my own two hands. Why should I suddenly become a landlord at my age? Besides, if it's working for Socialism and justice I'm in it just as much as you all are!"

The two young men who had appeared in the town one day, about the same time that the rebbe had arrived there, and the workers called them the "delegates," came from the big textile city. Their names were Boris and Adam. Adam belonged to the general Polish Socialist Party known by its initials as P.P.S., and Boris belonged to the Jewish Socialist Party Bund. The programs of both Parties were essentially the same; they stood for a very similar political and social ideology. The only difference was on the national question. The P.P.S. held that all the minorities in Poland, no matter what their religion was, belong to the Polish nation. While the "Bund" demanded national cultural autonomy for the Jews. There was a lot of heated discussion and argument between the two parties and their leaders and theoreticians over this point. And strangely, both parties were agreed in being cosmopolitan and internationalist in their propaganda. Both denounced nationalism as chauvinism, as a tool used by the bourgeoisie and the reactionaries to divide the working class,

177

and as a means by which the capitalists and the imperialists were able to organize wars that gave them fat profits on war supplies.

Boris and Adam came from very different homes and backgrounds and were very different in their characters. Boris's father was a Melamed, a Hebrew teacher of religion, and his mother was a reader of the prayers in the women's part of the synagogue, who read the prayers aloud so that the women who were illiterate could repeat them after her. There was never enough bread in the house. Boris, who had been Benjamin to his parents and was their sixth child, went to work at the age of twelve as a weaver's apprentice. The work was too hard for the boy, and he was put to work instead with a bookbinder. It was then that he discovered his passion for reading—books on general education. It brought him to Socialist literature, and to the Bund. He soon revealed himself as an effective speaker, a skillful debater, and a clever organizer. They sent him to a teachers' seminary, and he became a teacher in a Jewish school.

Adam came from a rich home. His father did big business with Russia and was fond of talking Russian. His mother was a beauty, a woman of education, who knew how to dress and bear herself with dignity, and she was a Polish patriot. His father and mother both came from rich devout Jewish homes, where the religious observances were strictly kept; and the parents spoke only Yiddish at home. They themselves were complete assimilationists.

Adam was brought up by a French governess. He found his way to the Polish Socialist Party in the university. He had then left his parents' home, but without giving up their assimilationist attitude.

It had not kept him from establishing contact with the Jewish workers' movement, and becoming acquainted with their problems, and even learning the Yiddish language.

Boris and Adam were friends, and worked well together, notwithstanding the difference in their Party programs on the point of Jewish national autonomy. One day Adam suggested that they should publicly debate this problem, and let the meeting afterwards express its own views in a discussion.

This was to be the debate. Reb Jacob's room was packed for the occasion, and there was an overflow into the side room and into the kitchen.

The old man had put a white cloth on the table, and had brought out all his chairs from the side room and the kitchen. Even then there wasn't enough seating for all, and many sat on the floor, mostly in couples, a boy and a girl together. Everybody chattered animatedly; it looked like a party. Except that the place was in semidarkness, the shutters were closed, and a cloth was hung across to keep the light from showing through the chinks. Everybody spoke in whispers so as not to attract attention outside, which might bring the police to investigate.

Reb Jacob didn't like this concealment. He made a suggestion: "I've got a bottle of brandy. We'll put it on the table here. Somebody go out and get a cake. I'll find some food for a snack. We'll turn up the lights. And stop whispering! One of you boys and girls—that couple over there—come to the table, and be bride and bridegroom. This is your engagement party. Can't I give a party in my house?"

Everybody laughed and clapped. And the couple whom Reb Jacob had picked on went to the table wondering how he had guessed that they were in love and wanted to get engaged and married, when they hadn't told even their closest friends.

Now the atmosphere was really like that at a party. People talked louder, with less restraint. They discussed things and argued and got heated over some point or other. Reb Jacob loved it. Like in the Beth Hamedrash when he was a young student, before his father died, and they put him to shoemaking to earn a living. The students in the Beth Hamedrash had argued in the same way about the interpretation of a passage in the Gemara or some other learned work. And here there were indeed among these factory workers, weavers, tailors, and artisans in other crafts, some who had previously been students in the Beth Hamedrash.

Nathan, who worked in Reb Zalman Finkelstein's weaving mill, a tall, stooping man with bad lungs and burning eyes, got up and addressed the gathering:

"Really, Comrades—we can't go on like this! All these private discussions! We've got a public debate here! Please keep silent. And then we'll begin."

Boris and Adam went to the table. The "bride and bridegroom" moved a little down the table to make room for them.

Adam began. He spoke a good Yiddish, but not easily, and it lacked the folk intimacy of the language. It was an acquired and studied Yiddish, a literary rather than a naturally spoken Yiddish. But he spoke clearly. He made his points. And with his academic training he presented a cogent reasoned case for his argument against cultural autonomy. Culture and language, he maintained, are two separate things—and a nation can create its culture in any language. The European nations had in the middle ages created their culture in Latin. The Jews after the biblical period had created their culture not in Hebrew but in many different languages, in the early periods in Aramaic, Greek, and Arabic. Then in the languages of the countries in which they lived.

"As for Yiddish," he went on, "we all know it is a mixed language, eighty percent Middle High German and Hebraisms and Slavisms, written in Hebrew characters."

He sensed the audiences disapproval of what he was saying, but instead of trying to win them with a retraction or a softening of his argument, he continued in the same strain:

"Isn't it an affront to this state and this people to refuse to accept the language and the ways of the country in which we live, and to demand autonomy for a language brought in from somewhere else, from a country that drove us out with hatred and with scorn, a country that is the enemy of this country where we live?

"There is a case for lingual autonomy," he said, "but only where a people belonging to a country have been cut off from it by the annexation of their particular area by another country with a different language. If they continue to inhabit this territory they are entitled to use their own language. But that is not the position with the Jew in Poland."

Boris argued that cultural autonomy for a minority was a benefit to the state as a whole, because it was good for the state that its people should be cultured and interested in cultural advance; and that was best possible in the natural language of the particular minority. It was oppression to demand that a people living in a country must abandon its own language and culture and adopt that of the ruling class, as though its own language and culture were inferior. It was an insult to that people which had created cultural values in its own language, which were not unimportant to mankind as a whole.

There had not been and there were not now any "native original languages" in a country belonging to any particular people, he contended. Every language derived from a common ancestry, from a common treasury, and every language was a mixture. A living language borrowed, to enrich itself; it developed and changed—in keeping with the changes in its life. And Yiddish, he said, is a language that came into existence and developed in its own way, as it had done till now, because it was the expression of Jewish life. To abandon Yiddish would mean for the Jewish people an end to its own natural life. It would be cruel suppression, violent strangulation of a people's life. The demand for cultural autonomy for the Yiddish language was right and justified, because Yiddish was the language in which the masses of the Jewish people lived their everyday life, and in which they produced their cultural values.

Long Nathan, in the chair, remarked drily that both speakers had been deviating from the strict principles of Marxism.

Next came the discussion, in which Joseph also took part. Concentrating on the idea of right and justice that Boris had emphasized, Joseph spoke of the concept of Socialism as an ethical movement, seeking social justice. He held that this was the true Socialism, and not preaching class war and so-called scientific Socialism according to the rigid rules laid down by Marx and Engels. Class war divided people where we should unite them, he said. And what could there be "scientific" about the problem of human relations, which Socialism essentially must deal with? The relationship between a man and his neighbor was not an exact science like mathematics. It was a matter of feeling, of conscience, of ethics. The best Socialists were the old Hebrew Prophets who had roused the people against oppression and injustice, against those who laid field to field, and ground down the face of the poor, and robbed the fatherless and the widow. "Scientific Socialism" with its dogmas and divisions and its antilibertarian doctrines was establishing a new orthodoxy and a new heresy-hunting, the "crime" of "deviationism," and he feared that the priests of Marxism would not be different from any other priests. They would want to stamp out opposition and independent thought, and impose a bureaucracy to enforce adherence to their dogmas. Instead of freedom it would bring a new slavery.

Murmurs of disagreement and protest rose all during Joseph's speech. But only among a few of the people. The majority soon decided that they were not a bit interested in what he was saying, and they stopped listening, paid no attention, conversed with their neighbors. He was talking, they said, like a *maggid*, a preacher in the synagogue.

Only Reb Jacob listened with shining eyes, drinking in every word, and he alone clapped loudly when Joseph finished, and sat down.

Adam and Boris replied briefly to the discussion, and then everybody sang the Bund hymn, beginning with "Brothers and sisters of want and toil," and concluding:

> *Heaven and earth our words will hear,*
> *And the stars shining bright and clear.*
> *We swear our oath, with blood and tear.*
> *We swear! We swear! We swear!*

The police didn't find out what was going on in Reb Jacob's room. But Wolf Jonachek did. He knew all about these Socialists who were meeting there and plotting strikes and revolution to overthrow the czar and the government and turn the whole world upside down. He had also heard reports that these same people had started interfering with his gang of thieves.

"I've let them carry on far too long," he said to his wife Golda. "They think there's nobody able to deal with them! I've got to teach them a lesson. I'll clear the Socialists out of our town!"

Wolf was spoiling for a fight. He was furious because his son Yankel, who had disappeared after that fight over the rebbe in whom Wolf had now lost faith, hadn't come home. He had no idea where he had gone.

So Wolf Jonachek let the leaders of the Socialist group know that he wanted to meet them. He appointed Reb Ozie's saloon as the meeting place. Boris knew what it meant; he knew it was a challenge he must not ignore. So he chose some of the best fighters in the group and sent Velvel with them as their spokesman.

Wolf Jonachek arrived first, and ordered a pot of beer, feeling that he was being kept waiting, and fuming because of it. He had another pot of beer, a third and a fourth. And still those Socialists hadn't arrived.

And then they were there. Five big fellows. "Youngsters!" Wolf sneered into his beard. "Mere boys!" He felt like putting them one by one across his knee, and smacking their bottoms.

He called them over to his table? "Have a beer with me!"

"Thank you, no! We don't drink!"

"Saints?"

"God forbid!"

"Then why don't you drink with me?"

Chelek, a reformed thief, who had once belonged to Wolf's gang, and was now working as a locksmith, blurted out:

"We don't drink with thieves and rogues!"

"Is that so!"

But Wolf decided to keep quiet for a while. He knew from their past association that Chelek had a heavy fist.

"All right then, if you won't drink, let's get down to business!"

He turned to Velvel:

"I can see you're the big man here. Very well, you tell me! Is it right what you're trying to do?—upset the government and dethrone the czar, and that everybody does what he likes, and there is no authority and no control? You want to do away with rich and poor! Everybody alike, you say, everybody the same! Now, do you call that right? Is Reb Zalman Finkelstein who built that big textile factory and runs it so successfully to be no better off than one of his workmen? Who would direct the factory and do all the business with the firms here and abroad who do their buying from him? Long Nathan? Would he do it? Would he? Would he be any better if he were on top? Anybody who is on top would be just the same as those who are on top now. That's the way of the world. Because we're human beings, and not angels!

"Now, another thing—me, my own personal affair. I'm a thief . . ."

He couldn't control himself any longer. He jumped up, and lifted his hand to Velvel, whom he had been addressing himself to all the time. That lifted fist brought Chelek at once to his feet, and down came Chelek's iron fist on Wolf Jonachek's face. Wolf started bleeding from his nose and mouth. He staggered. The next minute he got hold of Chelek's head with both his hands, meaning to use him as a battering ram against his companions. But Chelek shot out his leg and kicked Wolf in the groin. Wolf doubled up. He couldn't rise from the floor.

People came rushing up, wanting to help. Chelek and Velvel and the other three didn't even look at Wolf. They walked out.

10

That Saturday after the fight in the market place Yankel had gone away—anywhere, so long as he got away. He felt completely out of heart. The only relief from his black mood was the pain of the blows he had got from his father—in his ribs and on his swollen bruised lips.

"I wish he'd killed me," he kept saying to himself as he stumbled along. "I deserve it! What could have made me do such a thing?—pull out a knife and stab that poor man! He may die in hospital! And it'll be my fault! How can I think of Sheba now? She won't want to have anything to do with me, a cutthroat, a murderer!"

It was night now, but Yankel did not turn back to go home. He had decided to go and live and work in one of the neighboring villages. Which village? All the villages in the neighborhood had suffered from his father's thieving expeditions. They all knew him and his gang. The villagers would lynch him! Hadn't he been a thief himself and robbed them! How dare he show his face there!

There was one village where Yankel felt he could go—he had a peasant wench there. He could go to her, and she would look after him. Neither his father nor he had ever stolen a thing in that village. He would be safe there. So he went to the village, and he went straight to his wench. And there he stayed.

Malgosia was a big hefty young woman, with a broad squash nose.

"My dear!" she welcomed Yankel. "You haven't been here for a long time! What kept you away so long? But I'm glad you've come! My dear! My dear!"

Yankel didn't answer her. He was mum. The hut was small and poor and dark. It was a miserable place. The whole atmosphere was depressing. Malgosia's father was an old man, a very old man—he had been sixty or more when Malgosia was born; his wife had been fifty then, so she too was now an old woman. And she was almost blind. The hut was neglected. Their piece of land was not worked properly. The stable was empty—no cow, no horse, no pigs, no hay or straw.

The old people slept on a broken couch, covered with his sheepskin and a heap of rags to keep them warm. Malgosia slept on the floor by the stove. Yankel had to sleep at her side. There was no other place. And she gave him no peace all night, with her demands on him. She wouldn't leave him alone. It was nearly day before she fell asleep. And he couldn't sleep at all.

He wondered how he could get away, where he could go. There was no way out. He would have to stay here.

He stayed. He was still staying there when the winter was well advanced. Christmas was nearly on them. Yankel had relapsed into a dull stupor. He went about mum, deaf and dumb. He spoke to nobody. There was a sadness about his face and his whole appearance.

"You look ill!" Malgosia said to him one day. "Yet your body isn't ill. Your soul is sick! Your heart is suffering. You look like Jesus on the cross. Full of pain. You don't love me any more, Yahko! You're in love with somebody else! Tell me who she is! I won't mind! So long as you stay with me!"

So Yankel told her about Sheba, the rebbe's daughter, and

how he had never even spoken a word to her. She was beautiful and pure—like an angel in heaven! And he told Malgosia how he had stabbed a man in his hometown and had run away. He had come to her in the village to hide.

"So you don't love me any more, Yanko!" she said sadly. "And I love you so much!"

She told Yankel that she had had a child of his, and she had killed it.

"I had it in the stable," she said, "one night, before dawn. It was harvest time. I didn't know what to do with it. So I killed it. I chopped it up on the block, with an ax, and the dogs devoured it!"

Yankel shuddered. This terrible woman, he thought, could kill him too, if she became very angry with him, one night when he was sleeping.

He left her. He left the hut. He went to the old ruin in the village that had once been a blacksmith's forge. There he slept on the clay floor, beside what had once been the furnace.

One night—in deep winter with the snow up to his knees—Yankel had gone to the village, walking about for hours, because it was too cold in the forge, and he had no other place to sleep. There was nobody about, not a soul, not even a stray dog. The wind cut like a knife. He felt that he must knock at one of the sleeping huts and beg the people to let him in. Or he would die of the cold. His ears flamed. His feet were like blocks of wood. He thought of the night he had spent walking round near Sheba's window. And how he had afterwards gone home—it was Friday morning—and had put on the tephilin, and prayed. He started praying now. "Mah Tovu." "How goodly are Thy Tents!" The beginning of the morning prayers. They were the only words of the prayer book that he knew by heart, and he kept repeating those words aloud over and over again.

Suddenly a strong hand held him gripped round the neck.

"So it's you, Jew! I know you! You used to go around with that Malgosia, and live in her hut. What are you doing here!

187

You were going to break into our stable and steal our horses. Weren't you? But I've caught you! Where's your partner? I heard you talking to somebody! Where is he?"

"There's nobody else," Yankel said. "I'm by myself. I was talking to myself."

"That's a lie! I don't believe a word you say! There were two of you and the other one has got away! I'll see that you don't get away! Come with me!"

And Yankel followed his captor into the house.

All the people in the house were still up. There were three generations on their knees before an ikon in the corner, with a light burning in front of it—grandfather and grandmother, son and daughter-in-law, and the grandson, a boy of ten. The room was warm. They were saying their prayers before going to bed.

They now rose from their knees, and five pairs of eyes examined Yankel curiously. The tall farmhand was boasting to his master: "I caught him red-handed! He tried to dodge me and escape, like his partner, but I was too smart for him! Once I got my hands on him he couldn't get away! I heard the two of them talking. But the other one got away before I came up!"

The family gaped at Yankel, especially the ten year-old grandson and his young mother. She couldn't believe that this poor man was a thief who had meant to steal their horses.

"I know him!" the farmhand was explaining. "It's that Jew who's staying with old Paul and that daughter of his, Malgosia. A circumcized thief! And I know where he comes from! He's that red-bearded thief Wolf's son—everybody round here knows Wolf! He's the man who steals all our horses! The other one who got away must have been his father! That Wolf's a clever rogue!"

The old farmer had been watching Yankel, who stood, a lumpish oaf, looking very sorry for himself, not saying a word.

Then the old man said: "It's not true, Stash! He didn't come to steal our horses. No man in that state would. He's had a rough time. Out in that cold. He must have been frozen out there. He needs shelter. He probably wanted to ask us to take pity on him."

"He looks like suffering Jesus on the cross!" said the young grandson, crossing himself.

"You're right, boy!" said his grandfather. "He's a Jew—one of God's people! God's son!"

"Jesus was a Jew!" said the boy. "Our teacher told us that at school."

"Jesus was baptized!" the grandfather corrected the boy. "John the Baptist baptized him! He was a true Christian! As for you—" he went on, speaking to his farmhand, "I know how you always boast and exaggerate everything. It's all lies. You didn't catch this Jew stealing horses. He didn't come here to open our stable door. He came to ask for shelter from the cold outside!"

The old man went to the stove, which was well-heated, sat down, and rolled a cigarette. They all knew it meant that he was going to tell them a story.

"Once upon a time," he began, "there was a little Jewish tailor who used to come to our village, looking for work, repair work, mending trousers, jackets, smocks, spencers, sheepskins. Or a dress. No matter how old and how worn, he made something of it. Something we could wear. He stayed in our huts. He didn't charge much for his work. Poor people he charged nothing. He often gave them something. He ate only dry bread, which he brought with him, and his own knife, and his own pot for water. If we gave him an onion or a raddish he ate it with his bread. He comforted the suffering. He healed the sick. He consoled the bereaved. He played with our children and they loved him. He was before my time. My grandfather knew him. He used to tell me about him. He said he was a saint, a true saint.

"That Jewess Maria," he went on, "Andrei Victor's wife—whether he married her in Church or not I don't know, but she's his wife—she's that little tailor's great-granddaughter!

189

She's often in this village, helping people, like her great-grandfather used to do, helping the women at their work, teaching the children before they reach school age. She stays with Andrei's parents—good, honest people, good Catholics!

"Yes, this Maria continues the work that her great-grandfather did. She goes to the poor and the sick and the unfortunate, and helps them.

"And this Jew here," and he turned to his wife, "give him food, and make up a bed for him! No, you do it, Zosia!" he said to his daughter-in-law. "We wouldn't put a dog out on a night like this!

"Come!" he said to his wife, taking her arm. "Time for us to go to bed! Zosia will see to everything! Good night!"

But Zosia was a shrew. And she hated her father-in-law because he was still alive, and was the master of the house and the farm. If he died it would all be her husband's. And hers.

So as soon as the old people had gone she burst out furiously, just because her father-in-law had told her to, that she wasn't going to give lodging to a Jew, not to this thieving Jew, who as soon as they left him alone in the room would steal what he could and clear out.

"Kick him out, Stash!" she ordered. "Kick him out, and bolt the door against him!"

So Yankel wandered again through the freezing night. It was pitch black, and he couldn't see anything—no house, no road, no sky, no stars. The snow was up to his knees. But his hunger—he hadn't eaten all day—had gone. So had the sleepiness that had dazed him while he was in the warm cottage. His mind was full of the story the old peasant had told them about the little tailor. He remembered other stories he had heard people tell about the little tailor. The little tailor had met a cow, and had asked her why she was sad. Because her owner had sold her to a butcher for butcher's meat, she said. Because she was no longer giving milk. Then the tailor had gone to the peasant who owned the cow, and told him that his

190

cow would calf, and would give him a lot of milk, more than ever before. And it came to pass as he had said.

Another story was about the little tailor saying his prayers in the forest, and all the trees in the forest had prayed aloud with him, and the stones and the grass—and the birds had twittered, all the same prayers, all around him. Again Yankel kept repeating to himself the words of the prayer "Mah Tovu"—the only words he remembered by heart from the prayer book.

It seemed to him that it was summer, and he was in the forest, and the birds were twittering. He wanted to lie down under a tree and go to sleep. He was suddenly very tired again. But the little tailor stood at his side, and said: "No! Keep walking!" So he walked on, through the snow, though it seemed to him that he was walking in the forest in summer. And the little tailor was holding his arm, and guiding him. And then he was suddenly outside Malgosia's hut.

No! No! He would not go in! Not into the house!

The stable door stood open. The stable was empty. Except for the block on which Malgosia chopped wood, and the ax, leaning against it. He went into the stable, and stretched out on the ground. It was warmer in the stable. His eyes closed, and he slept.

Strange dreams came to him, mixed-up dreams, bits and pieces, a whirl of memories and fantasies. Suddenly there came to him in his dreams the picture of an infant lying on the block, and Malgosia chopping it to bits. He woke screaming. His eyes fell on the block and the ax. He rose, and shambled with a dull head to the door, and out into the village. The sky was a grayish-blue. The stars had gone. On the edge of the horizon the sun was beginning to rise. Yankel started walking again through the village.

The village was long astir. The peasants rose before dawn—winter as well as other times, though there was no fieldwork to be done—to clean the stables, milk the cows, feed the pigs, let the chickens out of the runs, collect the eggs, chop wood.

There was suddenly a sound of shots. And people went

running, men, women, and children, running in the direction from which the shots came—the house where the mayor lived. Women wept and screamed. A dead man lay in the snow, which was stained red with his blood.

"Those Socialists did it! The murderous revolutionaries! They've killed the mayor! Poor man! Left six children!"

But there were also other voices: "He was always on the side of the authorities! Always said they were right! Forgot that he was a Pole! Did everything they wanted for the Muscovites who took away our land from us! Our Poland! He handed over to them our boys and girls who risk their lives to win back our Fatherland! Handed them over to be shot or put in prison or sent to Siberia! He deserved to die!"

"But these revolutionaries," said others, "are not fighting only the Muscovites! They're also fighting the Polish squires and gentry—our own people! And they fight against the Church! They rebel against Christ and Heaven and God!"

"It's the fault of the squires and the gentry," some of the younger peasants put in. "They don't treat us right! We haven't enough land to make a living, to keep a cow and a few pigs. When we go to work for them on their estates they pay us next to nothing for a hard day's work. They have no pity for us! If they catch one of our women picking up fallen branches for firewood they have them flogged or sent to prison! Why should we stand up for them!"

Yankel paid no attention. He trudged past the crowd and the dead mayor of the village as though he hadn't heard or seen anything. He was thinking of the old farmer in that village hut who had talked about the little tailor. If he could find his way back to that hut the old farmer surely would give him a chunk of bread. But he couldn't remember where the hut was. Besides—that young woman who had ordered him to be kicked out, she wouldn't let him come in!

He stopped outside a whitewashed cottage with a thatched roof, and asked for a piece of bread. The young peasant at the door eyed him suspiciously. Then his look changed to one of awe.

"Please come in!" he said. He asked him to sit down at the table, and offered him a big chunk of brown bread, with plenty of butter, and cheese.

"Is there anything else you'd like?" he asked Yankel. But Yankel's head had dropped on the table, and he was asleep.

The young peasant stared at his sleeping visitor, wondering—was he only a tramp, who went through the country begging his bread? Or was he?—He dared not think! He crossed himself and muttered the Lord's Prayer. Then he went into the kitchen, and told his wife what he had in his mind.

"I think it's—he looks like Jesus Christ!"

His wife crossed herself: "Dear Jesus!" she cried. She dropped everything, and ran into the room where Yankel was fast asleep. Again she crossed herself, and said this was surely a saint—it might even be Jesus himself.

They didn't know whether to leave their visitor where he was, asleep at the table, or to wake him, and ask him to get into bed. They decided on a middle course—they made up a couch by the stove, and he picked up Yankel and carried him, still asleep, to the couch.

"You are right!" the woman said to her husband. "It is Jesus Christ, come down to earth just before Christmas, to be born again on earth. And he has wandered into our house!"

At that moment the baby, sleeping near the stove, woke and cried. The mother picked it up and gave it her breast.

All day, they both walked about on tiptoe, not to disturb their visitor who was fast asleep.

They decided not to disturb him. The holy man was surely aware of everything that was happening. If he didn't waken by himself it was because he didn't want to waken—not yet. So they let him sleep. They ate their meal. They did their work in the house and the stable. Then they said their prayers, and went to bed.

Yankel slept through the night and all the next day, till the evening. It was Christmas eve when he woke. He couldn't make out where he was; he had no idea what had happened to him. But he felt fresh and rested. He rose from his couch. He no longer looked so pale and agonized, but to the young peasant and his wife he was still the "holy man," Christ himself.

They had both put on their best dress—bright national costume. They felt embarrassed because they didn't know what to say to their visitor, how to address him. They wanted to wait for him to speak first. But Yankel didn't speak. He looked round the clean bright room. He was fascinated by the decorated Christmas tree, with the candles and fruits and sweets hanging on all the branches. His face lighted up with pleasure.

Then the church bells began to ring. The young peasant and his wife were perplexed—should they go to church? Would the holy man go with them? But he didn't move. If he wouldn't go then they shouldn't go either; they must stay with him.

The bells rang louder, calling them insistently. And as their holy visitor made no move they decided that he wanted to stay behind. They felt that they should go to church. Perhaps as their baby was sleeping in the cradle it would be best to let the holy man stay with it, and watch over it. They went to church.

Yankel sat still for a long time like a block of wood, making no attempt to move. Then gradually his mind began to clear. He started getting his bearings. He realized that he was in a peasant hut. He saw the baby in the cradle, and he thought it looked lovely. He wanted to kiss it. But he was afraid that it might waken it. So he walked away from the cradle. He couldn't take his eyes off the Christmas tree. Then he turned to the holy pictures on the wall, and his gaze was held by the picture of the Virgin. It seemed to him like a picture of Sheba. But thinking of Sheba hurt him too much. He felt that he had no right to think of her—he, a thief, who had stabbed a man and was now on the run from the police, a murderer!

He turned away. And he saw the statuette of Jesus, arms outstretched, inviting him to his embrace. The story he had heard the old peasant tell about the little tailor came into his mind, and he felt a warmth at his heart—the little tailor who had gone about doing good, healing the sick in body and mind, and those who like him had a guilty conscience. He felt the little tailor was near him, wanting to heal him, to comfort him, to put his arms round him. Hardly realizing what he was doing he moved toward the statuette and began to pray—the only words he remembered by heart—"Mah Tovu." "How goodly. . . ."

When the young peasant and his wife returned from church they found Yankel stretched on the floor, with his arms flung out towards the statuette. They crossed themselves, and muttered the Lord's Prayer.

With daybreak came an uproar. Screaming and shouting and banging. As though the village was on fire. Police and cossacks had arrived to find and arrest those who had shot the mayor, and all other insurrectionaries they could get their hands on. The police came with a list of names and addresses supplied by their spies. They went straight to each house on the list, opened cupboards and drawers, searched for illegal literature, tore up floorboards, slit open pillows and bedcovers, swore and cursed and knocked people about. The victims shouted and screamed, protesting against this disturbance on Christmas day. Most of the villagers had been still asleep, having come home late from the Christmas Eve service in church. Even then few had gone to bed. They had sat down to make a night of it, with a big Christmas dinner and plenty to drink.

The cossacks laid about them with their knouts. Crowds collected from all the neighboring houses, and shouted and protested. It began to look like a rising in the village. The younger peasants and many middle-aged flung themselves on the police and the cossacks. With the result that they too were arrested and driven to the town at the point of the sword.

But in some of the huts—including that where Yankel stayed—the people didn't hear all that noise and tumult, and slept through it till midday.

When his hosts heard what had happened they shrugged their shoulders. They were not interested in the political agitation in which some of the villagers engaged. They were the kind of people who kept to themselves. They gave all their attention to their work on the farm and in the house. They were content with their lot. They were young and they were still in love, completely absorbed in each other and in their baby. And now, the holy man staying in their home and transported them with joy. Even afterwards, in days and weeks to come, when the other villagers laughed and jeered at them for having believed in their "holy man" and told them that he was not holy at all, but was a Jew from the neighboring town, a thief and a rogue, and Malgosia's lover, their faith in him did not falter.

They remained convinced that he was a holy being and that he had come from heaven to earth in order to help people. They were sure of it, because they saw him always talking to the statuette of Christ, conducting a celestial conversation. They heard his muffled words, incomprehensible to them— "Mah Tovu."

Then one day, in the early spring, Yankel disappeared from their house, taking the statuette of Jesus with him.

Yankel's steps were leading him back to his home town. On the way he sat down several times on a stone or on the stump of a tree to rest, and he always brought out the Christ figure from under his coat, and fixed his eyes on it. To him, it was the little tailor.

He arrived in his home town late at night. Everybody was asleep. Not a living person in sight. All was cold and dark. The snow had been cleared away in the richer streets, but snow heaps still lay about in the poorer parts. A dog ran past howling. The wind rattled the shutters of the houses. The tall chimney stacks of the factories loomed up like giants. The weathercock on the roof of the town hall was revolving fast in the wind.

Presently Yankel saw people emerging from different side turnings, and hurry along, quietly, stealthily, keeping to the shadows of the houses. Men and women. The women had their heavy shawls over their faces. The men had their coat collars up to hide their feautres.

He came to the house where the rebbe lived. That was Sheba's window. He turned away quickly into the street leading to the Beth Hamedrash. He didn't want to go home in the middle of the night after having been away so long. And there was no other place he could go to. Except the Beth Hamedrash, which, he remembered, was open always, warm and lighted, always with a few old Jews sitting there, studying. He was suddenly filled with nostalgia for their voices chanting aloud from Talmud. The melody of the chanting had often drawn him to the Beth Hamedrash. He loved listening to it, though he didn't understand the words.

But when Yankel entered the Beth Hamedrash it was empty and almost in darkness. Only the flame of the Perpetual Light over the Holy Ark flickered—as though it too were on the point of going out. Its shadow rose and fell on the wall and the ceiling.

Yankel couldn't understand why there was nobody in the Beth Hamedrash now. As he remembered it there had always been a few people in the Beth Hamedrash, studying till daybreak. Shlomo had always been there.

It made him suddenly afraid. He felt like running out of the Beth Hamedrash. But his legs wouldn't carry him. Then he heard a noise, a movement—someone was crawling about under a table with a lighted candle. A young man with earlocks and a little beard. Yankel didn't recognize him. Nobody he knew.

"Who are you?" he called out.

"I'm the dybbuk that the rebbe here drove out. I'm a stranger in this town. I don't know anybody. So I came to the Beth Hamedrash."

Why are you crawling about under the table with a candle? You'll set the place on fire!"

"That's just what I want to do! I want to burn down the Beth Hamedrash! There's no longer any need for it!"

Yankel took away the lighted candle from the madman, and tried to put him outside. But he begged Yankel to let him stay; it was so cold outside.

"I'm a dybbuk!" he kept saying. "I've seen things! Things you people have never seen! I know things that you don't know! I know that this Beth Hamedrash is no longer needed. God doesn't want it! There is no God! Yes, there is a God, but not the God you think there is! He's quite different from what you imagine! He's a God of wrath! He is angry because people won't leave Him alone, because they keep praying to Him, worrying Him with their petitions about their silly little affairs. One comes along praying for something the complete opposite of what the other wants. What do you expect God to do then? Millions and millions of people, all praying for different conflicting things! Isn't it enough to make God angry? God is going to turn this world upside down! He's going to destroy it! He's going to kill the lot of you! He'll wipe you all off the fact of the earth! He goes on killing you, one by one! There's a man dying now on that bench over there! A man who spent his time thinking about God, speculating about God, trying to find out whether He is He isn't. And what sort of a God He is. Then he fell in love with the rebbe's daughter, that rebbe who drove me out, or said he drove me out. Because really he didn't! I'm still in me! When he saw that the rebbe's daughter doesn't want him he lost his will to live. Now he's over there on that bench, dying. On that bench over there. Maybe he's dead already. Come with me! I'll show him to you!"

He took Yankel by the hand and led him to a bench. There

was somebody lying there, moaning. Yankel held the candle near to him. It was Shlomo Chaye's Bujas. He called him softly: "Shlomo!"

But Shlomo didn't answer.

The shamash arrived at daybreak. As soon as he opened the door the madman ran up to him: "He's dead!"

"God the righteous Judge!" the shamash murmured. "He suffered enough! You take him by the legs!"

They both carried the dead Shlomo to the side room.

As the day advanced Jews began coming in to the Beth Hamedrash, with tallith and tephilin, for the morning service. But most of them seemed more interested in discussing affairs than in praying. Except for a few individuals who were really intent on their devotions.

Things were happening in the town—and in the outside world. There was a lot to talk about. The air was buzzing with news—great news, world-shaking news. Russia was on the boil. Poland was seething. People were bursting with eagerness to talk about all the rumors that were going about.

Then why come to synagogue to discuss these things? First, because for many years their footsteps had been directed toward the synagogue, morning and evening—it was familiar ground to them, their spiritual home. They were used to the synagogue routine. They put on their tallith and tephilin when they entered as a horse slips in the accustomed way into its harness. And second, because it was a big and convenient meeting place, where they could find their friends, and sit around and talk.

More people arrived. Some of the worshippers had finished their prayers and had gone. Gradually the hum of prayers rose louder, and only a few people here and there continued exchanging confidences about the events in the world. The third chazan was now starting the third service. Most of the time he rattled away, at top speed, almost gabbling his words except at certain places, at the Hallelujahs, or Boruch She-Omar, or Shema Yisroel, and at the Kedusha, where all responded loudly. Sometimes a devout worshipper hissed at a couple of talkers—"Quiet! Have respect for a House of Worship!"

Mordecai, "the chinless one," as they all called him, was standing leaning with his back against the Almemor; he was a skinny man, moving quickly like a squirrel, with ears pricked, and a scanty beard, where you could almost count each hair, showing his lack of a chin. He talked so fast that you could hardly make out what he was saying. He looked like a young man just married, but he had eight children, the oldest himself a young man already of marriageable age. Mordecai traded in anything and everything—he was a contact man, a go-between, a marriage broker. Near him stood Moishe, "the wise man," who was a fool—with a dull oxlike face, a black beard, and big bovine eyes. His trade was eggs. But he couldn't count, and when he was paid he usually gave the wrong change, nearly always to his own loss. There were also Ezekiel the Hebrew teacher, Hersh the pastry-cook, Meir the glazier—about a dozen Jews standing round in a circle, talking. What were they talking about? About the Socialists, the strikers, the politicals, the people who were plotting against the czar and his government.

"They're the scum of the earth! All the riff-raff of the town!" they chorused indignantly. "Filth! Sons and daughters of cobblers and tailors and weavers and locksmiths—the low-lifes, the dregs!"

Then they got suddenly frightened of their own daring— some of those Socialists might be listening. And they didn't stop at anything! All big fellows, who could use their fists. Look at the way they knocked out Wolf Jonachek—after the whole town and the police had gone about in fear of him!

The memory of what those Socialists had done to Wolf Jonachek roused their anger and made it flare up again.

"Blackguards! That's what they are! Got no fear of anybody! Scoundrels! Rogues! People who don't keep Judaism! Don't

200

keep the Sabbath! Eat forbidden food! Renegades, apostates! That's what they are! Even Joseph . . ."

"No!" There was a shocked hush. "Not Joseph!" Joseph was not the son of some cobbler or tailor or locksmith. He was the son of Reb Abraham and of Rachel! The little tailor's great-grandson! They wouldn't let anyone speak bad of the little tailor's descendants! His seed!

But there was one among them who threw caution to the winds.

"Yes, even Joseph!" he repeated. "He's no better than the rest of them. Who is this Joseph, after all! Once upon a time he used to study here in the Beth Hamedrash. But he stopped it long ago. Now he's a disbeliever, like all the others. His father and his mother were fine people. He comes of good stock. Descended from the little tailor himself. But he's no better than he should be! And his sister! She's even worse! Terrible! Lives with a Goy! They say that she's turned Christian. She killed her mother!"

"True! True!" the others chimed in. The troublemaker, encouraged by this approval, raised his voice more loudly than before against Joseph. "He's no better than the rest of them! Just as bad! The little tailor's descendants have brought shame to his name!"

The glazier held up his hand. "I won't hear another word! Not another word against the little tailor's descendants! This is something much more than a few young people who have strayed from the right road. If the whole of our younger generation—the whole town—has abandoned our way of life, the fault must be ours! We are all of us to blame! Our sins must be the cause of it, that this punishment has come upon us!"

Selig the postman sat near by, surrounded by some of his cronies. He had once been accused of opening letters that came for people from their children abroad, and where there was money enclosed, changing the figures to make the sum smaller, and keeping the rest. There had been some ugly

201

rumors about it, and there had been an investigation as a result of which he was cleared of the charges, and given back the license for the Jewish post, which still existed, as in the old days, when the town had been a very small place, and it was twelve miles to go to the post office in the big town.

Selig had all the latest news, and he was telling the people round him, some of the most respected Jews in the town, some of the things he had heard. He was telling them that the Socialists had thrown a bomb in Warsaw at the governor-general and had blown him to bits.

Several Jews from other groups came over to listen. But Selig the postman didn't go on. He had finished his story. That was all the news he had now.

A little further off there was another group talking politics. Near them sat a skinny young man poring into a learned rabbinical work. He was an orphan, a pauper, who practically lived in the Beth Hamedrash, one of the few who still came there to study. But many people had doubts about his piety. They said he had been reading philosophical works, and had come to question the existence of God. All they had to go on was the fact that he was engrossed in the Bible, especially in the Prophets, and gave them more time and attention than he gave the Talmud.

"What do you say about those Socialists, Zadock?" somebody in the group asked him, thinking he would get some fun out of teasing the boy.

"They preach what our holy Prophets preached," Zadock answered very earnestly. "Isaiah, Jeremiah, even further back, Moses himself!"

"Listen to him! Comparing those disbelieving Socialists to our holy Prophets! To Moses! Profanation! Blasphemy! He's a disbelieving Socialist himself! What's he doing in this Beth Hamedrash!"

Joseph came in just then. He had lately started frequenting the Beth Hamedrash again from time to time—he had fallen into fresh doubts about his doubts—and it was his old way of searching his soul, looking for answers to his questions. There

202

may have been some nostalgia too, nostalgia for those days of spiritual contentment when he had still been a good believing Jew, with perfect faith in God, and no doubts to plague and torment him.

Joseph looked pale and drawn, weary, on edge.

He saw that they were teasing the boy Zadok.

"Leave the lad alone!" he cried.

They stared at him. Behaving as though he was running the Beth Hamedrash!

And somehow Joseph thought he was. "This is my great-grandfather's Beth Hamedrash!" he protested. "I won't let you hurt the boy! My great-grandfather wouldn't have allowed it! You mustn't!"

And suddenly Joseph realized that he was talking to an empty Beth Hamedrash. Everybody round him had melted away. They were all crowding round the doorway. There was a stream of people, men and women, coming into the Beth Hamedrash. Dressed in their holiday best. A baby was crying. An elderly woman carried it on a pillow. Beside her walked a young woman, with a group of other women all round the two, like a bodyguard. They were going to have a circumcision in the Beth Hamedrash. Some of the men round the doorway were already smacking their lips—"There'll be brandy and cakes!"

The young mother took the infant from the older woman, who had carried it here all the way from her home.

"Stop crying!" the old woman said sternly to the child. "They did the same thing to your father and to your grandfather, and to his father and grandfather all the way back to the Patriarchs! They do it to all Jews! Of course, it'll hurt! So what! You can't be a Jew without being hurt!"

The young mother looked with pity at her baby son, and tried to hush him in her arms. But the baby only cried louder. Another woman, mother of many children, scolded the child.

"Listen to him! What are you making all that noise for? You're no better than your father was at your age. He had to through it, like every other Jewish man! All Jews must!"

203

A number of men were crowding round the mohel, and saying the prayers used at a circumcision. Beggars, always on the lookout for weddings and circumcisions were rubbing their hands. It meant alms. And it meant brandy and cakes.

The shamash called out: "Kvatter! Godfather!"

A young newlywed woman, the godmother, took the infant from the mother. It was still crying aloud.

"Kvatter!" the shamash repeated.

A young man came forward, took the infant from his wife, the godmother, and he passed it to the mohel.

The mohel placed the infant resting on his pillow on the knees of the sandek, an aged man with a white beard, wrapped in his tallith, seated in a big armchair that might have been a throne or at least a judge's seat. Elijah's chair. There was a footstool under his feet.

The mohel recited with great fervor the prayer: "This is the throne of Elijah. . . ." Then he carefully tested the edge of his knife, bent over the child, and performed the circumcision.

Everybody cried "Mazel Tov!" The baby was handed back to his mother, and the brandy and cakes were passed around.

11

It was still dark when Yankel walked out of the Beth Hamedrash. His mind was in a complete whirl. When he had left the village with the Christ statuette under his coat, but the little tailor in his heart, he had thought that now everything would go right, and he would be a changed man, a better man, the kind of man he would like to be. That hope had been a steady flame lighting his way. But when he came out of the Beth Hamedrash, that hope was dead—like Shlomo whom he had just seen die.

Yankel suddenly grew afraid of what his father and mother would say when he came back home. But he did not turn back. He went straight on. It was daybreak when he got to the house. His heart beat like a hammer when he recognized the familiar tumble-down building and the stable, with the cart standing outside. No one stirred. He pushed open the stable door. Empty! Not a horse there! Not one! The windows of the house were still shuttered. His hand shook when he lifted it to knock on the door. His mother opened it, in her nightdress, with a white cap on her head. She shrieked when she saw Yankel, as if he had come back from the dead—a ghost. She was falling, when he caught her in his arms, lifted her and laid her down on the bed.

"Mother!" he kept repeating. Till at last she realized that it was not a ghost, but flesh and blood—her son.

"Yankel!" she sobbed. "Yankel, my child!"

She told him of the terrible thing that had happened to his father, to Wolf Jonachek:

"I warned him not to go that night. He wouldn't listen to me. He said he must go. There were some fine horses on that estate, he said. When he got there, everybody on the estate was waiting for him with iron bars and axes. They killed him! They hacked him to bits! He was not buried as people are buried. They dug a hole for him by the cemetery wall. He hadn't even his son to say Kaddish for him!"

Yankel's mother had completely changed, since her husband had died. She had become very religious. She had shaved off her hair and wore a cap right down over her ears. She kept her eyes modestly fixed all the time on the ground.

She was happy to see that Yankel too had changed—that he now wore a beard, and put on his tephilin and said his prayers every day, and behaved generally like a good Jew, like a rabbi.

Yet Yankel grew more sad and dejected every day. Though he tried to keep it from his mother, she saw it, and she worried about it. But not enough to affect her great pride in her son, whom she now began to regard as a saint. She looked up to him. She thanked God for having such a son. She deplored it that she couldn't read, because the mother of such a son should be able to read all the prayers in Hebrew. She took down her fat prayer book, and kept repeating "Reboneh Shel Olam . . ." "Lord God, Creator of the Universe." And other words that rose to her lips. She often wept, sobbed her heart out, till she felt eased—and she concluded that it meant tha God had heard her prayer.

She kept the house spotlessly clean. How could Yank have people come to him if his home were not clean and tid

She scrubbed and scoured the floor, she washed the linen, sewed, and ironed. It was all a way of serving him. She had the walls and the ceiling whitewashed, after years of neglect. She bought paper flowers to give color to the home. Things were not easy for her. Wolf's death had left her very poor. The thieves who had worked under Wolf and who now worked under one of Wolf's lieutenants wanted to help her, offered to pay her a percentage on all their takings. She refused to have anything to do with them. She wouldn't allow them into the house. She took in washing. She went, at her age, scrubbing floors in other people's houses. And she kept her own home scrupulously clean and tidy. Always with a clean cloth on the table for a meal, and a salt cellar with salt in it.

Zlatte came to see Yankel, happy that he had returned. But he stared at her as though she were a stranger.

"What's the matter with you!" she screamed. "Don't you know me? I'm Zlatte!" She embraced him and kissed him: "Yankel! Yankel! I'm so glad you're back!" There were tears in her eyes.

Zlatte's devotion to him and her untiring attention gradually won Yankel, and he began to look forward to her coming. Now she spoke to him not only of how much she loved him, but of doing something practical to provide for his future. The first thing to do was to learn a trade, she said, become an artisan, and earn an honest living by his work. She suggested that he should become a shoemaker.

"Let's go to Reb Jacob, the shoemaker. He's a good man! He'll teach you shoemaking. He's not the kind of man who would exploit you. As soon as you can do any useful work he'll pay you what you're worth. In a year you'll be a good shoemaker, earning a good living."

She took his arm and stroked it. She snuggled against him. "And I've got some money toward a home and a workshop. everal hundred roubles . . ."

"You mean you've got a dowry?" said Yankel smiling.

"No, Yankel! It isn't my money! Most of it is money that you gave me. Every time when we met and you had a lot of money in your pocket, you gave me some. And I always banked it. I put it into the bank in both our names. It's as much your account as mine. And most of it is your money."

They went both of them to see Reb Jacob. And it was as Zlatte said. Yankel learned shoemaking.

Yankel was delighted at the change. "You see, mother," he said to her, "I'm no longer a thief. I'm a workman, a craftsman, an artisan earning an honest living. Like the little tailor. He used to go about in the villages mending the peasants' clothing. And to this day the peasants in all the villages around here remember him and speak well of him."

"Yes," said his mother, "he was a saintly man."

One morning Yankel woke full of a vivid dream. The little tailor had come to him in the night, and had said: "Coarse linen is stronger than silk, and better for the body—it absorbs the perspiration. Gold comes from the ground. Stone is nothing."

Yankel puzzled over the possible meaning of his dream. He couldn't understand what it meant. And then he suddenly remembered the statuette that he had brought from the village and had hidden in the loft. He went up now to the loft, and brought down the statuette under his coat, and went to work.

Reb Jacob soon saw that Yankel's mind wasn't on his work. He looked fuddled.

"What's wrong, Yankel?" Reb Jacob asked him. "What's happened?"

Then Yankel told Reb Jacob his dream.

"Can't you understand it?" Reb Jacob smiled benevolently. "It's so simple. You want me to explain and interpret the dream to you? Right! 'Coarse linen is stronger than silk, and better for the body—it absorbs the perspiration.' You asked my advice about Zlatte. That's the meaning of your dream. Zlatte is the coarse linen, much better for you than the deli cate, silklike girl you've been dreaming about. 'Gold com from the ground.' The same meaning. It's the common ear you dig up gold from. 'Stone is nothing.' That I can't under-stand. I'm only a working man! I can't understand everything. I can't think what it means. Come on, off with your coat, and get on with your work! Perhaps the idea will come to me."

Yankel hesitated—then he took the statuette from under his coat and put it down on the workbench.

Reb Jacob stared at it: "What may that mean, Yankel? What are you carrying the Christian god around with you for? You're not . . ."

So Yankel told Reb Jacob the whole story how the statuette had come to him.

"Now I see it," said Reb Jacob. "It's quite simple! A Jew believes in God, not in a stone. That's what the little tailor came to tell you. Take the statuette back to the people it belongs to. Or if you won't go to that village again, give it to the first Christian you come across, anyone."

The spring sun was already high in the heavens, but the shops in the town were still shut, though it was an ordinary weekday. The factories and the workshops were closed. The workers had stopped work. It was their holiday—the Festival of Labor! You could see them, dressed in their best, hurrying to their assembly points. Pious Jewish fathers and mothers begged their children not to go out into the streets, not to get caught in the May Day demonstrations. But the children took no notice. Many people barred and bolted their doors.

Soon the bands were heard, leading the processions con-verging from different directions toward the meeting place—the Polish Socialist anthem "Czewony Standard" (The Red Flag) and from another side the Yiddish Bundist "Shevuah" (The Oath) about the same Red Flag, which "with blood is red."

Young people and older people came running out from all he side turnings toward the music, toward the processions.

The sun poured down its golden rays from a clear, blue

spring sky. The birds twittered. Nature was itself in a holiday mood, like the workers.

Both processions stopped in the market place, each in a different corner, and the speeches started, the Jewish speakers in Yiddish, the Christian in Polish. Zlatte had brought Yankel—who had now shaved off his beard.

The Yiddish speakers were Boris, Nathan, Velvel, Joseph, and Hannah. Boris drew most applause: "Down with the Reaction! Down with Black Clericalism! Down with the Czar! Long Live the First of May! Long Live the Working Class International!"

When Joseph spoke Sheba stood at the back where he could not see her, her eyes fixed on his face. She devoured his every word.

But there were many in the crowd who found Joseph tedious, and wondered why he had been included among the speakers. Why was he always talking about the Hebrew Prophets? Did he think he was in a synagogue?

Only a few, like Sheba and Reb Jacob the shoemaker, and some of the former Beth Hamedrash students, thought that Joseph was wonderful.

Joseph's sister Miriam was also one of the speakers, at the other meeting, the Christian meeting, the meeting of the Polish Socialist Party. Here Andrei stood like Sheba at the Jewish meeting, listening enraptured as Miriam spoke, only he wasn't at the back like Sheba, but right in front, holding a red banner with the words P.P.S. on it in gold.

The town was like a battlefield—it was Civil War! The offensive was taken by the workers, by the conscious proletariat. And the defense consisted of the police and the manufacturers, and the clergy—the Christian priests and the rabbi and the Jewish clericals. Only the defenders were not in sight. They were in their trenches, in their dugouts. The factories were closed; the workers were on strike. Business was at a standstill. No goods were taken out or brought into the town. Prices went mad—they jumped up and down. The train services were irregular. The shopkeepers sat in thei shops and wondered what was going to happen next. Many kept their doors slightly ajar, looking as though they were closed, to deceive the strikers.

There was talk of a revolution. People said that the czar's government had resigned. That the czar had given way to the revolutionaries and had granted a constitution.

"Constitution!" This was the new magic word. At every step, in the street, in the market place, in the Beth Hamedrash every second and third word was "Constitution!" "The czar is no longer the ruler! Now he must govern as he is told to by the new democratic ministers appointed by Parliament, by the Duma! The new ministers have a program to help the people, to help the poor! They will introduce new laws that will abolish poverty!"

"Nonsense! How can you abolish poverty?"

"Like in America! They've got a president in America, and he has abolished poverty!"

"But we've got a czar."

"Then we'll get rid of the czar, and we'll also have a president!"

"And what about us Jews?"

"We Jews will be equal with everybody else. Just the same as in America! Everybody equal. A Jew can even become president in America. My daughter is in America with her husband, and that's what they've written to me. They've got a wonderful life there!"

"My son-in-law—you all knew him here—is still a tailor, just as he was when he lived here. Only here he starved. And there he lives like a lord!"

◆——◆——◆——◆——◆——◆

The revolutionary spirit, defiance, revolt, against the established traditions and forms invaded the souls of some of the most conservative, most pious Jews in the town. Reb Chaim Yossel's head was completely turned. People passing his shop were startled when they saw the door flung wide open, and

211

his wife Freida standing there, beside herself—her *sheitel* pushed down over her ears showing her gray hair beneath, her glasses broken—screaming:

"Help! Help! He's gone mad! He was the most devout Jew in the town and now he is blaspheming God! He used to fast every Monday and Thursday. He sat studying the Talmud day and night. Now he has put his tallith and tephilin on the fire! Help!"

Reb Chaim Yossel came rushing to the door like a madman, barefoot, bare-headed, his shirt open under his caftan showing his bare chest, his hair and beard all wild.

"Yes! It's true! I've burned my tallith and tephilin!" he cried. "Wool and leather, into the fire! Burn them! Destroy them!"

"He's gone mad!" his wife screamed. "Don't go near him! Avoid him like the plague! He deserves to be killed for the things he's saying!"

The crowd was getting ugly, and looked as though they meant to set about him. But Chaim Yossel picked up an ax that was always kept near the door, and everybody made off.

"You see that he's mad!" his wife repeated. "Ready to kill anybody! Shun him like the plague! Keep away from him!"

The workers in Reb Zalman Finkelstein's factory were on strike with the rest of the workers.

So Reb Zalman sat at home, and wondered what was going on. He couldn't make it out. He was a Hasid of the old school who had never had any trust in the local rebbe, and used to go on long pilgrimages to his own rebbe. He ran his house on patriarchal lines. His married sons all lived with him, in the same house, with their wives and their children. He loved jollity and song. So on the Sabbath, toward the end of the Sabbath, his house was packed with Hasidim of his own kind, and they kept Mlave Malka, with plenty of food and drink and the singing of jolly table hymns.

But now the house was silent and sad. Reb Zalman was pacing up and down in his own room, puzzled and angry. How could his workers do such a thing! He knew every one of them, and he knew their families, and the way they lived. He had been like a father to them, showed paternal interest in their welfare, helped them when they needed it. And now they had gone out on strike like all the others!

It was the same everywhere. The whole town was at a standstill. The railways and the postal services were also on strike. Nothing moved. The world was absolutely topsy-turvy, upside down! It could only mean the coming of the satanic kingdom, which must precede the Messianic era.

The house was silent. Reb Zalman's wife, their sons and daughters-in-law and their grandchildren were all going about scared, afraid to say a word.

The whole town was under a terror. The strikers had threatened that they would shoot anyone caught strike-breaking. And everybody knew they meant it.

After the May Day demonstration Sheba and Joseph went about together everywhere. She came to his house, and tried to win him with her kisses from the black mood that had settled on him since the May Day demonstration—because most of his comrades, including Boris, the leader, had objected strongly to his speech at the demonstration. Talking as he had done about the Hebrew Prophets was not what they wanted. It was not Socialism, they said, not revolution.

"I'm the odd man out," Joseph complained to Sheba. "They don't want me! They won't listen to me! Their approach is different. If it wasn't for Boris, they would kick me out of the Executive and expel me from the Party."

Sheba felt sorry for him, and would have liked to comfort him, but she couldn't deny what he was saying. She knew that he was right in what he said. His comrades didn't like his attitude, his talk about ethics and justice and about the Hebrew Prophets and righteousness. They wanted class war, fighting, and the overthrow of the capitalist class. "Down with the bourgeoisie! Down with the exploiters!"

"Can't they see", Joseph said to Sheba, "that there can be no proper society without an ethical base to it, without justice and right, without peace among people and nations? Their idea is war—to overthrow the capitalists, the bourgeoisie, to replace their rule with the rule of the proletariat. And the world will be divided again—only those who were on top before will be below, and those who were below will be on top. There will still be oppression—only different people will be oppressed. There will still be privileged classes and un-privileged. Only those who are now privileged will become the unprivileged. The new state will crush them in just the same way as the old state crushes the workers now. There will be power. And power is bad. Those who wield power grow to love power for its own sake. No, Sheba, our fight must be not to transfer power from one group to another, but to abolish power!"

"You're right, Joseph. I agree with you absolutely. But those others don't! They want power, in their own hands!"

"What am I to do?" Joseph asked her, feeling baffled. "Whom am I to go to if not to the oppressed and the suffering? When I see their faces pinched with want, when I see the humiliation in their eyes, I feel that my place is with them. And when they march, with the red flag of brotherhood, sing-ing 'Down with tyranny!' singing songs of freedom, I want to join them, to march with them, to be at their side!

"Then I start talking to them about the Prophets! And they don't like it. I want to show them that the justice they seek is a part of our religion, is in our sacred books. But Marxism has told them that religion is wrong! So everything I say is wrong! Can't they see that religion, faith, belief in a higher Power is the very spirit of man, and that if Socialism is established without it there will be no soul, no spirit in it—only the bare materialistic. We will go back to the animal stage!"

"The trouble is," said Sheba, "that they have seen so many

religious people observing only the outward forms of religion, not its spirit. They worry about the exact minute when the Sabbath begins and ends, about every minutiae of kosher and treif, but very little about the spirit behind these observances. Even their praying is an unthinking and unfeeling repetition of set formulas, with no real devout fervor. They just gabble words!"

"You're quite right," Joseph agreed. "I've been going sometimes to the Beth Hamedrash lately, and I've seen it—just as you say. So many of them pray without any heart or soul, just repeat the words, and chatter in between about their affairs, during the prayers. My place isn't there either. So where do I belong?"

"I'll tell you where you belong, Joseph," Sheba answered him. "You belong in your studio. In that room where you paint your pictures. I see what you want to say in the blue of your skies, in the green of your fields, in the stream that wanders through your fields, in your rising sun. I see it in your paintings of flowers and fruit, in your hills, and in your people who seem to be alive on your canvas, more alive than in reality."

"No, my pictures don't say what I want to say, Sheba. I'm not big enough for that. It's impertinence for me to think that I can really paint—I've never studied art, I've never gone to art school, I've never worked in an artist's studio. I'm just an amateur."

One day when Sheba came to Joseph's house she found him getting ready to go out.

"You're going to a meeting?"

"Yes."

"Will you be long?"

"I don't know how long they'll keep me."

Outside he began to wonder whether he should really go to the meeting, or return to the house and stay with Sheba. What good would it do for him to go to the meeting? Nobody there would listen to him. And perhaps they were right. If an organized movement with a clear program kept changing its

215

direction every time somebody with an individual point of view came along, it would never get anywhere. It was silly to expect the Party to listen to his lone voice. He felt that this was the last Party meeting he would be asked to go to.

Then he started debating with himself, as he often did—whether it was right that he should insist as he did on his own personal point of view. Wasn't there a destiny that ruled the world, and decided how the world should go? How then could his one voice saying "No!" influence the course of events? The path didn't deviate because he didn't want to walk along that path. The path still went its appointed way.

"No, that's wrong! There is no Destiny that rules out a man's free will! The Torah says a man has free will! He is not a slave, but a free agent!"

Joseph was so excited by this thought that he didn't realize that he was talking aloud to himself in the street. He hurried on. He was sure now that this was the last time he would be going to a meeting. Whether they expelled him or not, he had made up his mind—he would resign from the Executive and would leave the Party. But they would probably save him the trouble. They would turn the meeting into a disciplinary court and vote for his expulsion.

"I won't go," he said to himself. "It'll be easier if I send them a letter, telling them that I'm leaving the Party, and why.

Then he thought it over. No, he decided against it. That would be the way of a coward. He wasn't ashamed of his opinions. "I'll state them openly, and let them expel me!"

The Party now had its own home. It no longer had to meet in secret in old Reb Jacob's cobbler's workship. It met openly.

Joseph's instinct had been right. His expulsion was one of the first items on the agenda of the meeting. Every member of the Executive was present, Boris the chairman, Nathan the secretary, Velvel, and Hannah.

Boris's feelings toward Joseph were friendly—respect and

216

affection. Nathan was entirely hostile. Velvel was a rigidly disciplined Party man, who couldn't understand why they had ever admitted anyone as erratic as Joseph to the Party. Even the fact that everybody was present except Joseph—that he always came late—showed the kind of man he was. No discipline! Irresponsible!

Velvel looked at his watch, and said grimly:

"You see how this fine gentleman treats us. Keeps us waiting! No respect for the Party! What else did you expect when you admitted him? His father was a rich merchant. He was brought up in a bourgeois home. He probably inherited a lot of money. And he spends his time painting pictures. He's religious too. Used to study in the Beth Hamedrash. Still goes there. And when he speaks at our Labor demonstrations he talks about the Prophets of the Bible! Like a synagogue preacher! We give him our platform for his propaganda against our own beliefs. I move we expel him!"

Joseph's entrance completely put out Comrade Velvel. He looked down his nose, and broke off. All the other members of the Executive were at a loss what to say or do. Most of them held Joseph in high respect. Most of them were personally fond of him. Yet they felt that Nathan and Velvel were right when they accused him of preaching doctrines in conflict with their Marxist teachings.

The chairman motioned Joseph to his usual place at the table.

"You're very late, Comrade", he said. "We've been waiting for you. Now you're here, let's get on with our business."

Joseph remained standing. "I'm sorry I'm late," he began. "I meant no disrespect. But I haven't come to take part in a meeting in the ordinary way. I have come to present myself to you for trial and judgment."

There was a short silence. Then Boris said: "Very well!" And turning to the secretary he added: "We'll take the question first. The other items on the agenda will wait."

Boris continued: "Comrade Hannah and Comrade Velvel will join me to constitute the Court."

Addressing Joseph in a stern judicial tone Boris began:

"We should have done this a long time ago. We have felt long ago that you were not of our way of thinking on many things, and that we ought to exclude you from our Executive and from our Party. You are a utopian idealist. Our Party is Marxist. We are historic materialists. We are engaged in a class struggle in the economic and political field. Our aim is the establishment of a Socialist society on the lines laid down by Marx and Engels. But we have been tolerant with you, because we respect you as a man, as an idealist, as a thinking person, intelligent and sincere. But you do not fit in with our Party program. We had hoped, and I most of all, that you would come to realize your error. But now it is not only a matter of theory and beliefs. You have been doing things and saying things behind our backs that are contrary to all that we do and say. Tell me, did you go into a discussion about our strike with one of the employers where we are striking?"

Joseph was taken aback:

"I ran into Beirach the tailor, and I exchanged a few words with him; I said the strikers' demands were just."

"Another question: Did you warn the provocateur Meirowitch that he was to be shot?"

"Yes."

Everybody stared at Joseph. Boris, the chairman, caught his breath. Then trying to speak calmly, he said:

"And did you think that by doing that you were endangering the lives and certainly the freedom of our activist comrades?"

"I was convinced that Meirowitch, who had been a member of this Executive, did not deserve to be shot. He was not a traitor to our cause. All that happened is that we can say he was not a hero. It depends on how much heroism you can expect from any man. Not everybody can be as brave as the next man. They tortured Meirowitch, treated him terribly in prison. And they got out of him the names of a few members of the Party. Belonging to the Party is a crime in this country, but it isn't one of the most serious crimes. There is no severe punishment for it. Membership in an illegal organization

218

means a short term of imprisonment. Who of us in Meirowitch's place would have been more of a hero? When they released him from prison he came to us and told us what had happened. He made a voluntary confession. He wept because of it. He was a broken man. It was not something he had done deliberately, had planned to do—to betray his comrades. We must consider the circumstances in which he was placed. How he suffered. I would have agreed to his expulsion from the Party. But not to have him shot. So I warned him. I urged him to leave the town, to go into hiding somewhere. Not only because I wanted to prevent shedding innocent blood, but also because I wanted to keep our Socialist ideal.

The three judges retired. When they returned, Boris, as the presiding judge, addressed the meeting.

"The accused thinks," he said, "that Socialism is sacred only to him. He is wrong. It means more to us than it does to him. It is to us dearer than life itself. We are ready to sacrifice our liberty and our lives for it. Where the accused has gone wrong is in believing that Socialist ideals can be achieved without bloodshed. We don't want bloodshed. It's the other side—our rulers imprison us and torture us, and shoot and hang us. The prisons are full of our people. The road to Siberia is one long line of chained prisoners being sent to exile. Many rot and die there. Any one of us may be arrested any moment and sent that same way."

He paused. Then looking straight at Joseph he addressed him direct:

"You deserve the same sentence that we passed on Meirowitch. But we took into account the fact that you are sincere and naive, and also our own fault in having let you stay in the Party till now. We should have expelled you long ago. The sentence of the Court is therefore this: You are expelled from the Executive and from the Party for ever, permanently!"

It was autumn. The leaves were turning yellow and falling. There seemed to be a sad sighing in the skies.

Suddenly a panic broke out among the members of the Socialist Party. News spread that Father Gapon, a priest, who had been a leader of the Socialist movement, had been discovered to have been a government spy. He had betrayed the Party in leading a workers' demonstration into a trap, into a police ambush, and they were shot down. The czar had withdrawn the constitution. Father Gapon had given the police the membership lists of the Party, and the police were now going about arresting right and left.

There was a sudden police swoop in the town. They went from house to house, with a list, and arrested every member of the Party—except Joseph. And the most puzzled man— because he had been spared—was Joseph. He couldn't understand it.

The town soon changed back to its old normal ways. The smoke rose again from the factory chimneys, the workers returned to their work on the old conditions—long hours and a sense of humiliation because they had lost.

There was no more singing of revolutionary songs in Beirach's tailoring workshop. If anyone started it Beirach shouted: "Stop it! Where do you think you are! In the land of the constitution? There's no constitution!"

So one or two hummed softly, almost under their breath, not the militant, defiant marching songs, but the sad Labor dirges:

> *Dear friends, when I die,*
> *Bring to my grave our flag!*

Or:

> *We are hunted and driven,*
> *Hated more and more!*
> *And all because we love*
> *The suffering, toiling poor!*

Or this:

> *Black clouds in the sky,*
> *And the wind blowing wild.*
> *From Siberia your father sends*
> *You greetings, my child!*

As things got worse, some of the workers lost heart and looked for ways of bettering themselves. Especially the radical intellectuals. They found other employment in offices, in business administrations. Or they married rich men's daughters and went into business themselves. One or two opened workshops and exploited their workers mercilessly. Some became Zionists. Some became religious. The ex-Socialists who became masters or foremen or factory managers were the hardest taskmasters.

Then rumors spread of pogroms in Russia. And before long refugees from those pogroms arrived in the town, destitute, fleeing from death, telling terrible tales of the horrors they had witnessed. The hopes of the revolution, of the constitution, of betterment for the Jews and for all the workers had vanished.

Joseph felt it keenly. He began to torment himself with the thought that he shared some of the guilt for what had happened. Because he had been disloyal to the Party, because he had betrayed the Party's decision to kill Meirowitch and had enabled him to escape the sentence the Party had pronounced against him. Perhaps it was true that Meirowitch had been a spy, having come into the Party to discover who the members were and to give their names to the police, so that they all had been arrested, except him. Joseph saw this fact as evidence for his fears—that Meirowitch had, out of gratitude for the warning he had given him, withheld his name from the police.

221

Joseph decided that now the only course of action open to him was to execute upon himself the death sentence that the Party court had agreed upon in their verdict, but had set aside out of consideration for him, because he was so naive. It meant that in their judgment he was a plain naive fool, who in his folly and simplicity had brought about the arrest and imprisonment of many of his comrades. There was nothing else to do, he decided, but to execute the judgment that had been passed upon him.

The only difficulty was his opposition to capital punishment. How could he kill himself when he was against killing anyone?

There was also Sheba to consider. The blow would be too much for her. What right had he to destroy her life?

And there was also the driving force of the artist in him that could not reconcile itself to the idea of stopping work. It all tormented him terribly—what should he do about this sense of guilt?

Joseph was no coward. It was not death he was afraid of. Death was to him a part of life—the two belonged to each other. If you live, you must die. It was the natural conclusion. All one.

He decided that the right thing for him to do would be to go to the police and tell them that he had been a member of the Socialist Party and of its Executive, and ask to be arrested like the others.

Sheba found him in great distress when she came to the house. He had risen early, but had kept pacing up and down the room, debating his decision with himself. He hadn't washed or shaved or dressed. He was in his slippers.

It was most unusual for Joseph. Every time Sheba had come to the house before this, even as early as eight o'clock in the morning, she had always found him already at work, drawing or painting. Was he ill?

"No," he wasn't ill, he answered her question. "I've been up for hours. I've got a very serious problem on my mind. I couldn't do a thing because of it. Wait a moment, and I'll go and wash and shave."

When Joseph had washed and shaved and dressed Sheba wanted him to eat his breakfast.

"I'm not hungry," he protested. But she insisted. She took him by the hand and led him to the dining room, put a cloth on the table and got him his breakfast—a couple of boiled eggs, coffee, rolls and butter. She made him eat. He ate, half-heartedly. And then he started thinking again, moodily.

"What's wrong, Joseph?"

Finally Joseph told her what had been worrying him, and what he had decided to do.

"If your conscience says you must do this, then you must," she told him. "If it's the only way in which you can find peace, you must give yourself up to the police. Have no fear for me. I would gladly go with you to prison, but they wouldn't let us be together. But no matter where they send you, in whatever town you are in prison, even in Siberia, I will be there—I'll be near you. I'll come to see you whenever they allow it."

Joseph decided that before giving himself up to the police he must see his sister Miriam. So he went to the village where she lived with Andreï.

The road to the village was lined with chestnut trees. The leaves had already turned yellow; some were brown, and some ruddy, and many had fallen to the ground, to which all that lives and grows and dies must come. It was the month of Elul, in the days of the Selichot prayers, preceding the penitential days of Rosh Hashanah and Yom Kippur, the Day of Atonement.

Though Joseph was no longer religious, he felt again the old awe that had made him think in the old days when he was a youngster and believed, that the whole world was trembling with fear before the approaching Days of Judgment.

A peasant who recognized Joseph and knew he was Miriam's brother, stopped him at the entrance to the village, and told him there had been a big police raid on the village—police and cossacks had swooped down, on several neighboring villages too, and had arrested a lot of young people, and some of the older ones, and had driven them before them like cattle to the town, using their knouts and rifle-butts on them without mercy. Some of the older people had collapsed under the blows, and several had died.

It was just at harvest time, and the whole crop had been left unharvested in the fields. Now winter was coming, and there would be no food for the people and no hay for the beasts.

In one village the peasants had resisted, had fought the Russian czar's police and cossacks with scythes and sickles and axes and iron bars. Even the old grandmother had fought—as at the time of the Polish Insurrection. Then the police and the cossacs had fired. Some of the young peasants had revolvers and fired back.

"It was a real battle!" said the old peasant. "Like a real war. Blood flowed. Old Gregor who had fought in the Insurrection tore off his shirt and exposed his bare chest, and cried: 'Shoot, you dirty swine!' And one of the dirty swine had split his skull with his sword. But our scythes and sickles mowed down many of the police and the cossacks. 'Down with the Muscovites! Down with the czar! Long live Poland!' that was the cry of our people.

"We fought bravely!" the peasant went on sadly. "But the cossacks on their horses rode into us, with their swords flashing, and they cut down many of us, and we were trampled under their horses' hooves, and many of us were shot.

"In some villages the peasants met the police and the cossacks with crucifixes and holy pictures, and they knelt down and prayed, and they called out: 'We are believing Christians. We are not rebels!' It didn't help them! The devils rode them down! The crucifixes and the holy pictures were trampled under the horses' hooves.

"Many of our people are in prison now. They are hanging them and shooting them! And deporting them to Siberia!

"Your sister and Andrei are safe," the peasant went on. "They escaped. They are in hiding. I don't know where. But Andrei's parents know. They'll tell you."

Andrei's father, Stanislav, told Joseph that Miram and Andrei were hiding in the house of the mayor, the new mayor who had replaced the one who had been shot. The police had

224

been looking for them but hadn't found them. They had dragged him, Stanislav, several times to police headquarters in the town, questioned him and beaten him—he showed Joseph his bruises.

"But if they had killed me I wouldn't have told them where they are hiding. They caught both my two younger sons, Bronek and Michalek, and they are now in prison."

Andrei's mother came in holding a baby, Miriam and Andrei's child, in her arms. A few weeks old.

Joseph found Miriam and Andrei in a small partitioned corner of the Mayor's stable, among the horses and cows. They were safer there because the police trusted the Mayor, considered him loyal, and didn't search too closely in his house. They had been in the stable, but went away satisfied that there were only horses and cows there.

The old woman took Joseph into the hiding place by lifting out two boards in what seemed a solid wall against which the cows stood swishing their tails. It was pitch dark there, and the air was heavy. There was only a small slit that had been made in the outside wall to admit a little fresh air. There was a heap of straw on the ground to sit on and sleep on.

Miriam and Andrei had already got used to the darkness of the place. But to Joseph it was as though he had gone blind.

Miriam hugged Joseph and kissed him. Then she took the baby from the grandmother and put it to her breast to suck.

Joseph found it hard to breathe the foul air. Everybody spoke in whispers, not to be overheard. Miriam fed the child and handed it back to the grandmother.

If anyone had asked Joseph whether he was religious he would have answered that he was a freethinker and did not believe in any of the Jewish religious observances. Yet it hurt him to think that his sister's child had a Christian father. He asked if it was a boy, and when they told him it was, he dared not ask if it was circumcised, because he was sure it wasn't.

He told Miriam why he had come: "To find out if you were safe. And to say goodbye."

Miriam assumed that Joseph was going back to Warsaw. "I

hope you'll be happy in Warsaw," she said. "But keep away from the comrades. Don't try to rejoin the Party. I know the sentence of the Party court—you are permanently expelled from the Party. The decision has been communicated to every Party organization. They know it in Warsaw, as I know it here. If you ask me, the Party court was very lenient. If we had been in power, if we were the government, you wouldn't have got off so easily."

"You're right," said Joseph. "I deserve much more severe punishment. I know. That is why I have decided to give myself up to the police. I'm going to tell them that I was a member of the Party and a member of the Executive, and that I want to go to prison like all the others. That's why I have come here now to say goodbye.

"You're mad! You've taken leave of your senses! You're out of your mind!" Miriam held Joseph by the lapels. "What good do you think you'll be doing anyone by this foolhardy heroism! Whom will it help?"

"Me," said Joseph. "It will help me. My first thought was to execute on myself the death sentence that the Party court had passed on Meirowitch. But I'm against the death penalty. So I'm giving myself up to the police. Let them do with me what they will. I can't have it on my conscience any more, that so many comrades are now in prison because of me, and I am free!"

"But it wasn't becasue of you, Joseph! The police found your membership list and the minutes of your meetings in the home of your secretary Comrade Nathan. They didn't arrest you because it was recorded in the minutes that you had been expelled from the Party, and that you were of no use to the Party, but rather a danger to the Party. Meirowitch was no spy, he was no traitor—you did no harm by warning him. On the contrary, you saved the Party from committing an act of injustice."

Joseph's face cleared. A great weight had lifted from him. He stood speechless with relief.

"So you see," said Miriam, "there is no need for your expia-

226

tion. There's nothing to expiate. You've nothing on your conscience. Go home, Joseph! And keep out of the way of the Party. Don't try to help us. You'll only commit some other blunder. My advice to you is—sell the house that we inherited from our parents and go to live in Warsaw. Take Sheba with you. Marry her! About your art—I'm no judge of that, but I'm sure you've got talent. You'll have bigger opportunities for your art in Warsaw."

On his way home, near the entrance to the town, Joseph came to the cemetery. He hadn't been there for a long time. He didn't believe in the cult of visiting the graves of the departed. He believed that with their death his parents' mortal remains, their bodies, had nothing more to do with him. Their spirit lived on in his memory, every time he thought of them—and he thought of them often. All the same, as he was so near the cemetery, passing it, he felt that he should go in and visit his parents' graves.

It was getting dark. The western sky was lit up by the roseate flush. The sun was setting. The wind was soughing through the branches of the tall poplars. Against all his rationalist beliefs he felt a sense of fear and awe.

He told the watchman at the gate that he knew where his graves were, and that he would find his way there himself. He found them—three in a row, next to each other: the little tailor, his grandfather Reb Melech, and his father, Reb Abraham. The little tailor's tombstone had already begun to sink into the ground. Reb Melech's was showing signs of age. His father's tombstone was still like new. He sat down on it and plunged into heavy thoughts.

Suddenly he had a vision—a small town, or perhaps a village. Everything there was strange and fantastic. The sky was a wonderful bright blue, a dazzling azure, blinding with its brightness. The earth was covered with a luminous shining green. Little streams ran through the fields, silver and golden, red and blue, yellow and black. And lovely little houses, all of glass and crystal, reflecting the colors of the rainbow. Trees and flowers round each house. There was a holiday—the people were all happy and rejoicing. The children were playing.

In one of these glass and crystal houses, shimmering with bright gold and green light, a little old Jew with a thin goatee beard, and his face radiant with humility and love of his fellow men, sat at a table of mother of pearl. At his side sat an old hunchback woman, but her eyes shone with chaste modesty, piety, and boundless loyalty and devotion. And two other couples—his father and mother, his grandfather and grandmother. And more people were there, lots of people, men and women, old and young, some very young. And old Reb Jacob, the cobbler, was among them. Also his sister Miriam and Andrei, and Nathan, the lanky Secretary of the Party, and Andrei's parents, and workers and artisans and peasants, many of them, from the town and the surrounding villages. He saw himself there too, sitting at the table with Sheba.

The little tailor was talking to all these people, addressing them—his saintly great-grandfather! He was telling them about the poverty that people had suffered here years ago, when the town had been a small place, and people had worked hard, worked long hours, starting in winter early in the morning, when it was still dark. Because the rich had given no thought to the plight of the poor, had been cruel and selfish, cold and callous to the sufferings and the needs of other human beings. Now, he was saying, this is all over—it is the Sabbath of Sabbaths, because Messiah has come, and has redeemed the world from all sorrow and pain. Isaiah's prophecy of the end of days was fulfilled . . . .

Glossary

AL CHAIT: Penitential Prayer—"For the sin wherein we have sinned, God of Forgiveness, forgive us"—read on Yom Kippur, the Day of Atonement.

ALMEMOR: The reading desk, or pulpit, in the synagogue, usually in the middle, but also often in front of the Ark of the Law.

ARK OF THE LAW: Chest in the synagogue in which are kept the Scrolls of the Law used in the synagogue service, and toward which the congregation turns in prayer.

BAAL KORAH: The reader (usually the *chazan*, but not necessarily) of the Sedra, the weekly portion of the Pentateuch.

BETH HAMEDRASH: "House of Study" in a Jewish community, where Jews study religious lore, especially the Talmud. Many times, the Beth Hamedrash is the synagogue.

BEZALEL BEN URI: The architect of the Tabernacle (see Exodus 31).

CHAZAK!: "Be strong and of good courage." Recited by the congregation at the end of the reading of any of the books of the Pentateuch just concluded.

CHEVRA KADISHA: Holy Brotherhood—the community organization among the Ashkenazi Jews responsible for the burial of the dead in accordance with traditional custom.

CHUMASHIM: The Five Books of Moses.

DREIDEL: A spinning top, like the tee-totum, with Hebrew letters on the four sides—the initials of the miracle commemorated by the Hanukkah and Purim festivals. Played especially by children.

ELUL: The sixth month of the Hebrew calendar. The month of penitential preparation for Rosh Hashanah and Yom Kippur, which follow immediately after.

GALUT: Exile—applied to the dispersal of Jews after the Roman destruction of the Temple.

GEMARA: Talmud.

HEDER: Elementary Jewish school.

KVATTER!: Godfather—who passes the infant to the Sandek, who holds the infant on his knees during the circumcision.

LAG B'OMER: Jewish holiday falling on the thirty-third day of the *omer* (the seven-week period between Passover and Shavuoth) commemorating the staying of the plague that struck down many of the students of the historical figure Rabbi Akiba.

LATKES: Potato pancakes.

L'CHAIM!: A toast meaning "To Life!"

MAZEL TOV: A congratulatory phrase wishing good luck.

MEZUZAH: A small scroll of parchment inscribed with Deuteronomy 6:4–9 and 11:13–21 and placed in a case fixed to the doorpost by Jewish families as a sign and reminder of their faith.

MIDRASH: Rabbinical exegesis of the Bible, based on the Talmud.

MISHNA: The oldest collection, apart from the Pentateuch, of

Jewish legislative writings and tradition. It forms the basic portion of the Talmud.

MITHNAGID: Means literally "opponent." Generally means non-Hasidic Jews.

MLAVE MALKA: The festive meal eaten at the end of the Sabbath.

MOAZ TZUR: Hymn sung on Hanukkah at the kindling of the Hanukkah lights.

MOHEL: Qualified person performing the rite of circumcision.

MUSAF: Second part of the synagogue service on Sabbaths and festivals, after the reading of the Law.

PAROCHES: The curtain hanging in front of the Ark of the Law—usually richly embroidered.

ROSH HASHANAH: The Jewish New Year—Day of Judgment on which all mortals are judged before the Heavenly Throne.

SANDEK: Usually a venerable man who holds the infant on his knees during the circumcision.

SCHADENFREUDE: Joy at another's misfortune.

SELICHOT: Penitential prayers.

SHACHRIS: Morning service in the synagogue.

SHAMMES: The sexton of a synagogue.

SHECHINA: The Divine Presence.

SHULCHAN ARUCH: Code of Jewish Law compiled by Joseph Caro (sixteenth century).

SHTREIMEL: Fur hat worn by Hasidim.

SIYUM HASEPHER: Celebration at the conclusion of the copying of a Scroll of the Law.

TALLITH: A shawl with fringed corners traditionally worn over the head or shoulders by Jewish men during services in the synagogue.

TEKIAH GEDOLAH: The long-drawn blast of the Shofar (ram's horn) blown in the synagogue in Elul and on Yom Kippur and Rosh Hashanah.

TEPHILIN: Phylacteries—two small leather boxes containing pieces of parchment with scriptural passages, worn on the left arm and forehead during morning weekday prayers (see Exodus 13).

THIRTY-SIX SAINTS: *Lamed Vav*. The belief that in every generation there are thirty-six righteous men unknown to the world, by whose merit the world exists.

TISHRI: The seventh month of the Hebrew calendar. The first two days are Rosh Hashanah, and the tenth day is Yom Kippur.

TREIF: Nonkosher food.

VEHI BINSOA: "And it came to pass when the Ark set forward." Recited by the congregation when the Ark is opened and the Scroll is taken to the pulpit for reading the portion of the week.